Ama age of sixteen—a vast epic, starring all her friends as the characters, written secretly during algebra class. She's never since used algebra, but her books have been nominated for many awards, including the RITA®, Romantic Times Reviewers' Choice Award, the Booksellers' Best, the National Readers' Choice Award and the Holt Medallion. She lives in Oklahoma with her husband, one dog and one cat.

THE GOVERNESS'S CONVENIENT MARRIAGE

Amanda McCabe

MILLS & BOON

First Published in Great Britain 2018
by Mills & Boon, an imprint of HarperCollins*Publishers*
1 London Bridge Street, London, SE1 9GF

© 2018 Ammanda McCabe

ISBN: 978-0-263-93326-0

MIX
Paper from
responsible sources
FSC
www.fsc.org
FSC˘ C007454

This book is produced from independently certified FSC™ paper
to ensure responsible forest management.
For more information visit www.harpercollins.co.uk/green.

Printed and bound in Spain
by CPI, Barcelona

Prologue

Scotland—1882

Lady Alexandra Mannerly hurried down the back stairs of her father's hunting lodge, trying to tiptoe so no one would see she had escaped her governess. Even in Scotland, where life was much more free than London or at her father's ducal seat in Kent, she was supposed to have lessons in the mornings. But she did not *want* lessons. She was nearly thirteen now. Surely she deserved to be free? At least for a little while?

And besides—she knew exactly where she wanted to go now. Who she wanted to see.

She could hear the clatter of the kitchens, the cook shouting for more salmon to make mousse for dinner, the maids dropping pans, her brother, Charles, begging for cakes. Her father was out shooting for the day, as he always did in Scotland, and her mother was locked in her chamber with a tisane for her headache, as *she* always did in Scotland. Alex knew her governess would like a free hour to flirt with the butler, so Alex was free for a little while.

She slipped out through the back door unseen and ran through the kitchen garden to the gate. The brisk, cool wind, smelling of the green hills, caught at her loose, slippery pale curls and the skirts of her blue-muslin dress, biting through her jacket, but she didn't care. She could run now, run and run with no one to stop her!

The weeks they spent in Scotland every early autumn were her favourite of all the year. In England, she always felt so shy, so nervous of everything, so sure she was not being a proper duke's daughter. That was what her mother lectured her about all the time—what a duke's daughter should do.

In Scotland, no one was looking at her. She was just Alex, especially when she escaped to run outside and make her own friends. One friend in particular.

She pushed the gate closed behind her and ran through the thicket of woods. She could hear the wind whistling through the branches, rustling the drying leaves. From far off, she could hear the bang of the guns, but she knew they wouldn't come near. Her father wouldn't be home for hours, when there would be dinner, bagpipes and dancing, which she and Charles would spy on from above-stairs.

Beyond the woods wound the river, rushing fast over the rocks, a silvery tumble that made its own music, flowing down icy-cold from the heather-purple hills above.

And waiting for her was just the person she sought so eagerly. Malcolm Gordston.

Well—maybe he wasn't *waiting*, not for her anyway. He was fishing, as he did nearly every day from the same large, flat rock, casting his line into the water and coming up with salmon for the cook's mousse.

Alex stood very still for a moment, hidden behind a tree, and watched him. He was older than her by several years and thus quite ancient, yet he fascinated her. The son of one of the crofters on her father's estate, he was unlike anyone she had ever met. So handsome, tall and strong, with dark gold hair that was too long for any London fashion and features as sternly carved as the rocks around the river. His rough, working clothes never seemed to matter; he was too much like some long-ago king, even in patched trousers and old boots.

And he was always kind to her when they met.

He spoke to her as if she was herself, Alex, not Lady Alexandra. Not a child who couldn't understand anything. She especially liked it when he told her old stories, legends of the Scottish hills, which his grandmother had once told him.

She ran towards the rock and he waved at her with a smile. 'My lady,' he called. 'Come for another fishing lesson?'

'Oh, yes,' Alex answered eagerly. 'I'm sure I can do better this time.' Last week she had only caught a tiny sparling, fit just for throwing back. She wanted to do more in front of him, see pride in his icy pale blue eyes.

'I'm sure you can.' He handed her his extra rod and the bucket of cut bait, small strips of slimy herring. She knew just what to do, thanks to his lessons, and threaded the slippery bit on to her hook.

He gave her an approving nod. 'You're no squeamish lass afraid to get her hands dirty.'

Alex laughed. 'Faint heart never caught fat salmon, right, Malcolm?'

She cast her line into the water and for a long time they sat together in silence, the peace of the hills and the river wrapped around them. She felt so close to him then, so comfortable. She never felt that way anywhere else.

'How is your father this week, Malcolm?' she

asked. She knew from listening to the maids' gossip that Mr Gordston was not well, had not been well since his wife died last year. Alex felt terrible about it for Malcolm, worried about his family woes, but he always kept such emotions at a distance.

His jaw tightened. 'He's getting better, I think. The cooler weather affects his chest right now and he misses my mam. But we get the work done.'

'Should I bring him one of our cook's herbal tisanes?' Alex asked. 'My mother is ailing whenever we come to Scotland and she says they do her good.'

Malcolm gave a strange, wry smile. 'You're a kind lass, my lady. But some herbal concoction can't help what ails my father now.'

Alex was worried by his tone and wanted to ask more, but she felt a sharp tug on her line. 'I've got a bite, Malcolm!' she cried.

He grinned at her. 'Don't jerk hard on it, my lady. Reel him in easy-like, see. Nice and smooth. Don't let him wriggle free.'

She followed his instructions and pulled up a lovely, fat salmon, her first real catch. And Malcolm had seen her do it! 'Look! Malcolm, I did it!'

'Of course you did, my lady,' he said with a

laugh. He so rarely laughed and it was a wonderful sound, deep and merry. She wished she could hear it again and again.

She was so overcome with joy at the perfect moment, so wonderfully giddy just with being so close to him, that she bounced up on her toes and kissed his cheek. It felt slightly rough under her lips and he smelled wonderful, of fresh air and crisp greenery and just like—himself.

'Oh, Malcolm,' she gasped. 'I do hope we can be together here, just like this, always!'

She knew as soon as the words escaped that she should not have said them. His face went pale and he frowned, his earlier sunny laughter completely vanished. He drew back, his hands gentle as he held her away. Alex shivered, suddenly cold, wishing with all her might she could call back the last few minutes. Change it all.

'I—I just…' she stammered, feeling so very unsure. She longed to run away, but her feet seemed frozen to the earth.

Malcolm ran his hand through his hair. 'Lady Alexandra—you are the daughter of a duke. I can certainly help you learn how to fish…'

'But you cannot be my friend,' she answered quietly.

'You are a very kind young lady,' he said, in that terribly quiet, sweet tone people used far too often to placate her. She couldn't bear it from him, as well. Especially not him. 'One day soon you will take your proper place in the world and you won't want to waste time with a ghillie's son like me.'

Alex knew, deep down in her most secret heart, that was not true. She knew what was expected of her as a duke's daughter—her mother spoke of little else. Her governess drilled it into her. She was to bring honour to her family name, to marry well, lead society. But the thought of that made her feel terrified. She wanted to be free, to sit on the bank of a river just like this one, be part of nature, no one looking at her, expecting things she could not give.

To talk to Malcolm for as long as she wanted. For ever. He was the only one who seemed to just see *her*. And yet he did not, not really. To him, just like everyone else, she was the Duke's daughter.

She hugged Malcolm again, even tighter, afraid it was the last time. The thought that she might never see him again, at least not like this, alone, easy and fun, made her want to sob. Malcolm hugged her back.

'Let go of my daughter at once, you dirty cur!' A sudden shout, as loud and shocking as the crack of a whip, shattered the perfect moment.

Alex jumped back to see her father looming on the rise of the bank above them. He was tall, the capes of his tweed greatcoat flapping like an ominous bird, his face bright scarlet. She couldn't stop shaking with fear.

'Papa!' she cried. Malcolm moved away from her, sweeping his cap into his hand.

The Duke strode towards them and grabbed her arm, barely glancing at Malcolm. His hand was painful on her skin, bruising, yet she was so frozen she could barely feel it. 'Come with me right now, young lady. Your behaviour is disgraceful.'

Through her fear, she felt a flash of burning anger. 'It is not like that!' she protested. She glanced back at Malcolm, who gave her a small shake of his head.

'Your Grace, Lady Alexandra is not to blame…' he began.

The Duke whirled around on him, his face turning even more red. His eyes bulged, almost as if they would pop free. Alex had to stifle a hysterical giggle. 'You are just lucky that I do not thrash you where you stand! If I did not have to take my silly daughter home, believe me, I would. And I shall if I ever see you near her again. As it is, you should go home now and see to your worthless father.'

Alex had one more glimpse of Malcolm's face, his handsome features twisted with fury, before her father dragged her away. A cart waited on the lane just beyond the rise and he pushed her up into it roughly.

Alex couldn't hold back the tears any longer. They burst from her in rough sobs and she buried her face in her hands. Her father ignored her, of course, steering the horse towards their house, but she couldn't stop crying. That last, terrible sight of Malcolm, the fear of what he would think of her now—it made her want to sink into the earth and vanish.

The house was silent when they arrived, as if even the stones and glass knew she was in disgrace. That she had lost her friend. The hall, all cold flagstone floors, animal heads staring down glassily from the walls, echoed with heartless carelessness. She glimpsed a maid peeking over the balustrade from the top floor, a tea tray meant for Alex's mother in her hands, but then she vanished. Alex's brother was hiding in the attics, as usual, her mother resting with a headache.

'Go to your chamber, Alexandra,' her father said tightly. He tossed his coat on to a tall wooden chair and strode away.

But Alex had to try once more. 'Papa, you must not blame Malcolm! He was only—'

The Duke whirled on her, his eyes burning. He pointed one long, shaking finger at her, making her fall a step back. 'You know what is expected of you, Alexandra, how the family name must never be disgraced. Your cavorting with a farm boy will bring gossip and it must end. Now. Besides, his family is not respectable. They will soon be gone. If I hear of you seeing him again, the consequences for you both will be even more severe, I promise you.'

Alex's eyes ached and she was determined not to let him see her cry again. He would *never* see her cry again, would never know what she was really feeling. She ran up the stairs, past the rows of silent closed doors, to her chamber. Once she had loved that room; it was small, but in the corner of the old stone hunting lodge so boasting windows on two sides to let in the rolling countryside. Her white bed, draped in yellow tulle, her dolls stacked in the corner, her little white dressing table with its antique mirror, she had loved it all, found it a sanctuary from her family's silence. Today it was only another prison.

She threw herself on the bed and buried her head in the pillows, trying not to howl. She remembered the sun-splashed river, Malcolm's smile, the touch of his hand. He had been a good friend to her, maybe her only real friend. She couldn't leave things the way they were. She had to see him, to say she was sorry, if only she could sneak past her father.

She quickly wiped at her eyes and went to peer out the window. The sun was starting to sink in the sky, the familiar purple, dull-pink Scottish sunset gathering in. Her father would be in his library for hours, until dinner. She would have to hurry if she wanted to find Malcolm and apologise to him. See him one more time.

She wrapped herself up in a long, dark cloak and crept out of her room, praying she would not be seen.

The croft was silent as Malcolm approached it, no smoke curling from the chimney, no one working in the small kitchen garden to gather the last of the vegetables. It was just as he had left it that morning, yet he had hoped, as he always foolishly hoped, that something would change.

The Duke's words, that he had to see to his own house now, echoed in his mind, ominous and chilling. He had long known that the Duke, not a soft or kind man, would be patient no longer, but he hadn't expected that moment to come just then. Because of Lady Alexandra.

Malcolm shook his head as he studied the overgrown path of weeds that had once been a vegetable garden. Alexandra was a lovely girl, pretty and kind, eager to learn all kinds of new things around her, full of questions. At first, when he met her trying hopelessly to fish and offered to teach her, it had been out of pity. Yet he came to look forward to their afternoons together, to enjoy their conversations, hearing her laughter and chatter. She was extraordinary, entirely unworthy of her father. Surely she would do wonderful things in her future.

But now that friendship had brought trouble to his door. He only wished he could have protected her, kept her that sweet innocent he adored so much.

Malcolm shook his head and sighed. She would have to learn of the real world soon enough; everyone was forced to it sooner or later.

He took off his muddy old boots and left them with the basket of fish near the door. Despite his own efforts, he could see all the signs of neglect on the cottage. The peeling paint, the loose shutters, the tangled garden.

When his mother had been alive, it had always been bright and clean and welcoming. How Malcolm tried his best to keep it up, to keep his father from being evicted by the Duke. It was the only way Malcolm could escape, if his father was all right. The only way he could take the apprenticeship he had been promised as a draper's assistant in the city. He could be more than a farmer, if he worked hard there. Could win Mairie's hand at last. Only if his father could recover.

Mairie. Some of the glow from his afternoon with her faded as he looked up at the loose tiles on the roof. Her father would never give her to a poor crofter's son; she would never so give herself. And Malcolm wanted more for himself, as well. The vicar who had been teaching him for years said he was smart and quick, and could build his own business if he wanted. Maybe one day he and Mairie could make something together. They both had their own interests at heart, the interests of moving forward in the world, which was all that really mattered in a relationship.

He thought of that morning, fishing with Lady Alexandra, so quiet and sweet and clean. He wanted to build a life like that, a life where everything could be fine and good. A life just like *her*. He knew he shouldn't think that way; Mairie was more appropriate for him, was within his reach, only just. Someone like Alexandra, never. The terrible ending to their fishing meeting showed him that so clearly.

He pushed open the front door, loose on its hinges. Inside the small room, it smelled of smoke and mildew, of old whisky. When his mother was there, the floor was always swept, the furniture dusted, the air smelling of fresh herbs. He remembered when his father would come home in the evening, the way he would catch his mother up in his arms and kiss her until she laughed.

His parents had loved each other so much. Too much. His father had lost his way without her. Malcolm vowed never to love anyone like that, never to lose so much. He would never be helpless like that, never live his parents' mistakes.

'Pa?' he called. There was no answer.

He found his father up in the loft, sprawled across his bed. Still wearing yesterday's stained clothes, reeking of cheap whisky, his skin greyish and clammy, his jaw unshaven. An empty bottle had fallen to the dusty floor.

None of that was unusual any more. What was strange was the crumpled paper that lay next to the bottle. Malcolm scooped it up and read it quickly, anger burning higher and higher inside of him.

It was an eviction notice. Signed by the Duke of Waverton.

Malcolm remembered the sting of going last week to see the Duke, his hat in hand, to beg for time for his father. Time to gather the rent money.

The Duke had only watched him, stony-faced, and said he would do what he could, but he could not help those who would not help themselves for very long.

Now, he had tossed Malcolm's father out. Now, at their family's most vulnerable moment.

One day, Malcolm vowed as he tucked the blankets around his father, the shoe would be on the other foot and the Duke would beg *him* for help. And Malcolm would never give it.

Near the gate that led to one of the tenants' farms, Alex was surprised to see a glimpse of bright red against the grey-green of the fields. She looked closer and saw it was Mairie Mc-Gregor, the daughter of one of the shopkeepers in the village, perched on the gate. Alex always rather envied Mairie, for her beautiful, long dark hair and velvety-brown eyes, so different from Alex's own pale looks.

Today, Mairie's black hair fell free down her back and she wore a bright blue skirt and red shawl, looped loosely around her shoulders. And she was not alone. A man was beside her, leaning on the gate as he gazed up at her, their hands entwined. Their heads were bent together as they spoke together intently, seriously. Mairie tenderly touched his cheek and he turned his head to kiss her fingers.

It was Malcolm. Malcolm kissing Mairie Mc-Gregor.

Shocked, Alex tried to step back, to hide, even though she knew they could not see her. They were obviously much too wrapped up in each other to see anything else. And she felt the sinking, cold ice of disappointment.

Mairie jumped down from the gate and walked away, tossing a strangely angry look back at Malcolm as she left.

Impulsively, Alex called out to Malcolm as he started to follow Mairie.

'Malcolm!' she called. 'Please, just a moment.'

He glanced back at her, but his expression was anything but welcoming. She had never seen him look so cold, so hard, so—so much older. 'We can't be seen together, my lady. You've already got me in enough trouble.'

'I—I didn't mean to, please believe me,' she said, desperate. 'I am ever so sorry. I didn't think my father would see and—'

He cut her off with a wave of his hand. 'It doesn't matter. His Grace has done his worst by my family. Now I have to make my own way. And you have to make yours.'

Alex was baffled. 'What has he done? I can

go to him, explain…' But even she knew her father would never listen. Never care.

'Just take of yourself now, Lady Alexandra. That's all any of us can do.' For just a flashing instant, his hardness seemed to melt. He took her hand in his and squeezed it, holding on to it for one precious moment. 'Never let them change you, no matter what.'

'Malcolm!' Mairie called and that hard mask came over him again. He gave Alex a bow and left her standing there alone in the middle of the road.

Alex tightened her hand over the feeling of his touch and shivered. She knew then she would never see him again.

Chapter One

⸺⟡⸺

Miss Grantley's School for Young Ladies
—spring 1888

'Alex! Alex, are you awake? Let us in, quickly, before we're caught.'

Lady Alexandra Mannerly wasn't asleep, despite the fact that it was hours past the decreed lights out. She was huddled under her blankets, reading—no, *devouring*—*The Ghosts of Wakefield Forest*, a forbidden novel loaned to her by her friend Emily Fortescue, who had smuggled it back from London. Em, whose father was distinctly unstrict, quite unlike Alex's father, the Duke of Waverton. *He* insisted Alex be the perfect ducal daughter at all times, which didn't include reading scandalous romantic novels.

But her parents couldn't spy on her at Miss Grantley's at every moment. And Alex had friends who knew how to get around almost every rule without getting into trouble. She herself could never have been so brave before coming to school. She hated trouble, because trouble brought attention and attention made her heart race, her mind freeze, her tongue tie. Made her want to run away.

So being a duke's daughter was rarely fun at all. And it would surely get worse next year, when she made her debut at a grand ball at Waverton House on Green Park and began the search for a high-ranking husband. But not yet. Not quite yet.

'Alex! Are you there? We see your light!'

Alex tossed back the bedclothes and hurried to the door, her bare feet cold on the wooden floor. Her best friends, Emily Fortescue and Diana Martin, were waiting there, wrapped in their dressing gowns, dragging an enormous hamper between them. Giggling, they raced inside before Miss Merrill, the hall governess, could catch them. If they were found sneaking out together again, they would be in real trouble.

Yet Alex didn't seem to mind trouble so much when it was brought by Diana and Em.

'What are you two doing here?' she whispered, locking the door behind them.

'What do you think?' Diana answered. 'Midnight picnic!'

'Father sent a lovely hamper today. I couldn't possibly eat all this myself,' Emily said as she spread a blanket on the polished floor. Her father, who had started in business as a wine merchant and branched out to open one of London's first department stores, was always sending Emily lovely things. Hampers, fashionable hats, books.

'Isn't Mr F. lovely?' Diana sighed. 'My parents only seem to send foot warmers and peppermints.' Di's father had been a high-ranking diplomat in India, but it was true he never sent anything exotic like Punjab muslins.

'There's Brie cheese and some wonderful pâté. Tea sandwiches, *petit fours*,' Emily said, laying it all out on their blanket. 'And Lindt chocolates! Your favourites, Alex.'

'Oh, it is! How blissful,' Alex said. She couldn't resist taking one immediately, popping it into her mouth.

'What are you doing up so late?' Diana asked as she opened a bottle of ginger beer.

'Reading, of course,' Alex said. 'Did you think I had a *boy* in here? Jimmy Wilkins, maybe?' Jimmy Wilkins was the son of the local squire, handsome if a bit spotty, and, as the only male under sixty and over thirteen for miles near the school, the object of many pashes.

'If you did such a wildly naughty thing, Lady

Alexandra, I would *know* you had come down with a terrible fever,' Emily said.

Alex took another chocolate. 'Oh, I don't know. If I married Jimmy now, there would be no need for a Season. I could live near here at his nice, quiet manor house, and read all the time and ride out with the local hunt in the autumn. Heaven.'

'Oh, Alex, a Season will be fun!' Emily said. 'Think of the gowns, the dances, the tea parties, the theatre. The strange people we can laugh at in corners.'

'That's easy for you to say,' Diana declared. 'Your father actually wants you to go into business with him, he doesn't care if you marry. It can all be a lark to you.'

Alex gave her a sympathetic nod. They all knew Di wanted to be a writer, but her parents were much more conventional than Mr F. and wanted Diana to marry suitably. As did Alex's parents, of course. But to the Duke and Duchess, *suitable* meant another duke, if an eligible one could be found, or an earl at the least. Maybe even a German prince, as all the English ones were taken.

The thought filled her with terror. She recalled, just for an instant, that boy she had known so long ago, a poor crofter's son who'd looked like an ancient king, who'd smiled at her with the warmth of the sun. Until their painful parting. How long ago that seemed now. How impossible.

'Alex's Season will be the loveliest of all!' Emily said. 'You're the goddaughter of the Princess of Wales, her own namesake. Just think of all the grand people who will come to your parties.'

'Don't remind me,' Alex muttered. It was true the Princess was a good godmother, always sending splendid presents for birthdays and writing sweet letters, and Princess Alexandra would want to help make Alex's debut a success. But it only made Alex want to run away even more.

Diana squeezed her hand. 'Don't think of it now, Alex darling, it's all so terribly far away. You might marry Jimmy Wilkins in the meantime! But here, have another chocolate and tell us what you're reading.'

'*The Ghosts of Wakefield Forest*, of course,' Alex said, happily obeying the order to have another treat. 'It's so thrilling!'

'Have you got to the scene where Arabella meets the Count?' Emily asked.

'Not yet and don't tell me!' Alex said with a laugh. Em did tend to get carried away by her enthusiasm for stories and give away endings. 'Did your father send more books this week?'

'No, but he did send these.' Emily pulled a pile of fashion papers from the bottom of the hamper.

'Oh, this one's from Paris!' Diana cried happily. She grabbed one to pore over the sketches. She loved fashion and was always knowledgeable about the latest trends. 'Are these the new sleeves for summer? How cunning. Look at this ribbon trim.'

'Yes, and the hats are enormous compared to last year. Father is quite worried the costs will be ridiculous, with all these feathers and flowers. Alex, you must tell the Princess to start wearing small, plain bonnets immediately.'

Alex laughed. 'I'll write to her tomorrow.' She scanned one of the papers, caught by a sketch of a grand building. All of five storeys, with classical statues of goddesses at every corner and as many windows as Hardwicke Hall gleaming. 'Gordston's Department Store is opening a new branch in Paris?'

Emily made a face. 'Yes, and Father is furious! Mr Gordston seems to beat him at every post lately. The man seems unstoppable.'

'Even my mother loves Gordston's hat counter and she always said she would *never* buy ready-made,' Alex said. She tried not to sigh when she recalled she had once known a Gordston, too, in those golden days in Scotland. Memories were always so sad now.

She read over the breathless descriptions of the new Paris store, its marble floors from Italy, its gilded lifts operated by young ladies in red-velvet suits, its shocking new cosmetics counter. It was just as giddy in writing about the store's owner and his 'godlike face' and 'intoxicating laugh', hinting about his romances with actresses and countesses and American heiresses.

'Is he really as handsome as all that, Em?' Diana asked. Emily was the only girl at school who had ever met the notorious Mr Gordston.

Emily's head tilted as if she contemplated this question carefully. 'He is—interesting.'

'I think he sounds like a character in a novel,' Diana said. 'So dashing! So rich. Maybe I'll meet him in London and marry *him* instead of some dull diplomat or clergyman or army officer like my parents hope.'

'You would be much happier with the officer,' Emily said firmly. 'Now, here, girls! Eat up before we have to sneak out again.'

Alex turned the page on the paper and froze in shock. There, staring up at her in a grainy black-and-white image, was Malcolm. *Her* Malcolm, from Scotland, the one young man she could never quite forget, despite the terrible way they'd parted. Gordston's was not owned by some unknown Scotsman after all. He was at a race-track, standing near the railing with a lady in trailing lace and one of those enormous feathered hats. She gazed up at him adoringly, while he gave a half-smile into the distance. So tall, so gorgeous, so utterly unapproachable.

She read the headline.

The delight of every lady's eye!

She read on.

But is the handsome millionaire ready to take the plunge with Lady Deanston? She looks ready, but our sources say he never will be. Although a titled lady at his side could only improve his standing in society...

Malcolm was the owner of Gordston's? The famous man about town, with all the most beautiful ladies in love with him? Alex was surprised, but not really shocked. He had always been special indeed. The wonder was he had ever looked at her at all, with such sophisticated ladies just waiting for him out in the world.

Afraid she might start to cry, Alex carefully folded the paper and set it aside. She had never told even Emily and Diana about Malcolm. He was her own little secret, to be taken out and looked at like a precious jewel when everything got too overwhelming. And now he was *the* Malcolm Gordston, further away from her than ever. Maybe one day she would talk about him, but not soon. She didn't even have the words.

Alex lay back on their picnic blanket and listened to her friends' laughter, their chatter about new French fashions and the relative merits of different chocolates. There, with the night gathered close beyond the curtains and silence in the schools' halls, they were tucked away in their own warm, safe little world. How she loved it here at Miss Grantley's, where she was only another young lady among her friends, only Alex! If only they could stay right there. If only she could be just Alex for ever. Alex who remembered her very own Malcolm.

'I wish this would never end,' she said. 'That we could go on this way always.'

Emily and Diana lay down beside her. 'We can't stay at Miss Grantley's for ever,' Em said, touching her hand. 'But we will always, always be friends.'

'Are you sure?' Alex whispered, all too aware of how fast things changed in the world beyond the school gates.

'Oh, yes,' Diana declared. 'No matter where we go, or what happens to us, we will always have each other.'

Sarah M. 33

will not ?aim. . . . .
we go . . . .
lucy said Josephine

Chapter Two

London—spring 1889

Alex glanced over her shoulder as she tiptoed down the stairs of Waverton House. She held her hat and gloves, hoping she could stuff them behind a potted palm or one of the statues glaring down from their niches, if someone should see her. The enormous house was quiet—for the moment.

Her mother, the Duchess, was napping, her father was locked with his business managers in the library and her brother, Charles, was who knew where. He always left right after breakfast and returned in the dead of night, the lucky boy. Even the maids were quiet, their morning duties in the drawing room and music room finished and their evening tasks not yet begun.

Charlie could escape, but Alex was always

there, practising at the piano, waiting for callers, having fittings, listening to her mother list eligible suitors. None of them was department-store owners, no matter how rich, of course. She was being slowly smothered by it all, by the velvet curtains puddling on the Aubusson rugs, the silk walls, the portraits of all the Wavertons alive and dead staring down at her.

Having a Season was even more exhausting than she had feared—and more lonely. She was surrounded by people almost all the time, but she hardly ever saw her old friends from Miss Grantley's. That was why she was creeping down the stairs now.

Luckily, just as she was sure she would start screaming with it all, Emily's note had arrived, asking her to meet them for a Blues and Royals concert in Hyde Park. She hadn't seen Diana and Em except for balls and dinners, where they could only snatch a few whispers, in weeks. Surely a day with them, laughing in the fresh air, with no one around who knew or cared she was the Duke of Waverton's daughter, was just the respite she needed.

Unfortunately, just as she was almost to the bottom of the stairs and nearly free, the library door opened and her father and his business managers emerged. It was far too late to flee back up the stairs. She followed her original plan of shoving her hat behind a vase of ivy and ostrich feathers and tried to look casual.

She peeked down over the carved and gilded balustrade at her father. The Duke was as tall and grandly moustachioed as always, a formidable presence she had always been frightened of, especially after Scotland. But in that moment, when he thought himself alone, he seemed rather grey-faced and distracted. As the businessmen shuffled out, a blur of black suits, silvery pomaded hair and leather valises, the Duke glanced up and saw Alex there. He smiled wearily, no curiosity or scolding glint in his eyes, and she was glad it was him and not Mama who had seen her. He wouldn't notice she was wearing her new blue walking suit for a supposed afternoon at home.

'Hullo, my Flower,' he said. He used her old nickname, one he hadn't said much since she came back from school, but still he looked tired. Distant. 'What are you up to today?'

Alex thought fast. 'Just fetching my workbox from the morning room.' She paused, studying her father's strained expression. Had he heard she had sent money to her charities again and was unhappy about it? Her parents approved of benevolence on the part of a lady, but only to a point. A point not nearly far enough for her. Or maybe it really was business. Charlie had mentioned their father was thinking of selling his Scottish shooting box. 'Is everything quite all right?'

'Oh, yes, yes, just talking to my silly estate managers, nothing for you to think about.' He stepped closer to the staircase, reaching up to pat her hand where it rested on the balustrade. 'Tell me, Flower, how would you like to visit Paris?'

Alex felt a small leap of excitement in her stomach and smiled. 'For the Exhibition? Oh, I should love it! Everyone has been talking about nothing else lately. All that beautiful art...'

'Perhaps there will be a *bit* of art, of course, but mostly it would be an official visit. We have been asked by the Prince of Wales himself to be part of his visit to the city. And to loan the Eastern Star for an exhibition in the Indian Pavilion.'

Alex glanced at her mother's portrait at the head of the stairs, the Duchess in her blue-and-white satin Worth gown, the Eastern Star sapphire in her upswept hair. It was her mother's favourite jewel, a famous piece the Duke's father had brought back from India, bought from a maharajah under mysterious circumstances. 'Have you talked to Mama about that?' she asked doubtfully.

'Not yet. It was just presented to me as an idea.

And I think it is quite a fine one, as I'm sure will your mother.' He patted her hand again, staring up at her intently. 'There are so many people flocking to Paris right now. It could be a marvellous opportunity for you, Flower.'

Alex felt suddenly cold and wanted to snatch back her hand. 'Opportunity?'

'Yes. So many royal personages are there right now. You are so pretty, Alexandra, you would grace any royal court in the world. It would be a good connection for our family, could see you secure for your life.'

'I—I'm not sure I want to leave England, Papa.'

'And I would miss you! But with so many railroads these days, a visit to any corner of Europe would take no time at all.' His hand tightened on hers. 'We are Wavertons, you know, my dear. Our first duty is always what is best for the family.'

Alex knew that. She had *always* known that, ever since she was in leading strings. It had been hammered into her when she'd been separated from Malcolm. The Mannerlys had been in England since the eleven hundreds, had been dukes for centuries. Every generation had to make the family name stronger, bring it glory. It was their purpose. 'Of course.'

'You are a good daughter, Alexandra. We

only want the best, the *very* best, for you. Royal connections…'

'Do we not have royal connections? The Princess…'

'Your godmother has always been kind and her help will be invaluable to obtain the right introductions in Paris. I only want to ask you to make the very most of them. Seeing you well settled, and soon, would be the greatest comfort to your mother and me.'

Something in his voice, some edge of sharp desperation she had never heard there before, alarmed her. 'Papa, is something amiss?'

His smile widened, but it did not quite reach his eyes. 'Certainly not! I just wanted to tell you about Paris, Flower. It will be a splendid time.' He patted her hand once more and retreated back into his library, closing the door behind him.

Alex grabbed her hat and dashed down the stairs, unsettled by what had just happened, though she couldn't say why she would feel that way. It had been just a quick conversation with her father, him telling her what she had always known—she had to make a fine marriage. But it didn't feel like that was all it was.

She paused for just an instant in front of a silver-framed mirror to pin on her hat. She made a face at herself in the glass. Surely if she was not a duke's daughter, there would be no hope of her landing a prince and she wouldn't have to worry! She was small, too slender to look quite right in fashionable gowns, and pale, with large eyes in a pointed face and blonde curls that wouldn't stay in their pins. Not like Emily with her thick chestnut hair to her waist, or Diana and her auburn waves. With a sigh, she stabbed in her hat pins, drew the small net veil over her forehead and spun away from the glass.

Before anyone could stop her, she ran out to the lane just beyond the park and hailed a hansom cab. Maybe it was finally having the chance to see her friends again, but she felt a bit of a rebellious streak coming on, a restlessness. She dared not take a deep breath until the carriage door shut behind her and they rolled into traffic, leaving Waverton House behind.

She laughed, feeling free, though she knew she had to make the very most of it. If her parents had their way, she would be packed off to some German duchy forthwith.

Alex shuddered at the thought. She stared out the grimy window at the streets flashing past, the crowds, the carriages, the bright gleam of shop windows. It wasn't that she would mind seeing the world beyond London; in fact, it would be fascinating. She was excited to be going to Paris, whatever the reason. In between official engagements, there would surely be time to see some museums, shops, the wonders of the Exhibition, like the Eiffel Tower and Mr Edison's electric lights. Maybe even the Wild West Show!

Yet she had met princes and duchesses from Germany and Austria. If she felt smothered by life as the daughter of an English duke, that was ten times worse. The etiquette that ruled every movement in a German court, oversaw every moment, would never go away. How would it feel to be trapped in such a world for the rest of her life?

Neither, though, could she bear to think about letting her family down. Since the nursery, she had been taught that the good of the family was paramount. They had been dukes since the time of Queen Anne, devoted to royal service and rewarded for that devotion in turn. The Wavertons had one of the most respected titles in the kingdom.

But also ever since the nursery she had been plagued with a shyness, an overpowering desire to disappear into the background, that made that duty a blasted hard one! She had always known she would have to marry one day, but why did it have to be to some German prince?

'Ugh!' she groaned aloud. The very thought made her want to run away immediately to live alone in a hut on some snowy mountainside, if such a place could be found.

But she had no more time to think about her limited options as the hansom stopped at the gates of the park and she glimpsed her friends waiting. Diana had her sketchbook out, no doubt studying the ladies' hats, and Emily and Christopher Blakely, Alex's cousin and their not-very-strict-at-all chaperon, were arguing about something, as they usually did when they met. Chris was Alex's favourite relative, always so light-hearted, so quick with a laugh, so handsome with his blond hair so like her own, but somehow much smoother and lovelier. She couldn't understand why he and Em always seemed to be at odds.

'Alexandra, there you are!' Emily called as Alex stepped down from the carriage. 'We'd almost given up on you.'

'I'm so sorry I'm late,' Alex said. 'I'm afraid my father caught me as I was trying to sneak out and insisted on talking to me.'

'I *am* sorry, old bean,' Chris said as he kissed her cheek. 'A ducal lecture must be tiresome indeed. My own fa's are bad enough.'

'It wasn't a lecture, exactly,' Alex said. She considered sharing her concerns, but then decided not to. She didn't want to spoil the sunny afternoon. 'In fact, it was rather nice—we're going to Paris, it seems.'

'Oh, Paris!' Diana sighed as she tucked away her sketchbook. 'How heavenly. You are so lucky, Alex.'

'Maybe I'll see you there,' Emily said. 'Father wants to expand the business to Paris and I've been trying to persuade him to let me go there. We have to compete with Gordston's!'

Chris offered Alex his arm and they followed Diana and Emily as they joined the flow of people headed towards the bandstand. It was indeed a glorious spring day, the trees bursting into pale green, the flowerbeds bright with yellow-and-red blossoms, the crowds in their finest as they flocked to listen to the merry band music. How different it was from the people she saw at the round of parties and in her parents' drawing room! It was all so fascinating, so full of wonderful, vivid life.

'How is William?' she asked Chris. His brother, William—now *Sir* William—Blakely, had been working with the Foreign Office in India and was due home any day. Will, unlike Chris, had always frightened her just a bit. He was always kind to her, but so very darkly handsome, so solemn and businesslike and strong, he intimidated her.

'He's home now and promised to be at your

grand ball next week,' Chris said. 'But they already have him working all hours and, really, who can blame him for wanting to escape our parents as much as possible.'

Alex groaned. 'He has my sympathies.' Her aunt, her mother's sister, and her husband had not been happy for years. Her uncle tended to be loud and overbearing to get his points across and her aunt silent and passive. It was not a happy example of marriage, which was yet another reason Alex grew frightened when her parents pressed so for her to marry soon. 'I can't wait to see Will again, but tell him he absolutely doesn't have to come to the ball. It will be a dreadful crush, no fun at all.'

'*Fun* doesn't seem a concern to Will. Just work, work, work, that's all he thinks about.'

Alex laughed and nudged him with her elbow. 'Unlike his brother.'

Chris put on a stern expression, making her laugh even more. 'Someone has to maintain the family presence in society, Alexandra.'

'Yes, and you do that very well. Your name is always in the gossip pages.' The crowd grew thicker as they came closer to the bandstand, people pressing in on every side. Alex's hat was knocked loose from a pin and she clutched at it as she tried to hold on to Chris.

'I see some places closer to the front!' Emily called. Alex tried to follow her, to keep Em's large, pink-feathered hat in view, but the knots of people gathered around her ever tighter and tighter. Her arm slipped out of Chris's and she desperately reached out for him, but like Em he slipped away. She was alone, drowning in a sea of strangers.

She felt so cold, so stricken with a sudden giddy rush of panic that she wanted to scream. Her hat was almost knocked off her head and, as she grabbed at it, someone ran into her from behind, making her stumble. The people in front of her moved as she tumbled into them, but that left a patch of gravel clear for her to fall towards it.

Time seemed to slow down, to freeze with the fear, and her hands shot out to catch herself. She braced herself for the jolt of pain.

Before she could land, someone seized her around the waist and lifted her up—up and up, off the ground entirely. Everything around her spun like a stained-glass window, the green trees, the yellow flowers, the reds and blues and browns of the ladies' hats, all blurred together. Alex couldn't catch her breath.

When she finally landed on her feet again, clutching at her hat, she found herself facing the most astonishing man she had ever seen. For one giddy instant, she wondered if she had indeed hit her head and landed in a book of Norse sagas.

He was very tall, so tall he blotted out the sunlight, and was a silhouette haloed in its golden glow. His shoulders were so broad under the perfect cut of his fine hunter-green wool coat, and his hair, falling to an unfashionably long length from beneath his stiff-crowned silk hat, was a glorious red-gold colour. His nose was slightly crooked, as if it had once been broken and healed badly, but that didn't diminish from his sharp-cut cheekbones, his square jaw. He stared down at her from eyes so icy and pale blue they glowed.

She tottered on her feet, disorientated, and he held on to her by her waist, most improper. Most—interesting. He frowned—in concern, or irritation?—as he looked down at her. 'Are you injured, miss?' he asked, his voice deep and rich, touched with a Scots burr that made him seem even more otherworldly.

He reminded her of something, but what? It was just there, just beyond the edges of her mind, but it kept slipping away. Maybe she had dreamed of him once or something, he seemed quite unreal.

'I—I...' she gasped, feeling foolish, as she seemed to have forgotten all words.

'You can't breathe, it's no wonder, all these

glaikit people everywhere,' he said. 'Eh!' he shouted. 'Everyone move and give a lady some space to breathe.'

The crowd immediately cleared around them, of course. Who wouldn't, at the sound of such a voice? That brogue, so full of authority and menace, as if Hyde Park was a battlefield. Thor with a Scots accent. It almost made her want to giggle and she wondered if she was getting hysterical.

'Let's find you a place to sit down,' he said, gently taking her arm. His hand, ungloved, felt warm and steady, something to depend on in a dizzy world.

'My friends...' she said, suddenly remembering Emily and Diana. Where had they vanished? She glanced over her shoulder, but couldn't see them anywhere. The crowd had closed behind her again.

'We'll find them in just a wee,' he said. Her gaze was drawn to his lips, strangely sensual and soft for such a hard man. He frowned as if he was concerned. 'You look very pale.'

'I do feel a bit—startled,' Alex admitted. He led her gently to a bench under the shade of a tree, somewhat away from the crowded paths. The bench's inhabitants moved after a stern glare from Thor and he helped Alex sit down.

'I don't think I was expecting quite so many people here today.'

'Ach, a sunny day, a bit of free music, enough to turn things into a stampede ground in this *aidle* city. Let me fetch you something cool to drink.'

Before Alex could protest, he turned and strode quickly, long-legged, towards a stand selling ginger beer. She drew in a deep breath, trying to steady herself after the last few astonishing minutes. Surely she hadn't felt quite so much excitement in—well, ever! She had been so sure her life would never change, that she would smother in her parents' house, and now she had fallen and been nearly trampled, and then rescued by a Norse god who used the oddest words. No wonder she felt dizzy.

She craned her neck to study her rescuer as he waited in the refreshment line. He certainly *was* handsome. She was sure she had never seen him before, or anyone quite like him. He was so tall, so powerful-looking, so golden-amber, he looked nothing like the young men she danced with every evening, sat next to at dinner and listened to them talk about cricket. She was quite sure Thor never talked about cricket, or if he did she didn't want to know about it and spoil the fantasy she was indulging in.

He did wear the finest, most fashionable clothes, his sack coat of dark green wool with velvet lapels perfectly tailored, a gold watch chain over a luxurious ivory brocade waistcoat, boots polished to a gleam, and he seemed perfectly comfortable in them. Yet something about him made the finery seem a bit incongruous, like it wasn't his favourite attire. She could see him striding across the moor in shirtsleeves and tweed trousers, high boots, his hair shining in the sun.

Yes, he definitely didn't seem like he belonged in the city. The—what was it he called it? *Aidle* city.

He came back with a glass of the ginger beer and Alex sipped at it gratefully. Its tart coolness, fizzy on her tongue, seemed to steady her.

'Thank you,' she said, hardly daring to look at him for fear she would be dazzled witless again. 'You have been very kind. I feel so foolish.'

'Not at all,' he answered in his rough, warm voice. 'Anyone would want to faint in such a crowd. I would never have walked this way today if I had known.'

'So you aren't here to listen to the music?'

'I was on my way to work. I like to walk on fine days.'

Alex was dying of curiosity to know what he

did for work, but she wasn't sure it was entirely polite to ask. Aside from her uncle and cousin Will, both at the Foreign Office, she really had no relative who had work they *went* to. She decided he must be a poet, or maybe a spy. No, a royal Stuart, come to claim his throne! It was surely something terribly dashing and romantic.

She felt her hat slip again from its pins and pulled it entirely off, leaving soft curls of her hair to fall free against her neck and temples. She stared ruefully down at the bit of millinery, the scrap of blue velvet and net, now quite bedraggled. 'I'm afraid it's ruined.'

He studied the hat in her gloved hands with a small frown, his head tilted. He smelled heavenly as he leaned closer, like a green, summery forest. 'That shape is out of fashion, anyway. You need something with a larger brim, maybe with a scoop here over the eye, with a cluster of feathers. The colour is good, though, especially with your eyes.'

Alex gave a startled laugh. 'You know about ladies' hats, then, sir?'

He sat back on the bench beside her, his arms crossed over his chest. 'It's my job.'

He worked in *millinery*? Alex could hardly have been more astonished if he said he was just about to jump to the moon. It seemed so—

strange. He was surely the most masculine man she had ever encountered, so full of quiet confidence and strength.

'What do you think of my walking suit, then?' she asked, sitting up straighter and grinning at him, startled by her sudden boldness. It was very unlike her. Usually, she just tried to blend into the woodwork. 'Am I terribly out of fashion?'

He studied her carefully, those ice-blue eyes intent on only her, and she was almost sorry she had asked. She felt so hot and flustered under his gaze, and was sure her cheeks had gone bright red. She quickly gulped down the last of her drink.

'The colour is also good,' he answered. 'And the cut. Its fine cloth and the velvet and silk go well together. But the trim is all wrong. A fur collar would be just right, or some gilded embroidery, like Princess Alexandra wears now.'

'Princess Alexandra?' Alex said, thinking of her godmother, who was indeed always perfectly dressed.

'Everyone follows what she wears.'

'Yes, I know. She's always very elegant. But I don't look much like her. Would her style suit me?'

He studied her carefully, from her disarranged hair to the tips of her kid walking boots, and Alex had to look away. To will her heart to beat slower. 'Your colouring is different from the Princess, of course, but you have the same delicacy. The same—distance.'

Alex didn't feel 'distant' from him at all. She felt much, much too close. 'Distance?'

His icy eyes narrowed. 'Like you're not of this world. My old nanna, my grandmother, would have said you were a fairy queen of winter.'

'Of winter?' Alex asked, intrigued.

'Aye. All pale and delicate outside, full of icy storms, curses and danger inside.'

She laughed. 'I think I'm the least dangerous person there is.'

He shook his head. 'I shouldn't contradict a female—but I think you're wrong. You're definitely of the winter fairy folk.'

She didn't know how to admit that sitting here with him on this bench was by far the bravest thing she had ever done. She rather liked imagining being of the fairy folk, able to do as she liked when she liked. Just as she enjoyed thinking of him as a god of the Norse country. It all took her out of her dutiful life, the life where she was never quite right, never quite enough, for a moment. It took her out of the ordinary day, out of being Lady Alexandra.

'I will have to buy a new hat immediately,

then,' she said. 'A winter fairy can't go around being dowdy. What would you suggest? Something like that? She looks in the stylish way.' She gestured at a passing lady, who wore a gown of purple-and-cream-striped silk that was improbably close-fitting and an enormous cartwheel of a hat laden with fruit.

He didn't even glance at her, just kept watching Alex, something seeming to sharpen in his eyes. He didn't move closer, but it suddenly felt as if he had, as if his heat and strength surrounded her. 'I could buy you the most fashionable hat you've ever seen, if you would have supper with me tonight at the Criterion.'

And the light-hearted moment shifted, like a grey cloud shifting in front of the sun. Alex sat up straighter, shivering. Even she knew about the Criterion. It was luxurious, all satin-wrapped and filled with French champagne, with private dining rooms where gentlemen took their actress and opera-dancer friends. She heard whispers about it all at balls and teas, quickly quieted when she came near. This gorgeous man thought she was an—an *actress*?

She felt outraged and wanted to laugh, all at the same time.

'You—you think…' she gasped.

She could see immediately that he realised his

mistake. Once again, he did not seem to physically move, yet he was very far away from her. He took off his hat and ran his hand through his amber hair. 'Forgive me. I should never have assumed...'

'You assumed because I was alone for a moment, I am a woman of—loose morals?' she whispered, still unsure what she was feeling. Embarrassment, yes, burning hot, but also filled with a strange, hysterical mirth. And disappointment, that her brief dream with this handsome man was gone so quickly. 'I assure you I am not. I didn't realise your kindness was based on such a notion.' She quickly rose to her feet, glad she was steady now.

He stood up beside her and she instinctively stepped back. 'Of course not,' he said, his accent even heavier. 'It is just that you're so—so...'

'So?' So bold, so outrageous, so—not herself?

'Beautiful,' he blurted out.

Alex felt her face turn even hotter. He thought her *beautiful*? Just her, Alex, not the Duke's daughter? 'I must go!'

'Let me help you find your friends.'

'No!' she cried. She was tempted to stay right there, standing with him, so she knew she had to run. She spun around and dashed away, not daring to look back. She lost herself in the crowd, hearing the brassy strains of music, of the laughter in the air. It all made her feel even more as if she was caught in a dream, where nothing in her real life existed any longer.

It was only when she heard Chris calling her name that she realised she had dropped her hat. She glanced back, hoping to see her rescuer, no matter how improper he was. And that was when it struck her, where she had seen him before. Not in her dreams. Oh, she was such a *fool* not have known him immediately!

He was Malcolm, her Malcolm. The sweet, handsome boy who had once taught her to fish. Yet there was no trace of that lad in him any more. Now he was the owner of Gordston's Department Store, he had become arrogant, so sure everything belonged to him, just like the beautiful women he was with in the newspapers.

She thought she would drown in memories, the humiliation she felt when they parted. How had she ever considered him her friend? He never had been and he truly was not now. They were worlds apart.

But she still wanted to cry when she remembered the sweetness of what once was, even if it was all just a girlish dream.

'*Dobber!*' Malcolm Gordston muttered as he watched the winter fairy disappear into the crowd. He sat back heavily on the bench, wishing he could slap himself. He had indeed been a first-class fool. Anyone with eyes should have seen right away that she was a lady. Probably even one with a capital L. Her refinement, her voice, her clothes, so finely made and yet subtle, her gentleness—aye, it all said lady, loud and clear.

And yet the moment he had touched her, he had been overcome by a wave of longing like he had never known before. A need for her softness, her sweetness. It wasn't like him at all, the tough offspring of a crofter on the Duke of Waverton's Scottish shooting estate, longing for a delicate fairy. He had worked his way up from a ghillie's muddy son to being one of the richest men in England and not by giving in to any longing for softness and refinement.

Nor had he done it by being ignorant of human nature. He'd learned how to read every nuance of people, to know what they desired before even they could see it and then provide it—for a price. Men and women, they were far more transparent in their wants, needs and deepest fears than they realised. It was his key to never going back to his miserable childhood, where one man was ruined at the mere whim of another.

It was his most invaluable tool in his professional life and in his limited personal time, as well. He liked women, liked the way their minds worked in such subtle, slippery, fascinating ways, so much more complex than most men, shrewder, sharper. Like him, they had to make their way up in a world not designed for them, through back doors. And in return, they seemed to like him, too. Female company was not hard to find.

But all his judgement seemed to have fled when he looked into a pair of heather-coloured eyes. Fairy eyes indeed, so large in her pale, pointed fey face, changeable blue-purple-green, set off by feathery, sooty lashes. He had never seen anyone quite like her. So small and delicate, pale curls escaping from that terrible hat, the silvery, unexpected sound of her sudden laughter. The way she felt under his touch, so light and frail, trembling as if she would sprout sparkling wings and fly away at any moment.

He was enchanted, in a fairy-story sense of the word, taken out of himself. And fairies were dangerous creatures. Always flying away as soon as you touched them. Always putting a curse on your home.

When he was a wee lad, after his mother died and his father went off drinking every night, his nanna would make him supper and tell him tales of the fairies, the winter and summer folk. When he held the lady's hand in his, smelled her light, pale green lily-of-the-valley perfume, he whimsically wondered if he was seeing the pale winter queen set down in Hyde Park.

And he was never a man to be whimsical. He had learned that from his childhood. Never leave your heart open. Never be helpless.

It had made him take a foolish misstep, a rare misjudgement of a person. He had wanted her so much, he made himself believe she was available when she so clearly was not. He had a solid rule in romance—never dabble with an innocent. There was only pain and confusion in that for everyone involved. He stayed with women like himself, who knew the rules of engagement. He had built his life up by hard work to exactly where he wanted it. He wouldn't let anything tear it down now. And he knew very well a woman like that was not for the likes of a Gordston.

But, just for a moment, as he sat beside her and watched her smile, he almost would have been willing to watch his kingdom burn down.

Surely it was a lucky thing she had run away. It just didn't feel so lucky yet.

Malcolm laughed again and put his hat back on before he made his way through the crowd towards the park gates. As usual, because of his height and the long, quick stride he needed to get where he was going fast, the knots of people unravelled before him. He rarely noticed it any longer; his mind was always on the next task, the next new idea. Yet today, he scanned the bright crowd, looking for a pale woman in blue. She wasn't there, of course, yet he couldn't seem to stop himself.

At last he left the park and being on the clatter of the streets was like waking up to himself. There was work to be done. There was *always* work to be done.

Gordston's Department Store was busy, as usual. Malcolm dashed up the marble front steps and through the gleam of the revolving doors into the lobby. Black-and-white stone floors were waiting, the gleam of glass counters, displaying every temptation from kid gloves to crystal perfume bottles to Belgian chocolates, beckoned. The salespeople greeted him with smiles, the customers with curious glances, but he saw none of it today.

He took his own lift straight to the offices on the top floor. It was a different world from the shimmer and perfume of the sales floors, still luxurious with dark-panelled walls and thick Persian carpets underfoot, but with the buzz of low voices and tap of typewriters rather than laughter and the murmur of fountains. The air smelled of paper and ink instead of rose scent and violet powder. The buzz of efficiency and commerce, his forte.

He went to his own office at the end of the corridor and had only a moment to drape his coat and hat on the rack before his secretary, Miss Mersey, appeared. Like everyone else on the top floor, she was efficiency itself in her white shirtwaist and black skirt, her greying hair pinned atop her head, her spectacles in place on her stern nose. She had been with him almost since he opened the store and he could not do without her.

'Good morning, Mr Gordston,' she said, snapping open her notebook. 'Mr Jones has yesterday's sales figures almost ready for you from the accounting office.'

'Almost?' Malcolm said as he sat down behind his desk. It was all in order, the stacks of reports where they were meant to be, his gold pen and blotter lined up.

'It seems there was a small discrepancy with the glove counter, which is being sorted out. I have the travel arrangements finished for Paris, as well. The repairs to the yacht will be finished by Friday, so everything is quite on schedule. The latest reports from Monsieur Jerome's architecture office are on your desk, as you see. The store will be finished on time and you will be able to depart for the grand opening as planned.'

'You mean *we* will be able to depart.'

For once, a tiny gleam of interest pierced Miss Mersey's admirably steely exterior. 'We, Mr Gordston?'

'Of course. I could never manage my business in Paris without you.'

'But the store here…'

'Mr Jones will be perfectly able to oversee things for a few weeks. If you can bear to tear yourself away for a time by the Seine. Maybe dine in a café or two, a new hat…'

Miss Mersey's brow arched over her spectacles. 'I think I could bear that, Mr Gordston, for the sake of my employment.'

'Certainly. Now, Miss Mersey, about the new shipment of muslins from India…'

Once all the morning business was concluded, Miss Mersey closed her notebook and turned to leave, a stack of letters in her hand to be typewritten.

'Miss Mersey,' he called impulsively.

'Mr Gordston?'

'Do you happen to know of a customer who is a young lady, very petite, with pale blonde hair? Terrible taste in hats?'

Miss Mersey tapped her pencil thoughtfully on her notebook's leather cover. She had a prodigious memory, almost as good as Malcolm's own, and could remember every detail of every regular customer, their orders and perfumes and likes and dislikes. But that description was probably too vague even for her. 'There is Miss Petersham. She is blonde and ordered that odd parrot hat last month. Or Lady Minnie Grant? Mrs Gibson?'

Malcolm shook his head. He knew all those ladies and none of them was his fairy. 'If she's been in, I doubt she's a regular.'

Miss Mersey's brows went even higher. 'She, Mr Gordston?'

'Just someone I met in the park. I was—curious.'

'Curious, Mr Gordston?'

He tossed down his pen. 'Yes. That's all, Miss Mersey, thank you.'

'Of course. Oh, I almost forgot. This came for you. An invitation to Lady Cannon's garden party.'

Malcolm glanced down at the engraved card she handed him. 'How boring.'

'Just so. But it's one of the most sought-after events of the Season and Lady Cannon is a very good customer. Perhaps just a tiny little short appearance?'

He knew she was right and gave a brusque nod. 'Just a tiny one.'

Miss Mersey gave a delicate little cough. 'About the lady—I could make enquiries among the staff? Maybe they have noticed her.'

'No,' he snapped irritably, because what he really wanted to do was shout *Yes, of course, find her!* And that would be a mistake. 'Thank you, Miss Mersey.'

She sniffed and spun around to leave the office, the door clicking shut behind her. No matter how miffed she was, she would never *slam*. Malcolm reached for the architect's drawings of the Paris store and tried to concentrate on the important business at hand, expanding Gordston's on to the Continent.

Yet he couldn't quite get a pair of wide, heather-coloured eyes out of his mind.

Chapter Three

'Alexandra! Aren't you ready yet? We will be terribly late,' Alex's mother called from the dressing room doorway.

Alex studied her mother's reflection in the mirror as her maid put the finishing touches on her hair. The Duchess was tugging on her gloves, straightening her hat, as impeccably dressed as usual in a green-and-white-striped gown, pearls and amethysts in her ears, blonde hair barely touched with silver. Tall, statuesque, exactly what a duchess should be. Alex knew her own tiny, delicate looks had always been something of a puzzle to her mother.

Just like now. The Duchess tilted her head as she studied Alex's coiffure, her pale blue watered-silk dress. 'Oh, that's quite nice, Mary. You've done wonders with Lady Alexandra's hair.'

'Thank you, Your Grace,' Mary said, stabbing another pearl-headed pin into Alex's ruthlessly smoothed-down curls. Alex could still feel the sizzle from the hair tongs.

'I know such things take time, but we mustn't be late,' the Duchess said.

'I thought that was what you wanted, Mama,' Alex said. 'To be the last to arrive and make a grand entrance at the top of Lady Cannon's garden terrace.'

'Don't be ridiculous, Alexandra, we would never be so rude.' Her mother tsked. 'But to be seen is never a bad thing, of course. I have heard that a French *comte* will be in attendance! A French title is never optimum, they've become so sadly republican, but they do always sound so lovely.'

Alex cringed inside. Her parents were showing ever more eagerness to marry her off and it was keeping her awake at night worrying. Her grand debut ball was still several days away, her Season young. It made her nervous to wonder why there was such hurry.

Mary carefully placed her hat, a pale blue tricorn trimmed with white bows, on her hair and pinned it tight. Diana had assured her it was the latest fashion and Alex had to admit it *was* pretty.

It made her remember her sadly crushed dark

blue hat last month, dismissed by the most handsome, intriguing man she had ever seen. The man who had once been her Scottish Malcolm. Those fjord-icy eyes, that voice! Like something in a novel. Even though he had thought her a woman of loose character, she couldn't quite stop thinking about him. What had happened to him to make him change so terribly?

She sighed to remember him, her Thor, suddenly feeling a little pang that her life would take her in a different direction.

She reached for her gloves and reticule, and felt the weight of the book she had hidden there, just in case. She knew she wouldn't be able to hide away and read a few pages. Her mother would be watching her like a hawk.

She followed the Duchess out to the waiting carriage. At least it was a fine day for a garden party, she thought, as she arranged her skirts on the velvet-cushioned seat. The warm days had helped clear some of the miasma of coal smoke clinging to the rooftops and the sky was a lovely soft turquoise. She knew Lady Cannon's famous garden would be looking its finest—if only she could be free to explore it.

As her mother listed who was to be in attendance at the party, who Alex should speak to at length and who to show mere politeness, Alex

studied the streets outside the carriage window.
The allure of the bookseller's window, with its
rows of new volumes, the glow of silk ribbons
at the modiste, the lush purple violets and pure
white carnations at a flower stall. When they
passed the gates to the park, she thought of Thor
again. The way he caught her before she fell,
holding her so close, closer than she had ever
been to a man, the warm, green summer scent
of him. His smile, so unexpectedly sweet in his
harsh, handsome face. Why couldn't he still be
the man she remembered? Why did she still want
to be near him, despite everything?

What would it be like, she wondered, to be a
truly wicked woman? To do as she liked without a thought to what people would think. She
sometimes had daydreams about skipping right
over marriage to independent widowhood. Her
own house, time that was all her own. Was that
the same as being wicked?

'Alexandra, are you listening to me?' her
mother demanded.

'Of course, Mama,' Alex murmured. She wondered what her mother would think of Thor and
his outrageous assumptions. It was fascinating
to imagine. She turned to smile brightly at her
mother, who frowned quizzically in return.

'You are always so distracted, my dear,' the

Duchess said. 'It is so important that you pay close attention at such soirées. Everyone will be watching you, you are a duke's daughter, meant to lead society. Every time you speak to someone it means so much. It must be correct.'

'I know, Mama,' she said. Good heavens, but she knew! 'I will not disappoint you.' She hoped. Disappointment was all she seemed to bring her family sometimes.

Her mother sighed. 'I know you will not. It's just that your father and I want so much for your happiness. With the right marriage, you could do so much. Use your advantages.'

Alex wondered if her mother had somehow sensed her dreams of independent widowhood. 'I want that, too.'

Her mother frowned. 'I did wonder if sending you to school was the right thing. No Waverton daughter had ever been educated outside of home. But you were such a shy child, so dreamy. Your father was sure making friends your own age would do you good.'

'And Miss Grantley's *was* good for me!' Alex hastened to assure her, as she always had when her mother expressed her doubts about the school.

The Duchess still looked uncertain, but the carriage had rolled to a stop in front of the Cannons' house, and she couldn't say more.

* * *

'Mr Gordston! How perfectly charming to see you again,' Lady Smythe-Tomas said, holding out her hand to be kissed. 'I'm so glad you did not miss Lady Cannon's garden party, it's always so amusing.'

Malcolm smiled at her and bowed over the fine pale lavender kid glove he knew had come from Gordston's own glove counter. Lady S.-T. was one of his best customers, and the first besides their hostess to greet him at the painfully genteel garden party. Not that there had been any lack of attention. Everyone stared, thinking themselves hidden behind teacups and parasols.

He glanced around at the groups gathered on the terrace, taking tea at small wrought-iron tables under the trees, strolling the flower-lined pathways. They all looked elegant, stylish in pastel gowns and feathered hats he could value to the shilling, smelling of attar of roses, smiling discreetly. A completely different world from the cold, harsh one he had known growing up.

It all made him think of the winter fairy, of her soft smile, her gentle touch. He had thought of her so often since their too-brief, too-embarrassing meeting, and he felt even more foolish than ever that he could have considered her less than a perfect lady. Everything about her had breathed gentleness and innocence, a castle tower high above the coal-streaked world. Just like this garden.

Lady S.-T. tapped his arm, bringing him back into that real world. She smiled up at him from beneath her wide-brimmed, lilac-trimmed hat. She was a widow of great fortune and whispered reputation, one of the great beauties of society with her masses of auburn hair and cat-like green eyes, her photograph displayed in shop windows along with Daisy Warwick and Princess Alexandra. Only a few people, like Malcolm, knew that slightly scandalous society lady was only a front for her work at the Foreign Office, for he sometimes passed on a titbit or two she might find useful. She was a great friend, someone whose company he much enjoyed—yet even her great beauty couldn't quite distract him from the pale fairy.

'Lady Cannon was quite naughty to invite you without telling me about it,' Lady Smythe-Tomas said. 'I would have so enjoyed being here early, to watch the stir your arrival no doubt created.'

Malcolm laughed. There had indeed been something of a 'stir' when he first stepped out of the French doors on to the terrace, a ripple of silence across the lush flowerbeds. 'I'm not sure why she sent the card. Miss Mersey insisted I accept.'

'Ah, the excellent Miss Mersey. She was quite right. You want as much publicity as possible for your new Paris venture. That was surely why Lady Cannon invited you. Everyone is astir with all things Paris now.'

'Including your own office?' Malcolm asked quietly.

Lady S.-T. tapped her gloved fingertip on her dimpled chin. 'I may be crossing the Channel very soon, yes. Strange things seem to be afoot along the Seine. Perhaps I will call on you at your new store?'

'You are always welcome.'

'You know what must happen if I do. I must seem utterly empty in the pocketbook.' She took his arm and led him down the terrace steps on to one of the gravel pathways. She nodded and waved to various acquaintances. 'In the meantime, I must show you who is who, though no doubt you already know! They all shop at Gordston's. Lady Amberson and Mrs Downley. Now, those hats could have come from nowhere else than your own milliner. Miss Chumleigh— now *she* could use a trip to your underpinnings department, such unfortunate posture. The Viscount Hexham over there, and Mrs Browne, his mistress, though they think they are terribly discreet. And Mr Evansley over there, though I do wonder why Lady Cannon would invite him. We should watch out for him. I have been tasked with keeping an eye on him most carefully.'

Malcolm studied the man she indicated. He looked quite inoffensive, small and pale with thinning blond hair, obviously thrilled to be there among the cream of society. 'Why is that?'

'I can't quite say yet, of course, but he has been known to associate with Mr Nixson. We don't know yet how deeply involved he might be in the business. Did you not refuse to get involved with that scheme not long ago?' she answered.

Nixson. Malcolm frowned to remember when the man had come to him to propose a business deal—one that was entirely illegal, not to mention immoral. Of course he had turned him down. But who knew who among society wouldn't be so wise to know what the man was about?

'But oh, look!' Lady S.-T. said happily. 'There is Christopher Blakely, how utterly charming. I was rather good friends with his brother, Sir William. We should say hello.'

She took Malcolm's arm and led him across the garden to greet Mr Blakely. As he and Lady S.-T. happily chatted, Malcolm studied the crowd around them, nodding to acquaintances, smiling at people who frowned at him, obviously wondering how he had been allowed into the party.

Then his attention was caught by some newcomers who appeared on the terrace with their hostess. A stately lady in a striped gown, with a younger lady behind her, small and delicate in pale blue, smiling politely. *The winter fairy.*

'Ah, the Duchess of Waverton,' Lady Smythe-Tomas murmured. 'I'm sure you've heard of the family? Too high in the instep for the scandalous Marlborough House set, though Her Grace has deigned to talk to me once or twice. It's a good thing, as they possess the Eastern Star sapphire, which would be a helpful decoy in Paris.'

Malcolm watched Lady Alexandra, his winter fairy who now had a name—and was a duke's daughter. Not just any duke's daughter, but Waverton's, the man who had once ruined his family. The sweet girl who had once sat beside him near the river. The one whose innocence he would have done anything to protect. Now she was here, right in front of him.

She was smiling and nodding as Lady Cannon greeted them, but she seemed strangely far away. 'A sapphire is involved in your plans?'

'Bait for a villain, of course. Luckily, the Duchess's nose is so far in the air she can't see her husband's business affairs dissolving right in front of her.' Lady S.-T. tilted her head, watching as the Duchess nodded to Lady Cannon. She drew her daughter forward and Alexandra looked startled for a moment before her smile was in place again. 'And that must be the daughter. They say the Wavertons have high hopes for her. She's very unusual-looking, isn't she? A bit rabbity and pale, maybe, but nothing the right clothes couldn't fix in a trice.'

'Pale and rabbity?' Malcolm scoffed. 'Fair, perhaps, but those eyes could never belong to a rabbit.'

Lady S.-T. gave him a long, considering glance. 'How can anyone see her eyes from here? But now I am most curious. Little debs aren't usually your style. Come, let's go greet them.'

Malcolm remembered all too well how his first encounter in the park with Lady Alexandra had ended. She certainly wouldn't want to see him now. 'Laura, don't be daft. No duchess wants to meet a shopkeeper.'

'You are no mere shopkeeper. You are Malcolm Gordston, one of the richest men in London, keeper of the treasures of Gordston's Department Store, where even the queen has bought a few things. Even a little rabbit is sure to be intrigued by that. And this party is too dull by half. Come along.'

She took his arm and pulled him along the path, back towards the terrace. He wasn't entirely reluctant to go with her. Or, if he was honest with himself, as he always was, not reluctant at all. Surely he couldn't embarrass Lady Alexandra so much when she was surrounded by her family and friends. And he was curious to know how it would feel to touch her hand again. Just for a moment.

Alexandra smiled at Lady Cannon, half-listening as her mother exchanged pleasantries with their hostess. She studied the garden, the crowd gathered there, arranged like a bright painting of an idyllic day. The Cannons' annual garden party was famous, for they had what was easily the largest private garden in town, and they always seemed to find the loveliest spring day to show it off.

Surrounded by a towering box hedge, thick enough to keep the noisy streets at bay, the flowerbeds overflowed with white, purple, golden-yellow, pink, crimson, as bright as the gowns of the fashionable ladies who exclaimed over them. Classical statues, white and impassive, gazed down at it all as if unimpressed.

A buffet tea was laid out in the small, pillared temple, a tempting array of dainty sandwiches and sugar-art cakes, which people nibbled on at small tables in the shade. Parasols twirled, laughter echoed against the soft music of a string quartet tucked into an arbour and Lady Cannon's little spaniels barked.

It was all most elegant and Alex wished she could explore it all. Could dash down the paths in search of her friends and whisper with them all day on one of the shady benches. But she knew she could not. She was on duty.

'How excited you must be about Paris, Lady Alexandra,' Lady Cannon said, drawing Alex's attention back to that duty.

'Oh, yes. It all sounds very agreeable,' Alex murmured.

'And so intriguing, with the Exposition going on!' Lady Cannon sighed. 'So many things to see from all over the world. I have told Lord Cannon we must go, but not until I have replenished my wardrobe. The styles are always so different in Paris.'

'Different, perhaps, but certainly not better,' the Duchess sniffed. 'I have seen the latest fashion papers and the new sleeves are quite immodest. All those frills and bows.'

'Oh, I don't know,' Lady Cannon said wistfully. 'They rather remind me of when I was a girl and sleeves really *meant* something in fashion. Oh, look, here is someone who is certain to know all the latest style news from France! Mr Gordston.'

Alex froze, certain she'd turned into a pillar of ice. Mr Gordston was here. Her Malcolm, who once she cared about so much and who had hurt her.

The icy shock quickly turned to burning embarrassment and she was sure her face was the colour of an apple. Oh, why couldn't the terrace be a magical one, the stone opening beneath her feet to swallow her up? She wondered wildly if she had time to flee, but she did not. Lady Smythe-Tomas, who held Mr Gordston's arm, waved at them with a merry smile and steered him inexorably towards the terrace steps.

It was the sight of Lady S.-T. as his companion that brought the icy feeling back again. She seemed exactly the sort of lady who belonged with a man like that, a lady who was everything Alex wasn't. A sophisticated widow, beautiful, witty, stylish, famous even. Free. Alex had looked at her images in the fashion papers, elegant portraits, group photographs of royal house parties, Lady S.-T. dancing, riding to hounds,

playing lawn tennis, and Alex had secretly envied her.

Not quite as much as she envied her right now,
though, as Lady S.-T. whispered something into
Mr Gordston's ear, which she could do because
she was also wretchedly tall, and he laughed.

'You invited Mr Gordston to your garden
party?' the Duchess murmured to Lady Cannon.

Lady Cannon's cheeks turned bright pink.
'Well—my husband asked me to, Your Grace.
They do say even the Prince of Wales has received him, privately, of course. And he does
add a certain—decorative flair, don't you think?'

Oh, yes, Alex *did* think so. Here in the calm of
the quiet garden, away from the pressing crowds
of Hyde Park, she had a moment to really study
him. She'd wondered, in her daydreams of him,
if his attraction would fade if she saw him again.
If it was only the unusual circumstances of their
meeting that made him so fascinating.

But that had not been it. He *was* fascinating.
So golden and powerful, so different from everyone else around them. And she could see that she
wasn't the only one who thought so. Heads swiv-
elled as he passed by, everyone watching him.

Alex forgot her urge to flee until he climbed
the terrace steps, almost to her side. Then she remembered every detail of their first meeting—

and her face burned again. But it was much too late to run away.

'Your Grace,' Lady Smythe-Tomas said, her voice full of laughter. 'I hear we are to be in Paris together!'

'Indeed, Lady Smythe-Tomas?' Alex's mother answered coolly. Alex knew her mother did not approve of the lady and her 'fast' friends. Not even the Prince of Wales was up to her mother's standards.

'Yes. Bertie and Princess Alexandra are always so kind to include their friends in their adventures. Mr Gordston here will also be in Paris, opening his latest investment on the Champs-Élysées.' She smiled up at Malcolm from under her feathered hat. 'Have you met Mr Gordston yet?'

'No, I have not,' the Duchess said shortly. Lady Cannon, who should have made the introductions, seemed to have frozen.

'Well, Your Grace, may I present Mr Malcolm Gordston?' Lady S.-T. said happily, seemingly impervious to any froideur, as if her elegant hat was a shield. 'And this is the Duchess's daughter, Lady Alexandra Mannerly.'

'How do you do, Your Grace?' he said with a bow, all perfectly correct.

'How do you do?' the Duchess murmured.

But Alex held her hand out to him. She couldn't seem to stop herself. Would he remember her? 'Mr Gordston. How do you do?' She prayed her voice wouldn't waver or dissolve into giggles. Luckily, it came out quiet but steady, like a normal person. 'We do hear so much about you. I'm glad to meet you.'

He took her hand. He wore no gloves and through the thin silk of hers she felt the heat of his touch, the rough strength of his fingers. Just as when they had touched in the park, a spark seemed to dance over her skin, hot and shocking, bringing life with it. Everything around him turned into a mere blur of colour and she couldn't look away from him.

He seemed to sense something odd, too. A frown flickered over his face and he looked rather discomfited, something she was sure he didn't often do. He seemed made of confidence and strength and surety. 'Lady Alexandra. How do you do?'

Alex's mother gave a small cough and it was like being dropped with a thud back on to the hard stone terrace. Everything that had turned hazy sharpened and Alex saw that Lady Cannon and Lady Smythe-Tomas were watching her with avid interest.

She knew she would be gossiped about, which

was the last thing she wanted. She stepped back, listening as Lady S.-T. and her mother exchanged news about Paris, and Lady Cannon was called away.

'Your Grace, have you tried the raspberry ice yet? It's quite divine,' Lady S.-T. said and smoothly led Alex's mother away under a cover of bright chatter that smothered any protest. Alex wished she knew that trick.

And now she was alone with Malcolm Gordston. They stared at each other for a long, silent moment and she wondered desperately what he was thinking. If he, too, was remembering their first meeting.

'Would you care for a stroll, Lady Alexandra?' he asked at last, his Scottish accent blurring his words.

'Thank you, that would be nice,' she answered. He offered his arm and she hesitated for a moment, wondering if that spark would fly through her again at his touch and she would burn to cinders. He frowned, as if he noticed her hesitation and mistook it, and she quickly slid her hand into the crook of his elbow.

She did not burn up, but she did find she enjoyed the feel of his arm under her touch. A lot. Too much, maybe. But there was no turning away now.

He led her down the steps to the pathway that wound past the flowerbeds. The rose-scented breeze caught at her hat, but luckily Mary had pinned it down firmly enough there were no new millinery disasters. He was so much taller than her, his stride so purposeful, that she felt quite protected. It was rather nice.

He cleared his throat, and Alex glanced up at him. 'I—I feel I must apologise, Lady Alexandra, for our last meeting. I must not have been quite myself that day.'

Alex thought surely he *was* himself in the park. It was here that he, that both of them, were constrained, unsure. She felt so shy, so flustered, which was silly. They came from different worlds; they could have no expectations of each other. Surely they should be free around one another? She wished she could be, anyway. That she could just be Alex with him, whoever that was, and not Lady Alexandra. Once she could do that with him. But no longer. He had changed.

'It is quite all right, Mr Gordston,' she said. 'It was an—an odd moment. And it was nice not feeling like a porcelain doll for a little while.'

They turned a corner on the twisting paths, into a small herb maze that was much quieter. 'Is that how you usually feel? Like a doll?'

'Sometimes,' Alex said, marvelling at how he

made her feel. Shy and yet bold at the same time. 'Many times. I'm told where to go, what to say, who to sit with, who to dance with…'

'Who to walk with in the garden?'

Alex laughed. 'Yes, usually. But this time I was rescued by Lady Smythe-Tomas.' She glanced back towards the terrace, now far distant, where Lady S.-T. was still chatting with her mother. 'She is so elegant, isn't she?'

'One of Gordston's best customers.'

And was she more than that? Alex found she didn't like the little green-eyed pang that came over her at the thought. 'Is she—friends with you? Old friends?'

He looked down at her with a crooked smile and she feared she had given too much away. 'Friends, yes, only. We're too similar to get along in any other way.'

'As we were once friends?' Alex blurted.

He frowned. 'Friends?'

'Do you not remember me? In Scotland? You taught me to fish. I never forgot.' And she had never seen him again after that day she saw him with Mairie McGregor. How high had he climbed since then.

'I did remember you later, after we met at the park. I felt so foolish for not realising right away.

You were quite a terror with a rod and reel back then. Are you still?'

'There isn't much call for it here in London.' Alex looked away, pretending to study the flowers. 'Look at you now, though. And Lady Smythe-Tomas shops at Gordston's, as does everyone! How did you come to own such a place? They say it's so elegant, all the latest fashions.'

'You haven't been there?'

Alex bit her lip. 'I don't often get to choose where to shop.'

'The porcelain doll?'

'Yes.'

He led her to bench under the shade of a looming oak tree and sat down next to her. 'Well, I didn't grow up dreaming of department stores. I was born in Scotland, a country lad, as you know.'

'Yes.' She remembered when she was a child, the craggy hills against the lavender sky, the cold, smoky air, running free over the moors. The excitement of fishing with Malcolm. 'I've never felt so gloriously free as when I was allowed to explore the hills.'

He watched her closely, his expression closed, unreadable. 'It's a bonnie place, nowhere else like it, in the hills. But it's no good for work. I was an apprentice at a draper's shop in Glasgow when I left. My father had recently died then.'

'Oh, I am sorry!' Alex cried. She remembered his father had not been well the last time they met.

'He missed my mother so much, it was probably a blessing he went quickly,' Malcolm said tonelessly. 'I found work a good way to forget.'

Alex fidgeted with her parasol, not sure what to say. 'And you found you liked that work?'

'Aye. I was surprised by it. As you said, I was used to exploring the hills, being free. But I liked meeting the customers, seeing the pleasure it gave them to find just the right fabric, the right style. I even liked keeping the accounts, seeing them all add up. It was a great satisfaction.'

'I do envy you,' Alex said. How lovely it would be to have a job to do, learn how to do it well and see its rewards.

But Malcolm looked surprised. 'Do you? It's long hours, learning from mistakes, hard work on your feet. Even now, with a new kind of store. Maybe even especially now.'

'That's why I envy you! You forge your own path. I have to always follow. I don't even know what I would be good at.' She didn't want to admit to him she had never tried anything. Emily was good at business, Diana at writing. All Alex had that was her own was the charity work she did and she did find great satisfaction in that.

'We're all put on our own path at birth and we have to follow,' he said. She thought she heard a tinge of bitterness in his tone and she knew the feeling too well.

'But you have not,' she said. 'You're here in London, a—a mercantile prince. Like a Medici or something! Not out on the moors, where you were born.' He had always reminded her of a powerful Renaissance prince, no matter where he was.

He laughed, a rich, golden sound, like summer sunshine. 'I like the sound of being a Medici. Do they spend their hours over accounts, do you think, as I do?'

Alex shook her head, remembering how she had imagined him a Norse god, thundering free in the world. 'I am sure they must have, to accumulate such a fortune. Between destroying their enemies, of course. You are truly lucky to have work you enjoy and I will hear nothing different.' She sat back on the bench, kicking her kid boots against her flounced hem, feeling strangely whimsical. 'I do sometimes wonder what work I would like to do. Perhaps I would be an actress, as you first took me for!'

A dull, dark red flush touched his glass-sharp

cheekbones. 'You are much too fine and good for such a thing. I was a fool to assume for even a minute.'

Alex thought of the girls at the charity school where she sometimes did her volunteer work, girls who had been caught in some terrible, inescapable circumstances before they found the haven of the school. Were they not 'fine and good', too? 'Some women, too many, have no choices at all. They could not be apprentices as you were.'

'No. I agree. My stores employ many dozens of people, lots of ladies among them. If I could just show you...'

'There you are, Alexandra,' she heard her mother say.

She looked up to see the Duchess hurrying towards them along the pathway. She smiled, but Alex could see the clouds in her eyes. 'Lady Ellsworth is here, we must say hello.'

'Of course, Mama.' Alex felt the mantle of duty fall back over her shoulders, heavy as smothering velvet. She stood up from the bench and smoothed her skirts.

She glanced back at Malcolm Gordston and wished she had not left him with a quarrel. Perhaps she would never see him again. The thought made her feel much too downcast, and she made herself smile. 'Good day, Mr Gordston. Thank you for the stroll.'

He stood and gave her a bow. 'Good day, Lady Alexandra.'

Her mother took her arm and drew her away. She said nothing, but Alex could feel the disapproval in every tense line of the Duchess's body. Alex had shirked her duty. She had wandered off with someone unsuitable instead of greeting her mother's friends. Instead of looking for someone eligible to flirt with. Not that her mother would ever say *flirt*.

Yet she wished more than anything she could have just gone on walking with Malcolm, talking of Scotland and shopkeeping, and even arguing about women's roles in the world. He was not a comfortable person at all. So tall, so roughly masculine, so filled with burning energy, he made her feel quite giddy.

And yet, being in his company felt oddly— easy. For just a moment, she could be herself, speak without worrying about her position and what her mother would say if Alex's words reached her ears. Malcolm Gordston listened to her and looked at her as if he saw *her*.

It was quite nice. More than nice. Alas, she feared her brief moments alone in his company were finished. Her mother wouldn't let her out of sight now. And Alex felt cold and sad, shivering as if it was December and not a fine, gardeny day.

She wondered if maybe, just maybe, Emily would fancy taking her on a little shopping trip…

Chapter Four

Malcolm tore off his fine coat and tossed it over a chair in his office before he loosened his elaborately tied cravat. Miss Mersey would be most disapproving when she saw he hadn't hung it up—the woman was like the protective, hen-like mother he'd never had and he secretly enjoyed it, but he couldn't worry about her now. He felt as though he was suffocating.

He pushed open the window and leaned out to stare at the street far below, breathing deeply of the sooty London air. The crowds swirled below, a sea of black bowler hats and feathered ladies' chapeaus, carriages halted in a traffic jam. It was always that way when he went out to society parties. He had to do such things for his business, but they felt heavy, damp, smothering. He would always prefer to be in his office or walking the sales floors, doing what he understood—working.

Yet for a while today, he hadn't minded being at a frivolous party at all. Because Lady Alexandra was there.

Her soft voice, her smile, the fleeting, birdlike touch of her hand, it had all made everyone else vanish for a while. He had wanted nothing more than to stay hidden behind the scented wall of flowers with her all day, talking to her, trying to make her laugh. He hadn't felt that way around a woman since—since Mairie. No, not even then. Mairie had been a lovely convenience. Alexandra was anything *but* convenient.

Malcolm shook his head, trying to drive out any memories that might surface of Mairie. She so rarely haunted his thoughts now, as she once had when they were young and foolish. She'd been the daughter of a local shopkeeper, all sparkling brown eyes and flirtatious laughter. They would walk the moors outside town, whispering secrets, laughing. Dreaming of the day they could raise themselves in life.

He'd asked her to come to Glasgow with him, but she refused, saying she couldn't hurt her father that way. She had walked away, angry with him, right before Alexandra had called out to him that day. She'd been quite right, of course.

He couldn't have given her the comfortable life she wanted then and he wouldn't be where he was now if he'd had a wife and family to worry about. But knowing that hadn't stopped the anger, the hurt. The knowledge he hadn't been good enough.

Lady Alexandra wasn't really like Mairie. She was small, shy, delicate, whereas Mairie had been full of laughter and energy, sparkly but hard on the inside. And despite his wealth now, Alexandra was more above him than Mairie ever had been. Yet when some of her reserve fell away, when she smiled at him, she had some of that zest for life. He felt himself being drawn in, tugged closer to her by some invisible, silvery thread, wanting to know more and more about her.

He knew that was completely impossible. He'd known that the instant he heard his winter fairy was the daughter of the Duke of Waverton. *Lady* Alexandra.

He pounded his fist hard on the windowsill. Why did it have to be Waverton? The *walloper* who had ruined his father's life when he fired him from his estate, impoverished them, cast Malcolm out into the world on his own. How had the villain ever had such a daughter as her?

He slammed the window shut and sat down at his desk, reaching for the architect's designs for the new Paris store, his crowning achievement. But work, usually his whole life, couldn't distract him. All he could see in his mind now was Lady Alexandra's smile, her heather-blue eyes. How he had longed to kiss her, until it was an actual physical ache inside. And that was the one thing he could never do. The thing all his ambition couldn't buy him.

Chapter Five

❦

Miss Grantley's school—one year later

'*Je serai, tu seras, il sera, nous serons...*'

The girls seated in a semi-circle around Alex's desk obediently repeated their French verbs after her, their faces shining with eagerness. She always thought her heart would burst with pride every time she saw them there, looking so much like she, Diana and Emily had during their own schooldays. Wearing the same uniform of white shirtwaists, blue skirts, red bows in their hair, so eager to learn, to know. So ready to burst out into the world.

So ignorant of what the world really held for them.

Alex wished she could hold them there in the classroom for years and years, protect them. She knew she could not. At the end of the year, these girls would graduate from Miss Grantley's. A few of them would go to Continental finishing schools, maybe even take classes at Lady Margaret Hall at Oxford, but most would go out into society, as Alex had. The best she could do was try to prepare them for what they would find.

She hoped they would not find what she had. Family scandal, when her father's bankruptcy and involvement in the attempted theft of the Eastern Star had been revealed in Paris, at the Exposition, in front of the Prince of Wales. The Duke of Waverton involved in jewel theft! And bankrupt, too!

But she had come out well in the end. Better than well—she was content. She loved her new work at Miss Grantley's, as a teacher. Just as she had in her charity work at the girls' home in London, she found she enjoyed helping young people. She liked listening to them, trying to help them find a confidence she herself had lacked at their age.

She liked being plain Miss Mannerly, teacher of French and literature. She could hide there, as she never could as Lady Alexandra, the Duke's daughter. The *disgraced* Duke's daughter.

'Very good,' she told the girls. 'Now, can you remember "to be"?'

As they recited, she handed out a stack of new books. *Mallarmé*, in French.

'What is this, Miss Mannerly?' one of the girls asked.

'A new novel, in French. I definitely think you are ready for a challenge,' Alex answered. 'We can translate it together.'

'A *novel*?' another girl whispered.

Alex laughed. 'Yes, but not a terribly scandalous one, even if it is French. Let's take a look at it together and see what we think of it all.'

For the rest of the class, they made their way through the first chapter, the girls translating very well. They did so well, that Alex found herself daydreaming a bit about the last time she was in Paris, for the Exposition. Eiffel's Tower, soaring like majestic lacework into the sky above the Seine. The boats that floated along the water, the sun sparkling off the waves; the music and colour of the exhibits, dancing in moonlit gardens, champagne and foie gras.

That glimpse of Malcolm Gordston in the midst of the grandeur of his store, those ice-blue eyes that seemed to laugh at her. The touch of his hand…

'Miss Mannerly, what does this mean?' one of the girls asked, pulling her away from the City of Lights, from memories of an unearthly handsome man she would never see again and into the prosaic reality of the teaching day. Alex almost laughed aloud at herself. She couldn't afford dreaminess any longer.

When the lesson was over and the girls filed out of the classroom, whispering and giggling together, Alex started tidying up. She pushed the chairs back into place, erased the lines written on the chalkboard, gave the plants some water, losing herself in the now-familiar chores. She *did* like it at Miss Grantley's, she thought as she shelved some of the books. The same halls and classrooms that had given her refuge when she came there as a shy schoolgirl gave her sanctuary now, a quiet haven of learning, smelling of books and chalk dust and the girls' perfume, a place where she could find herself again after the world overturned.

She put on her grey cardigan over her own shirtwaist and blue skirt, and stacked up some books to take back to her chamber. It was the end of her teaching day and not her evening to supervise the girls at dinner in the refectory, so she could have a quiet night of tea, toasted cheese and reading next to her own fireplace. She also had time to answer Diana's last letter from Vienna, where she lived at the embassy with William. She looked forward to it all immensely.

As she was turning down the lamp, there was a quick knock at the door and Miss Grantley herself hurried in. She was a lady probably around the age of Alex's own mother, tall and slim, with auburn hair pinned high atop her head and dark eyes behind gleaming spectacles, energy in her every step.

She smiled and said, 'Alexandra, my dear, do you have a small moment to talk?'

'Yes, of course, Miss Grantley. This was my last class of the day,' Alex answered. She wondered for a nervous moment if she had done something wrong, if the girls in her classes were not progressing satisfactorily, but Miss Grantley smiled kindly. 'Is something amiss?'

'No, not at all.' She gestured for them to sit in two of the chairs near the window, her burgundy-wool skirts falling gracefully around her. 'I do hope you've been enjoying your time back at the school?'

'Very much,' Alex said. 'I never realised before how rewarding teaching really is! To see the girls learning, it's very thrilling.'

Miss Grantley's smile widened. 'I always found it so. And all the girls do seem so fond of their Miss Mannerly! You've done wonders for them, especially the shy ones.'

Alex knew why that was—she was shy herself

and understood how it felt to feel so frightened in a sea of other girls. 'They are all quite lovely.' Except for the few that thought themselves bullies, but Alex had learned to deal with them.

'And you are not too terribly homesick? Missing your parents?'

Alex bit her lip. It would be hard to feel homesick for homes that were gone. The London house was sold; their country seat was closed. And her brother, Charles, who her parents had despaired for even before the crisis, had locked himself up at their old Scottish hunting box, which was kept when the town house was sold, but was in a rather dilapidated state. She thought of her parents, far away in Florence, the sad letters her mother sometimes wrote about their small rooms, their one maidservant, the lack of invitations that came their way. While Alex enjoyed her new life, her poor mother decidedly did not and it made her feel wretchedly guilty.

'I do miss them,' she said. 'But I like my work here. I owe you so much for giving me the position.'

'Not at all! I owe *you*, my dear. You are a natural teacher and having you here has been a great favour to me. Which is why I am rather sorry to ask for even more favours now.'

More favours? 'I am happy to help in any way I can.'

Miss Grantley took a letter from her jacket pocket. It looked rather important, heavy cream stationery with a red seal. 'I have had a letter from a former pupil, Lady Bullard. You would not know her, she was several years ahead of you, but she was one of my most clever girls. She is married to one of the ambassador's staff in Paris now, a mother of two little girls herself, and still one of the school's greatest benefactors. She has written to me asking if I know of a good governess who might be willing to come to Paris for a few months. Someone to help make sure her daughters are ready to enter the school next year.'

Paris? Alex remembered her earlier daydreams, the memory of the beautiful pale houses, the pinkish sky and glorious green parks of the city. 'And you think I would be good at the task?'

Miss Grantley smiled. 'Of course! You have been to Paris, you speak excellent French. And your family knows the life of a diplomat. You would be perfect.'

As excited as the thought made her, she wasn't quite sure. She had not been a teacher for long, after all. 'I have never been a governess.'

'For all I have heard, Lady Bullard's girls are very intelligent, well-behaved little girls.' Miss

Grantley gently took Alex's hands and gave them a reassuring pat. 'I know you have doubts about going out into the world again, my dear. But I think it's time for you to make your way. Just dip a toe in, maybe.'

'If it would be a help to you…'

'It would. I think it could be a help to you, as well.' Miss Grantley handed her the letter and rose to her feet. 'Just think about it, Alexandra. There is no great hurry.'

Alex nodded. When she had gathered her books and made her way up to her own room on the top floor, she put on the kettle for tea and stared out the window as she waited for it to boil. The sun was just going down, turning the green lawns to emerald. But she didn't see the tennis courts, the girls straggling back towards the school in their white dresses. She saw Paris, as it was the last time she was there.

How beautiful it all was then, how exciting! A new world of electric lights, bicycling by the Seine, dining with the Prince and Princess of Wales, strange new art, beautiful gowns.

And the wonders of Gordston's Department Store, all marble and gilt and cool, powdery hush. The last time she glimpsed Malcolm Gordston, the Viking of her dreams.

She felt her cheeks turn hot at the memory.

How handsome he had been; how she had not been as polite as she should have been. He always made her feel so wretchedly flustered just to look at him!

What if—what if *he* was still in Paris? What if she happened to see him there, in a park or on the street? She closed her eyes and let her imagination run wild, let herself imagine walking along a Parisian pavement. Her handkerchief fluttered out of her hand, a man picked it up, smiling up at her as he rose. And it was Malcolm, his pale blue eyes shimmering, his laughter warm and rich. His hand reaching for hers…

Alex's eyes snapped open. The terrible thing was, she didn't know if she dreaded seeing him again—or if she longed for it with all her might.

Chapter Six

❧❧❧

Paris

Malcolm stared up at the displays in Gordston's shining picture windows, frowning as he studied every detail. The collection of gowns, hats and scarves was the finest of the new range of sportswear—for tennis, bicycling, even motoring, an array of white, green, blue, brown, around a bicycle, an archery set, golf clubs. All a modern young lady could need, full of action and movement.

Even with the Exposition closed, Gordston's Paris was busier than ever. Crowds were constantly streaming in and out of the revolving doors, footmen laden with packages trailing behind ladies in furs and wide-brimmed hats. Everything about the place gleamed and shimmered in the pastel Paris light, so clean and luxurious and perfect. And he had built it.

Usually, the sight of his stores filled him with quiet pride, with the burning need to do more, create more, *be* more. But today he felt somehow—hollow.

He studied the next window, a selection of the newest dinner gowns: fluttering chiffon, delicate floral print silk, lace and gauzy frills. He glanced back at the sportswear window, and the sight of the tweed bicycling suits made him think of the last time Lady Alexandra had appeared in his store. The only time, really.

He hadn't seen the winter fairy since that day, more than a year before, and yet he still couldn't help thinking about her. Far more than he should. She came into his thoughts, floating as if on a magical cloud, when he was going over accounts, or inspecting the sales counters, or talking to suppliers. Her rosy-pink lips, curved in a shy smile; her enormous, heather-coloured eyes; her delicate laugh. She popped up at the most inopportune times.

Just like now.

It was nonsense. They had only met a few brief times, yet he thought of her far more than any of the women who had been his dalliances. Actresses, bored married society ladies, all of them beauties, sophisticated, witty—none of them lingered like Lady Alexandra.

Malcolm studied a display of hats, not seeing the striped taffeta bows, the sweeps of egret feathers, the velvet flowers. He just saw her, her eyes peeping up at him from beneath her blue hat.

He knew the Duke of Waverton had gone into disgraced exile. After all his years of such fiery anger towards the man for what he'd done to Malcolm's family, the destruction he had wrought on so many poor people in his power, Malcolm hadn't had to lift a finger to ruin him. Waverton did it all on his own and good riddance to him. Malcolm had thought perhaps then the past could be in the past, though it didn't always feel like that. He couldn't always let go of his anger.

But Malcolm hadn't heard of what happened to Alexandra. Had she gone to Italy with her parents, living a meagre life in rented rooms? Was she sad, angry, ashamed? He hated to think of her that way.

If only she had come to him for help…

Which was an absurd thought. They barely knew each other. Why would a duke's daughter, even one in disgrace, come to a shopkeeper at all? Yet from that first day in Hyde Park, when he made an ass of himself, he'd felt an overwhelming protectiveness towards her. Perhaps it was her delicacy, or the memory of Mairie and how he couldn't help her. But something about Alexandra lingered, like a whiff of her soft perfume.

He heard a sharp cry from somewhere behind him, a burst of angry French words, and he turned to see a woman with a small child standing across the street. She clutched the child to her shoulder as a *gendarme* berated her. It seemed a great mismatch to Malcolm, the small, skinny woman, a girl really, in a faded, patched dress and jacket, the sniffling, grubby-faced child and the hulking policeman with his fat, red face and bristling whiskers. And if there was one thing Malcolm hated, it was a bully.

He strode across the street, dodging the elegant carriages. 'What is the problem here?' he demanded in French.

The *gendarme* spun around, obviously ready to shout at Malcolm to move along. But the sight of Malcolm's fine coat, his silk hat and gold watch, and the fact that Malcolm was even taller and broader than himself, seemed to change his mind.

'Begging is forbidden on this street, *monsieur*,' he said with a bow. 'I was just telling this creature to move along.'

'I wasn't begging!' the girl cried. 'I was just looking for work.'

'Here?' the *gendarme* scoffed. 'No one here

would hire one such as you. Move along to Pigalle.'

'I wouldn't be so quick to make such a judgement, if I were you, charged with protecting the public,' Malcolm said. He smiled at the girl, who held the child closer. 'What kind of work are you looking for, *mademoiselle*?'

'Sewing,' she answered slowly. 'I did embroidery at Paquin before I had the baby, speciality work. But I can also do plain sewing, stitching, alterations. I thought one of the stores…'

'A likely tale,' the *gendarme* shouted. 'I said be gone with you! And you, *monsieur*, this is really none of your concern.'

'On the contrary,' Malcolm said. 'I own that store across the street. And we are always looking for good seamstresses. If you would care to come with me, *mademoiselle*…'

'*Monsieur*, I must protest…' the *gendarme* spluttered. Malcolm ignored him, and gently took the girl's arm to lead her across the street. It felt as fragile as a matchstick under her thin sleeve. 'On your head be it if the store is robbed, then!'

The girl watched him suspiciously, holding herself stiffly as they went through the gilded revolving doors into Gordston's lobby. But she didn't run away and the baby quieted as they both took in the hushed, polished, violet-scented luxury.

'Do you really own all this?' she whispered.

'I do.'

'Then why would you want to help someone like me?'

Malcolm remembered their dirt-floor croft in Scotland, the thick smell of peat and boiled cabbage that always hung in the air, the helpless feeling of having nowhere to turn. 'We do always need seamstresses. Our workrooms are always busy. Especially if you really are adept at embroidery. I'd like to start our own original fashion line soon, not just copy the work of others.' He led her across the black-and-white marble floor to the lifts, ignoring the discreet glances of the black-clad salespeople behind the counters. They were all used to his 'strays'. Some of them had once been in such a position themselves.

'How do you know I can really do that?' she said as he led her into his own lift and the operator closed the doors behind them.

'I don't, of course. That's why I'm taking you to my secretary. She'll go to the head of the cutting rooms and you can show them your skills.'

The girl looked cautiously hopeful. 'But— but I have him,' she said, hoisting the now-silent child against her shoulder.

'They can look after him, too. How did you learn your embroidery skill? And I'm sorry, but I don't know your name. I am Monsieur Gordston, by the way.'

'I'm Elise. And I went to Mademoiselle Gardinier's school when I was younger. My *maman* was a laundress and when she died they took me in.'

'I see,' Malcolm said. Mademoiselle Gardinier's school, a branch of one started in London by a Mrs Poole, was famous among shopkeepers. She turned out excellent seamstresses, housekeepers and nannies from the pupils she gathered from poor families. He sometimes hired her graduates for both his stores. 'I have heard of them.'

'They are angels,' Elise said, smiling for the first time.

The lift door opened on the office floor, all dark-panelled walls like his office in London, deep-piled carpets keeping everything hushed. Miss Mersey stepped out of the typing room, a stack of papers in her hands. 'Mr Gordston?'

'Mademoiselle Elise here is an embroiderer, Miss Mersey,' he said. 'Can you take her down to the cutting room for an interview?'

'Of course. Oh, you poor thing! Come with me at once and let me find you some tea,' Miss

Mersey clucked, taking the child from Elise and leading them away. He knew that in her capable hands, Elise and the baby would quickly have a hot meal and baths, as well as a sewing audition. She was used to his ways by now. 'Don't forget, Mr Gordston! Miss Emily Fortescue has an appointment in half an hour.'

'Of course,' Malcolm answered, not letting her know he had rather forgotten. Miss Fortescue was the daughter of one of his chief business rivals, but now they were thinking of going into a partnership together and had requested a meeting to talk about it.

He also suddenly remembered that Miss Fortescue knew Lady Alexandra. They had been together the last time he saw his winter fairy, when they were shopping for bicycle suits in his store. Maybe—just maybe she would know where Alexandra had gone?

He went into his office and sat down behind the desk, staring at the mountain of paperwork that waited for him there. Yet he couldn't focus on it as he usually did, leaving the rest of the world behind in work. Instead he remembered Mairie, his infatuation for her when he was young, the way she had been lost in the world. And he thought of Alexandra, her sweet smile.

The way he wanted to lose himself in her goodness and never leave it.

Miss Mersey knocked briskly on the door and bustled into the office, folders of paperwork in her hands. She dropped them on the desk and folded her arms over her crisp, ecru shirtwaist.

'Mademoiselle Elise is settling in,' she said. 'It seems she was correct about her embroidery skills. She is very adept. I left her demonstrating a beautiful satin stitch.'

'What?' Malcolm said, finding his thoughts were still miles away from the store, where they should be. He could barely remember an hour ago. 'Oh, yes, that is good.'

Miss Mersey gave her head a rueful, and, he hoped, affectionate shake. 'You and your ways, Mr Gordston. You can't fight all the dangers, save all the lost ones.'

Malcolm remembered all the people he had grown up with, hungry, grubby-faced children, parents with barely the energy to pay attention to them after long days at work. He smiled at her and said, 'No, maybe not, but we can definitely help a few along the way.'

She tapped at the papers on his desk, which he saw were the afternoon post. 'You should answer these invitations. Some could be very valuable for the business. Like this salon at the Comtesse de Brissacs's *palais*. She is one of the leaders of Parisian fashion.'

Malcolm glanced down at the thick, glossy cards, impressively sealed with flowers and coronets. He knew being seen at such places was good for business; these were the ladies he needed to be seen patronising the store. But he dreaded such evenings. 'I'm no good at that sort of thing, Miss Mersey.'

'You can be good at it. You certainly are charming when you *want* to be,' she sighed. 'What you need is a wife. Someone adept at moving about in society, with good connections. Someone to organise a fine house for you, where you can entertain and run your social life properly. Someone who can organise *you*.'

'You do that!'

Miss Mersey shook her head. 'I am your work secretary. I can only organise your post. You need a hostess. And a companion to help you in your life.'

Malcolm tossed down his pen and sat back in his chair. Miss Mersey had lectured him about his need for a properly run household before and he didn't entirely disagree with her. The thought of a *real* home, warm and brightly lit and beautifully furnished, full of people, talk, music, rather than his usual rented lodgings, was appealing.

He remembered when he was child, creeping out of the cold, empty house after his mother died, peeking into other people's windows, spying on them as they ate together, laughed together by the fire. It might be nice to have a home again.

On the other hand—he had no idea how to have his own family. Those small, tantalising glimpses had always vanished much too quickly and there was only his own cold grate to return to, scraps of food, an empty bed and later long hours of hard work. Where could he even begin to make a lady, a real lady, happy?

He knew there were plenty who would marry him for his fortune and the unlimited supply of hats and gowns from the stores. But someone like Miss Mersey suggested, who could run a smooth, busy social life, plan a comfortable, stylish home? *And* put up with his bearish, Scottish ways? A woman who would not expect too much from him, would not expect love such as his parents had. The love that had destroyed them in the end.

Malcolm thought such a lady surely didn't exist. Certainly not in society drawing rooms.

He had a sudden flashing memory of Lady Alexandra, his winter fairy in her pale blue silk in the Cannons' garden, her gentle smile, her soft touch. Perhaps there was such a lady after all—but she was beyond his touch.

Ever since he could remember, he had been determined to control his own destiny, to not be weak like his father, to not let emotion destroy him. Perhaps one day he might marry for convenience, but he would be sure his heart was not involved in the transaction. It would be a matter entirely under his own control.

'I will take it under advisement, Miss Mersey,' he said.

She shook her head again. 'You definitely should. Before you are too old.' The house telephone, run from a switchboard in the basement and connecting all the different departments, rang, and she answered it. 'Miss Fortescue is on her way up for her appointment,' she said as she hung up.

'Thank you, Miss Mersey,' he answered, reaching for the file on the Fortescue business. 'If you could have coffee sent in?'

'Of course.' Miss Mersey hesitated for a moment. 'Now, Miss Fortescue would be a fine match—'

'No, Miss Mersey,' he cut her off. He and Emily Fortescue were much too similar to ever get along for more than an hour or so. They were both consumed with business. 'Miss Fortescue

is much too busy with her own concerns to organise mine.'

Miss Mersey pursed her lips and spun around
to march away. Within a few minutes, Emily Fortescue took her place, smiling as she reached for
Malcolm's hand. He could see why his secretary
would try to matchmake for her; Miss Fortescue
was a tall, slender beauty, with sparkling am-
ber-coloured eyes and dark chestnut hair bun-
dled in a psyche knot under her wide-brimmed
hat, dressed in a green velvet, fur-trimmed suit
that was the height of fashion. But she was like
a whirlwind of energy and business, and he saw
he was right to assume they were too much alike.

But he *had* seen her with Lady Alexandra.
How did they know each other?

'Mr Gordston, I must congratulate you on your
splendid new store!' She sat down across from
him, taking off her green kid gloves. 'It's even
grander than when I first visited during the Exposition. Your displays are amazing!'

Malcolm smiled at her. He found himself in a
position he rarely faced—not being able to say
what he really wanted to. He wanted to demand
to know how she was acquainted with Lady Alexandra, what his winter fairy was doing now,
how he could find her. But he wasn't in the habit

of alarming ladies with stalkerish demands. 'I am glad you approve.'

'Of course I do and I am quite envious. And you're having a grand opening party soon?'

'Yes, I hope you'll come. And your father, if he's in Paris.' Had they been sent an invitation? Surely they had, but he found he didn't know. This was surely one of those society wife duties Miss Mersey spoke of.

'I wouldn't miss it! I do hope you don't mind if I bring some friends?'

Malcolm felt a surge of excitement at the thought that her 'friends' might possibly include Lady Alexandra, seeing his store at its very finest. 'Certainly not. The more the merrier.'

She laughed. 'To show off your superior wares, of course.' Miss Mersey brought in the gleaming silver coffee service and Miss Fortescue gave her a bright smile. 'And you are thinking of opening a café and food hall on the top floor, yes? My father was most intrigued at your proposal to collaborate on such an effort.'

'I have no experience with such ventures yet, but many of my customers have asked for such an amenity. Fortescue's has a reputation for the greatest knowledge of fine wines and foodstuffs.'

'It is one of our specialties and the proposal does sound like it could be quite profitable. Have you any projected numbers I could look at yet? Capacity for the proposed space?'

After an hour of coffee and negotiating, Emily smiled and tucked the pages into her valise. 'We will have an answer for you very soon, Mr Gordston. In the meantime, I'm afraid I must dash, I have a tea meeting. It has been fascinating, as always.'

Malcolm rose with her and shook her hand, still wishing he knew a subtle and unsuspicious way to ask her about Alexandra. 'A pleasure to do business with you, Miss Fortescue. If you will give your friends' names to Miss Mersey, she can send them invitations to the party.'

'How kind! I'm quite sure Mr Christopher Blakely will come. You know the family? His brother, Sir William, is now a very high-up consul in Vienna. His wife always needs stylish new fashions.'

'Ah, yes. She writes about Continental fashions for some of the London papers, if I'm not mistaken.'

'You do have a good memory. My friend was Miss Diana Martin, now Lady Blakely, yes.'

'It's my job to remember such things.'

'And you are very good at it. Until your party, then, Mr Gordston!'

After she left, Malcolm found he couldn't quite settle down to his paperwork. He went back to the window, studying the fashionable parade of carriages and riders on horseback, the colourful garden of flowery hats, on the street below. Paris was always decked out in its finest, rain or shine, and the elegant procession usually inspired him.

A figure on the walkway caught his attention. She was alone, studying the Gordston's window displays. Unlike most of the stylish women swirling past in their lace and plumes, she wore a plain, tailored chocolate-brown skirt and jacket on her slim figure, a straw boater hat on her simple pinned-back knot of hair. But that hair was an unusual spun-silver colour, glowing in the light reflected from the window.

Malcolm stood up straighter, all his senses sharpening. Could it really be? He had imagined several times he'd seen her on the street or in a park, only to realise it was someone else entirely, that no other lady could really have such hair. He'd always been left feeling foolish, laughing at himself for being so eager to see a lady he had only met a handful of much-too-brief times.

But something about *this* time, this woman, was different. Something in the way she stood, so straight and still, as if poised to dash away, something about the way she tilted her head. Malcolm pushed open the window and leaned out to look closer, hoping she would glance up. That it would indeed be Lady Alexandra.

Emily Fortescue emerged from the store and called out something as she waved. The lady in brown ran to her and as they hugged she tilted her head back, and Malcolm saw that it really was her. He hadn't been imagining things. And she looked even lovelier than she had the last time he saw her, her cheeks glowing pink as she laughed.

The two women, giggling together, hurried away and it took all Malcolm's self-control not to call after her. Not to run downstairs and chase her through the streets.

'Mr Gordston!' Miss Mersey cried. 'Whatever are you doing with the window open? It's much too windy outside.'

Malcolm took one more look down the street, but Alexandra had vanished. He closed the window, telling himself that now he knew she was in Paris, now he knew she was friends with Miss Fortescue, surely he could find her once again.

'Not a thing, Miss Mersey,' he said, turning to smile at her. 'Could you ask Monsieur Albret to come to my office when he has a moment?'

Miss Mersey frowned. 'The head of security? Is there a problem?'

'Not at all, merely a task I might have for him. And we need to add a few names to the invitation list for the grand opening…'

Chapter Seven

Alex stared up at Gordston's Department Store, mesmerised. It was even more beautiful than she remembered it from the last time she had been there, shopping for bicycling clothes with Diana and Emily. The pale stone façade gleamed, with classical figures staring down at the street from each of the corners of the roof. The windows were diamond-like, framed in gold, filled with tempting and luscious things.

She did hate to remember the last time she'd been there, how Mr Gordston looked at her when she became so flustered and ran away. The way she grabbed Diana's hand and ran out, like a frightened little rabbit. Had he been thinking badly of her all this time, thinking she was just a snobby little madam? The thought pained her far more than it should, as he was a part of her old life now. Albeit a part of her old life she thought about far more often than she should.

Sometimes at night, when she lay alone in her narrow bed, images would come back to her. Memories of meeting Malcolm in the park, his pale blue eyes crinkling as he smiled down at her; walking with him in the garden, closed in their own sweet little world. The touch of his hand on her arm, making her feel as if she could leap up into the sky and fly away with the excitement. Older memories, too, of her childhood, when everything around her seemed so solid and unchanging, and he was the most handsome, kindest person she had ever met.

Now he was a wealthy, powerful businessman and she was just a governess. They were further apart than ever. She had changed, seen the shallow flash of life like that once she was forced to move into the world. Why could he not do the same?

Alex caught a glimpse of herself in the diamond-bright glow of the window and she grimaced. If a man like Mr Gordston had ever looked at her with admiration before, he wouldn't now. Not in her plain tailored suit and straw hat, with all the Parisian ladies parading past her in their trailing lace and cartwheel-sized hats swathed in tulle.

It was better if she didn't see him again. Yet she found herself half-hopefully, half-fearfully scanning the windows of the upper floors, wondering if he might be there. All she could see was the dazzle of the sunlight, which always seemed so gloriously rosy in Paris. Like magic, like a place where anything could happen.

'Alex! Darling, there you are,' she heard Emily call. She turned to see her friend flying out of the store's revolving doors and dashing down the marble steps. As always, Em was a whirlwind of energy, dressed in fur-edged forest-green velvet, with a green-and-gold hat perched on her mass of russet-coloured hair. Alex felt so tiny and drab next to her, but just as it had never failed when they were at Miss Grantley's, she still felt buoyed up and full of laughter when Em hugged her. It was impossible not to be happy when caught in Emily's whirlwind.

'Did I keep you waiting long?' Em said. She linked her arm in Alex's and led her down the crowded street, past all the fashionable people rushing in and out of milliners and perfumeries and patisseries, their arms full of boxes and packages. 'Shall we have some tea? I am quite parched.'

'I wasn't waiting long at all,' Alex said with a laugh. 'Lady Bullard is very generous. I have the whole afternoon off while she takes her daughters to the Louvre.'

'I still can't imagine it, Alex—you, a governess! It's too awful, too Jane Eyre–ish.' Emily ushered them into the plush, gilded hush of a teashop and they were soon seated on a velvet banquette in the corner, across from an elegant lady dining with two poodles in pearl collars.

'Not Jane-ish at all,' Alex said. 'For one thing, I've met no Mr Rochesters at all.'

'You poor dear! You must come out with me some time. We'll find you someone to sweep you away to Thornfield.'

'Oh, no. Remember how *that* turned out! Madwomen in the attic, conflagrations, clergymen. I've had enough of drama with my family to last me the rest of my life.' A silver tea service and tiered tray of glistening sweets were laid before them and Alex ate a raspberry tart with a contented sigh. 'Besides, I am perfectly happy as I am.'

'As a governess?' Emily took a sip of tea, looking doubtful.

'Yes. The girls are quite adorable and they love our little educational outings here in Paris. Plus, I am here, in France! Without my parents keeping me locked up in some hotel, not able to look around at all. I tell you, Em, it's bliss.'

Well—maybe not *bliss*. It was also rather lonely, not having someone to share the delights of the city with, to confide her worries and fears and delights to. But it was better than it was before.

She thought of Malcolm Gordston, high up in his shining castle of a store, and wondered who he had to confide in. What he thought of being in Paris. What kind of person was he now? Hard and cold, calculating?

'I can understand how nice it must be to be away from the ducals,' Emily said. 'Everything that happened during the Exposition was so shocking. And Miss Grantley is such a dear. She's always there to help any of us when we need it. But surely this isn't what you want for ever?'

'I don't know what I want to do, really,' Alex answered honestly. 'I feel like I have no idea what I *can* do, what I am, without having to be a duke's daughter. I'm not good at business, like you, or writing like Diana.'

'Oh, Alex, darling,' Emily said, reaching across the table to squeeze her hand. 'You are *you*. The kindest, sweetest lady I have ever known. I'm sure you've kept on with your charity work here in Paris, even with all your time taken up governessing.'

'Oh, yes,' Alex said enthusiastically. 'I have

found a school run much along the same lines as Mrs Poole's in London, by a woman named Mademoiselle Gardinier. She takes in girls off the streets and from desperately poor homes and teaches them sewing, cooking, childcare and then helps them find work. I have been doing a bit of teaching reading and English there when I can.'

Emily laughed. 'Of course you are! Because that is you, always helping others. Surely, Alex, with the right kind of marriage, you would have the time and financial wherewithal to do even more. Maybe even set up your own charitable school.'

'Where would I find this wealthy, generous man who wants to marry a disgraced, impoverished duke's daughter?'

'There are plenty such out there. A ducal connection is still a ducal connection and you are lovely and sweet, and would be an asset to any household.' Em tapped her long fingers on the starched tablecloth, making her emerald and topaz rings sparkle. 'Let me make a list...'

Alex laughed. 'No, Em. Not one of your lists!'

'Well, at least come out with me soon. I have an invitation to the grand opening soirée at Gordston's Department Store and you are invited, too. Everyone will be there! Even Chris Blakely is back from Vienna and is sure to have news of Di and Will. Do come with us.'

Go to Gordston's—where she was sure to see Malcolm? Alex looked away, trying to stop herself from blushing. From hoping. 'I don't have anything to wear to such a thing. All my evening gowns are out of date now.'

'I am sure they are lovely. Or I could loan you something! Or we could go buy something new. The new styles this year are so scrumptious, you should see the trims. Just think about it, darling. It will be such fun.'

'I couldn't let you buy me anything. And any of your frocks would be miles too long on me! But I will think about it. Lady Bullard has been urging me to take an evening off.'

'And she is quite right. You can't spend all your evenings with sticky-faced tykes.'

'They aren't sticky-faced! I make sure of it,' Alex said with a laugh. 'But tell me all *you* have been doing lately. It must be much more glamorous than teaching French verbs and table manners.'

Emily poured out more tea and took a tiny chocolate eclair from the tray. 'Just work, really. Father is trying to negotiate a collaboration with Gordston's, a food hall and café. That's what I was doing at the store today.'

Alex longed to ask Em more about the store, what Mr Gordston had been like, how he looked, what he said. But she didn't want her friend's suspicions to be aroused. She dabbed at her lips with a damask napkin, pretending only mild interest. 'Do you think it will go through?'

'I hope so. Mr Gordston plays his cards close, as always, but he does seem interested. He's a strange one.'

'How so?' Alex asked, deeply curious.

Emily shrugged. 'It's hard to say. I've learned to read most men through business deals rather well. What they want, what we can do for each other. But Mr Gordston keeps his own counsel. Has no weaknesses that I can see. But he is always honest in his dealings and when we are able to work out deals they are almost always profitable. Oh, now, look at that hat in the window! Quite hideous, isn't it?'

Alex was quite disappointed she could get no more out of Emily about Malcolm Gordston, but she laughed at the hat and they went on to talk about the new styles in sleeves, Diana's news from Vienna and other school friends. When they parted, she promised to think about coming to the party.

She took a shortcut towards the Bullards' street through a small park as it was such a lovely day as the evening gathered in. The light on the pale walls of the buildings glowed almost a coral colour, darkening the red geraniums in the window boxes, and amber lights blinked on behind the windows of the apartments, making her wonder what lives were being lived behind them. What stories were going on all around her.

How she loved Paris, Alex thought as she watched the vivid light dance over the cobblestones beneath her feet, inhaled the scent of fresh bread from the bakery chimneys, listened to the silken swish of ladies' skirts as they hurried by. Children shrieked with laughter as they chased each other down the park's pathways, the bright ribbons of their hats fluttering, their nannies calling after them.

Alex watched them wistfully for a moment. One of them, a little boy in a tiny blue-serge sailor suit, bumped into her.

'Pardon, madame!' he cried.

'Pas de problème,' she answered as he dashed away.

Emily had certainly been right about one thing—Alex did sometimes long for more. For a family of her own. A family that would be very different from the one she grew up in, where they were bound mostly by strong ties of name and duty, by family and position. She wanted children to love and nurture, who might love her in return. Who would always know they had a place to belong, just because of the person they were.

But all that seemed as far beyond her reach right now as the moon. And that thought made her feel cold, wistful.

She hurried on her way, turning down the Bullards' street of elegant apartment buildings and exclusive little shops, lined with chestnut trees and watchful concierges. The girls would be waiting for her after their nanny gave them their bath and supper, waiting for her to read them their stories and tuck them into bed. Then the rest of the night would stretch ahead for her, quiet and solitary.

One of the maids was waiting for her in the hall. *'Pardon, mademoiselle,'* she whispered, her eyes large and nervous.

Alex felt a jolt of worry as she unpinned her hat. 'What is it? Is Lady Bullard asking for me? Is one of the girls ill?'

'Oh, *non*, but you have a caller, waiting in the music room. He says…' Her voice dropped to a whisper, her hands twisting in her white apron. 'He says he is Monsieur le Duc!'

Chapter Eight

Alex carefully peered into the pale-blue-and-gold music room, half-shadowed in the dying daylight, and was shocked to see the maid was right—it was indeed Monsieur le Duc who waited there. Her father.

What could he be doing in Paris? She couldn't fathom it was anything good. Her parents had been settled in rented rooms in Florence since they were forced to leave England and they seldom wrote after she refused to join them there and instead took the job at Miss Grantley's. They had finally accepted her course, but she always sensed they would never approve.

He stood by one of the tall windows, staring out at the Parisian sunset, and he hadn't seen her yet. He looked so much different than when she last saw him. Though it had been only months, he looked years older, his hair more grey, his shoulders thin in his grey coat. He leaned on a gold-headed stick.

She felt such an urge to run to him, to wrap her arms around him as she had when she was a child. Back then, it seemed her father was a bulwark against the world, a strong defence that held her safe. But she was painfully aware that she was not a child any longer; she was a woman making her own way in the world and her parents were all too fallible. Human, just as she was herself. And she had disappointed them.

'Papa?' she called softly as she stepped into the room, nervously smoothing her skirt. 'Is it really you?'

He turned away from the window, his face expressionless for an instant, scored with fresh lines. Then he smiled. 'Alexandra, my dear Flower.' He came to her side, leaning on his stick, and kissed her cheek with his cool lips. 'How nice it is to see you again. You are looking well.'

'As are you, Papa,' Alex fibbed. She took his arm and led him to one of the satin sofas near the harp and the piano where her charges practised every morning. 'What are you doing in Paris? Is something amiss?'

'Oh, no. Just a quick visit. I'm on my way to meet with the attorneys in London and I thought I would come to see you on the journey.'

'I am very glad you did,' Alex answered. She was still doubtful, despite his reassuring words. There was tension about him, a wariness. 'Is Mama well?'

'The doctors have sent her for a stay in Baden-Baden, taking in the spa treatments for her health.'

'Her health!' Alex cried, alarmed. Her mother's last letter had complained about their accommodations, but nothing about her health.

'Yes. Our rooms are quite damp and her rheumatism and headaches have been paining her. She will feel better soon, I am sure, and perhaps we can move into the Tuscan countryside before winter.'

Alex nodded, and wondered how they were paying for Baden-Baden and Tuscany, if they were truly doing her mother good. 'And Charles?'

Her father sighed. 'Still in Scotland. He writes seldom.'

'Scotland. Yes.' Her brother, who had never been happy in London society anyway, had hidden away at their old hunting lodge as soon as the scandal broke. She always imagined him as quite the countryman there, growing a beard maybe, stalking the moors with his gun, drinking whisky by his fire at night. She doubted he could, or wanted to, find a proper wife there.

Thinking of Scotland made her remember Malcolm. Just like Charles, he could take on the trappings of position and city life, but he seemed a Scotsman at heart. Strong, brave, entirely himself.

Until it all fell to pieces around them.

'I am sorry, Papa,' she said. 'What can I do to help?'

He reached over and took her hand, holding it tightly. His signet ring pressed into her palm. 'I am glad you asked that, my dear. It's actually why I have come here.'

Alex was alarmed by the weariness in his voice. 'My wages…'

'No, Flower. A teacher's wages could never help us. But there is something you could do for us, your mother, Charles and me.'

'What is it?'

'You can, you must, marry,' he said insistently, firmly. The old father she remembered too well, the one who would brook no opposition.

'Marry?' she said, scared by the iron certainty in his voice. It was what she and Emily had just spoken about, marrying, what she had imagined as she watched the children playing in the park. But she was quite certain that her vague, longing dreams had nothing to do with what her father needed. 'But I have no suitors at present. Have you—have you someone in mind?'

'Not specifically, of course. My mind has been much preoccupied of late. But your mother and I talked about it before she left for Germany. Perhaps the variety of suitors might no longer be the same, but there are still plenty of gentlemen who would be honoured to have a wife such as you. A wife educated in all the finer things in life, who could help them establish a refined household.'

A *rich* man. Alex knew exactly what he meant. Once, they had wanted her to marry a prince. Now they wanted a wealthy *arriviste* who would happily buy a duke's daughter, even an impoverished one.

'I live a very quiet life here, Papa,' she said. 'I seldom meet any sort of eligible suitor at all.'

He waved this off. 'It can't be a difficult matter, surely! With all the people still gathered here in Paris after the Exposition. Businessmen of all sorts. Surely some of your old friends would take you about. Or even the Bullards. I hear they are respectable sorts.'

Alex remembered Emily urging her to go out. To go to the party at Gordston's. 'Papa, I am not sure…'

'Alexandra.' His hand tightened, his eyes dimming as he looked down at her. 'I would not ask you if it wasn't necessary. If there were a chance I could regain our fortunes, I would wait, even if you are no longer quite a debutante. But there is no time left. With the help of the right brother-in-law, your brother's estate could be saved, your mother could get all the medical care she needs. It is most urgent. We Wavertons always do our duty by each other, you know. I know you will not forget your place, not forget what you owe your family.'

Alex did know. Growing up, the first lesson she had always learned was that the ancient Waverton title came first. Always. Every member of the family was a part of it and had to learn it. She felt the unbearable emotional pressure of it bearing down on her again.

Her job teaching was a sort of glorious freedom. Now she felt the tightening knot of her name closing around her again. Her father was ruthless when he knew what he wanted. She remembered what happened to the Gordstons so long ago.

'I will look about, Papa,' she said.

Her father smiled sadly and patted her hand. 'Of course you will. I know you will always do your best for your family, Alexandra. Just as we try to do so by you. None of us wants to be alone in the world, which we surely would be if we forgot our duty to each other.'

Alone in the world. Yes. She knew he *would* cast her off if she did not do her duty now. It was a terrible feeling.

'Now, shall we go to dinner?' he said in a lighter tone, as if all was decided. 'Perhaps we could devise a list of suitable gentlemen. I am not without some influence still.'

Alex made herself smile in return. 'That sounds lovely, Papa. Let me just speak with Lady Bullard and change my gown.'

Up in her small chamber, Alex put her hat and gloves on the dressing table and stared at herself in the mirror. Her slippery, curling pale hair was escaping its pins again and there was a spot of dust on her shirtwaist. She sat down and pulled the pins out, shaking her hair free as a strange numbness came over her. She tried to envision her future, as she and Di and Em had whispered about when they were at school, but the picture came up blank. She couldn't fathom what it might be at all. Once she had thought there would be some faceless prince, far in the mists of the future. The classrooms and lessons, and wandering around Paris trying to build new dreams.

Now—now she had no idea. But when she closed her eyes, she had a strange image appear as if out of a cloud. Herself holding hands with Malcolm, her hair flying in the wind as they strolled over a heather-covered hill, laughing. Free, but not lonely. No longer lonely at all.

And when she opened her eyes, she wanted to cry for the lost beauty, the impossible joy, of such a moment. 'Why couldn't I have been born someone else?' she whispered. But she hadn't. She was still a Waverton and there was never any escaping that.

Alex held on to her father's arm as he led her up the wide, red-carpeted stairs to the main dining room of Le Grand Véfour. Véfour was one of the most venerable, most luxurious and still most fashionable places to be seen in Paris, a veritable palace on the rue de Beaujolais, swathed in crimson velvet, glittering with floor-to-ceiling mirrors, and crowned with a domed ceiling painted with a scene of classical gods feasting against a blue-and-gold sky. Life-sized gold sconces of more goddesses held aloft electric torches, illuminating the way to the dining room, the portraits and landscapes that glared down at them from the velvet walls.

It smelled delicious, of chocolate and delicately herbed sauces, and the sounds of an orchestra flowed through the air. As they moved past the tables, Alex saw countesses and princes, famous actresses, American heiresses, all laughing together.

It had been many months since she stepped into such a place and her stomach gave a nervous little flutter as she handed her cloak to a satin-liveried attendant. She pressed her hand against it, trying to steady herself, and glanced at her reflection in a silver-framed mirror. She had found a new world to live in, all too briefly, and now it seemed as far away as the moon. Did she really want all of this?

She had worn one of her best gowns she had kept from her old debutante life, a confection of white tulle, as shining as new snow, trimmed with dark blue velvet, and had borrowed a pair of kid gloves from Lady Bullard. Lady B. had also kindly loaned her maid to arrange Alex's hair and the girl, originally from Mademoiselle Gardinier's excellent school, had done a very good job, firmly anchoring the slippery curls into a fashionable pompadour tied with blue bows.

It was not so bad, Alex thought, trying to encourage herself. But the dress *was* from last year and she had only a small gold locket on a chain for jewellery.

She remembered the Eastern Star, the large sapphire her mother had always worn with such pride, but which had brought their family such bad luck. She was surely better off now. She patted at her hair, trying not to displace the fragile style, and smiled at her father as he appeared next to her. In his evening suit, he looked far more as she remembered him, not as thin and grey. But his eyes were still tired. He still knew she owed him her deepest familial duty.

'Shall we, my dear?' he said, offering his arm. 'I am having quite a yearning for their pigeon *en bécasse*.'

'Me, too,' Alex said with a laugh. She took his arm, feeling how thin he had become. She gave it a squeeze and an encouraging smile. 'And the hazelnut mousse. It has been much too long.'

As he led her into the golden magnificence of the main dining room, for a moment it was all as if nothing had changed. The classical frescoes on the walls, endlessly reflected in the mirrors, the sparkle of jewels and gleam of satin. She was with her father, the Duke of Waverton, and all was as it had always been. And she was sure she would drown under the opulence, the weight of the stares, the expectation.

But she took a deep breath and noticed a few of their old acquaintances nodding at them as they passed. Only one or two turned away, but many others stared in curiosity. Alex kept her head high, a smile on her lips, trying not to let that wretched blush into her cheeks. She didn't want anyone feeling pity for her.

Her father was stopped by old friends, Lord and Lady Avondale, and paused to chat with them for a moment while the maître d' led Alex to their table. Once, not so long ago, it would have been the best table there, near the dance floor where they would be seen, but tonight it was very nearly in the corner.

Alex didn't mind at all. She could sit there, somewhat away from attention, and watch everything that was happening. After so many months of quiet schoolroom life, it was quite overwhelming. All the light and noise, the tangled blend of music, laughter, the clink of heavy silver on fine porcelain, the scent of lilies and roses from the centrepieces, the richness of the ladies' perfumes.

She watched the couples twirling on the dance floor, the wondrous kaleidoscope of the women's gowns against the men's black suits. She wished Emily was there to explain all the new fashions! The velvet flowers trimming necklines, the lace ruffles on the sleeves.

And suddenly she rather thought it was actually *fun*. The music, the clothes, it was all so frivolous, so silly, so delightful. Had she really missed it, just a little bit? Perhaps she had, but she didn't want it for all the time. Not when there was a better way.

Her father joined her and the waiter in his red-and-gold tailcoat appeared with two glasses of champagne. Alex took a sip, laughing at the wonderful golden tickle of it. She had definitely missed champagne.

As her father sat down on the pale green brocade chair across from her, seemingly miles away over the crisp white-damask cloth, the forest of sparkling crystal and gleaming silver, it reminded her of her childhood, going down to kiss her parents at teatime, seeing them over acres of china, silver, silk, all the things that kept them apart. All the longings for real love she once had.

He studied the gilt-edged menu, and when he had ordered they chatted about inconsequential matters. How her mother had decorated their rooms in Florence, the weather in Paris of late, the people her mother was seeing at her spa. But Alex couldn't forget why he was really there—to find her a husband. Some of the bright pleasure of the evening seemed to dim at the memory and she peered suspiciously at every man who stopped to greet her father. She let the waiter refill her glass and quickly gulped it down.

'There is Sir Ronald Bascombe,' her father

said, gesturing towards a man who had just stepped into the dining room. He was stooped over a walking stick, tufts of grey hair sticking up around his head. 'A great fortune in shipping.'

'Oh, Papa, really,' Alex said, horrified. 'He must be ninety!'

'Well, what about his nephew, then?' Her father nodded at the boy who stood next to Sir Ronald, supporting the old man as he staggered across the room. He was tall and reedy, a shadow of peach fuzz on his smooth cheeks.

'And I think he must be twelve,' she said. 'Is it half-term at Eton?'

Her father gave a reluctant bark of laughter. 'Alexandra, this will never work without your full co-operation. I have your best interest at heart, too, you know. Don't you desire your own respectable household? A position in the world?'

Of course she did. She remembered the children she had seen in the park, playing in the afternoon sun, and she felt a sharp pang. She *did* want her own home and family. But not with someone like Sir Ronald or his nephew. It would be like a new prison, not a true family.

The waiters brought the first course, an aromatic lobster bisque. As he spooned the pale pink liquid carefully into her gilt-edged bowl, Alex glanced towards the entrance. A couple had just come in and the maître d' hurried to greet them. Even the dancers seemed to pause for an instant to look at them, all the soft golden light of the room centred directly on them.

Alex felt suddenly cold, floating, and everything else seemed to blur and fade around her. It was Malcolm Gordston who had just entered the restaurant, with Lady Smythe-Tomas on his arm. They looked as if they had just stepped from the fashion papers, the lady's coppery hair bound with loops of pearls and emeralds that matched her green-velvet gown, Malcolm looking every inch the Norse god Alex once imagined him, even in the usual black evening suit. No wonder everyone stopped to look at them.

Alex suddenly felt quite the drab in her old white dress. He was used to far more glamorous women all the time.

'Who the devil is that with Lady Smythe-Tomas?' her father said irritably.

'That's Mr Malcolm Gordston, of course, the owner of Gordston's Department Store,' Alex answered. 'Do you really not recognise him, Papa?' She didn't just mean from the famous stores, but from so long ago in Scotland. Yet even if her father did happen to remember a crofter's family, which she doubted he ever would, it had indeed been long years ago. Malcolm was a very different person now, powerful, wealthy, full of confidence. And her family was brought low.

'Your mother is the one who does all the shopping. How would I know a tradesman?' her father grumbled. But he studied Malcolm closely as the maître d' led them to a table near the dance floor. Lady Smythe-Tomas held on to Malcolm's arm, laughing up at him as he smiled warmly in return. 'He seems familiar somehow. Money, is there, in these department stores?'

'Yes,' Alex answered shortly. 'A lot.' As hard as she tried to stop herself, she couldn't help but stare at the couple just a bit, as they laughed and talked together. Lady S.-T. even reached out and gently touched his arm, pointing out something on the menu.

Suddenly, Malcolm glanced up and caught Alex looking. Her face grew hot and she turned sharply away, fussing with her napkin.

'He is not ninety, Alexandra my Flower,' her father said. 'Nor on holiday from Eton.'

Was her father actually suggesting she should chase after Malcolm Gordston? 'Papa, you just said you don't know tradesmen. And he's with Lady Smythe-Tomas, anyway. He wouldn't look at me.'

Her father's expression hardened. 'Times have changed, Alexandra, you know that as well as I do. And Laura Smythe-Tomas, lovely as she is, is not a duke's daughter.'

Alex did know times had changed. Very well. She reached for her wineglass as the waiter brought the fish course and tried not to stare at Malcolm and the beautiful Lady S.-T. She didn't want to even feel jealousy, let alone show it to the whole world! Yet she feared it was there, lurking in green-eyed splendour.

'Shall we dance, Alexandra?' her father said.

She glanced at him in surprise. Her father seldom danced. 'I—yes, of course.'

The orchestra was playing Strauss's 'Gartenlaube Waltz', and as she took her father's arm she saw that Malcolm was already on the dance floor, spinning with Lady S.-T.

Alex tried not to stare at them, tried not to be jealous, to wonder what he and Lady S.-T. were to each other—until one spin took her bumping right into them. She glanced up at Malcolm, stammering apologies, trying not to blush.

'Oh, what luck!' Lady Smythe-Tomas cried merrily. 'I have been so wanting to ask you something, Your Grace, and here you are right in front of me at last. Shall we dance and talk for a moment? Malcolm, you can partner Lady Alexandra, can you not?'

'Of course, it would be a delight,' Malcolm

said and Alex could read nothing from his polite tone.

His hand slid over her waist, warm and strong, the roughness of his fingertips catching on the tulle of her gown. Perhaps he had not expected to dance that night, just as she hadn't. The moment had burst on her in complete surprise, like bright white fireworks exploding in her head. He held out his other hand to take hers and she slid her fingers slowly over his. How small her hand looked against his! She stared at it in wonder, that touch of their hands, and for a moment she had no words. No breath even. She'd never really dreamed of such a moment, where time ticked to a stop. It was like a book. Like *Cinderella*, maybe.

And her pumpkin would soon return. She had to make the most of that moment.

The music quickened, swayed, and the couples around them swirled into motion. Malcolm gently tugged at her hand and she smiled at herself, standing there gaping at his hand like a fool. He spun her in a slow circle, their bodies pressed just a little closer than was proper by the crowd around them. She felt like she would float up into the air, giddy and free.

It had been so many months since she danced at all, but her feet seemed to remember the steps, the rhythm. It helped that Malcolm was a good dancer. He looked like a marauding Viking, even in his subdued evening dress, but he moved with a smooth, elegant grace. It was *fun* dancing with him, spinning and turning, and for a moment she even forgot to be shy of him.

'You are a fine dancer, Mr Gordston,' she said. 'I think I'm the envy of every lady here!'

And it was true. She saw many of the women on the dance floor studying them, their expressions unsmiling, pinched. She glimpsed Lady S.-T. dancing with the Duke and she was laughing, her movements light and careless, not looking towards Malcolm at all. Alex wondered if she was *with* Malcolm, or if something else was happening between them.

'All part of my rehabilitation from shop boy to society department stores,' he answered lightly, spinning her so fast she burst out laughing. 'How to dress, how to eat soup without slurping, how to dance without treading on toes...'

'You had good teachers. I've never felt so light, like I'm waltzing on a cloud!' They slipped easily around another couple and she held tightly to his shoulder, leaning closer. She smelled his scent, an expensive, enticing green-lemon smell of a warm summer day, and she remembered when they walked together at the garden party.

Enclosed in their own Eden. 'How have you been since we last met, Mr Gordston? I hear your store has become quite the wonder of the city.'

'We can barely keep the counters stocked before they're emptied, which isn't a state of affairs I can complain about. Paris has been very welcoming.' He smiled down at her, studying her for a long quiet moment with those intense pale blue eyes. He watched her for so long she felt her cheeks turning warm with that hateful blush and she stumbled a bit. 'And how are you enjoying the city of lights, Lady Alexandra? Are you here with your family?'

Alex glanced at her father. She wondered what exactly Malcolm had heard of the Wavertons' misfortunes. Surely he had caught the gossip, as everyone had. What did he think of them? Did he despise them, pity them? She decided she could only be honest with him. Those extraordinary eyes seemed to see everything, anyway. Seemed to see right through her, to her very heart. It was a most discomfiting feeling—for all her life, no one seemed to see *her* at all.

'My father lives in Italy right now, along with my mother,' she said. 'I am in Paris as governess to Lady Bullard's daughters.'

His brows arched in surprise. 'Governess?'

Alex made herself keep holding her head high,

keep smiling. Keep looking into those eyes, even as she ached to turn away. To hide from him. She couldn't bear it for him, of all people, to think badly of her. 'Yes. To two little girls, who luckily behave like utter angels—most of the time. I've really only seen parks and doll stores in Paris lately!'

The music slowed a bit and their steps swayed together. 'I feel like I must apologise, Lady Alexandra,' he said softly.

'Oh?' she said, suddenly worried. 'Did you step on my slipper? I barely felt it.'

He chuckled. 'Not at all. Dancing with you is as easy as dancing with a feather. I apologise because I did not remember when we danced together once in Scotland.'

'It was so long ago,' Alex said wistfully, thinking of those bright days when she ran free over the hillsides as a child. 'I'm sure I'm quite different.'

'Not so very much. You were like a little fairy then, too, all silver and gold, fluttering here and there. So fast no one could ever catch you.'

She smiled. 'My nanny always just told me I was too thin and delicate, and tried to force me to drink more milk. Not that it helped, I never got any taller. I wish I had known I was just one of the fairy folk!'

He gave her a crooked, enticing little smile she wished she could read. 'That you are. My grandmother used to tell me tales of your sort. How never to trust you, because you would just fly away, leaving only the memory of magic behind.'

'How wonderful! I often wished I *could* fly away. My brother and I were always looking for fairy circles on the moors and we never saw one. If I could have summoned them merely with magical words...'

'And you were always running out to the fields, asking questions.'

'Yes. I must have been rather a nuisance. I remember you and your father, too. You were always so patient with Charles and me, you even let me try a bit of scything in the fields. It's a wonder I still have all my toes after that!'

He laughed. 'You weren't so bad. If governessing doesn't work out for you...'

'It would be a desperate farmer indeed who hired me.' She thought of those days when she first knew him, his tanned cheeks, his wide smile, his steady hand as he helped her over the hillside. What had happened to him, that boy, to make him what he was now? 'And how is your father? Do you see him much since you went off to learn shopkeeping?'

His laughter faded, his expression closing like

a shutter snapping down. Her heart sank to see it. 'He died many years ago. Soon after I went to work at the draper's shop.'

'Oh,' she whispered, sure she should have remembered that. He had told her so before, of course. She felt terrible. 'Oh, I am sorry. No wonder I never saw you again after that one autumn. And then we stopped going to Scotland altogether. I never knew why and I missed it very much. Charles lives there now, he's so terribly lucky, I think.' She was afraid she was babbling, but she couldn't make herself stop. Something felt different between them, as if the air had shifted into a colder breeze, and she didn't know why.

He said nothing, just glided her gracefully through the figures of the dance, his hands warm through her thin gown. She peeked up at him and he looked rather distant. Angry, even.

She thought of how he had looked that magical autumn in Scotland, that laughing boy. He had changed much indeed! They all had, of course; they were no longer children, unknowing of the world outside.

Suddenly, she remembered something else about that autumn. That day she had glimpsed Malcolm at the gate—and he hadn't been alone. He'd been with a girl, a beautiful creature named Mairie, with a cloud of long, waving dark hair, wrapped in a bright red shawl. Alex had been so desperate to apologise to him after her father's rage had focused on his family and he'd had someone else, someone far more beautiful, to comfort him.

She studied Malcolm carefully now, as they danced in the luxurious surroundings of the finest restaurant in Paris, so far from Scotland. What had happened to her? Had he ever felt that tenderness again, or was it buried so deep beneath *this* Malcolm Gordston, this wealthy Viking of the business world, that he was utterly vanished? That thought made her feel terribly sad.

'How far we have all come,' she murmured.

'And yet not nearly far enough,' he answered and she puzzled over what he could mean. The music swirled to a stop and she reluctantly let go of him and stepped back. It felt even colder despite that overheated room.

'Would you care for a breath of fresh air?' he asked, gesturing to the tall glass doors that led out to a terrace and the Véfour's famous garden, where she could see a few couples strolling in the soft gleam of light reflected from the dining room. 'The smell of all these infernal hothouse lilies is quite overwhelming. Your cheeks look flushed.'

Alex pressed her gloved hand to her cheek. She was certainly tempted to go out there, to not lose this moment with him quite yet. She glanced at her father, who was talking with a table of his old friends across the gilded room. Lady S.-T. was still with him, chattering brightly.

'Won't Lady Smythe-Tomas miss you?' she asked.

Malcolm looked at the lady and smiled. 'I doubt it. She's much too busy. I promise I won't keep you outside too long.'

'I wouldn't let you. I couldn't miss the Véfour's famous croquembouche, could I?' Alex nodded decisively. She was no longer completely under the weight of her old life. She could give in to her own wants, if she so dared. And Malcolm made her feel bolder than she ever had before.

He offered her his arm and led her out the doors, opened by the liveried waiters on to the terrace. The white marble shimmered in the night, cold and glassy-smooth under her satin shoes, softened by banks of potted palms, cosy arrangements of wicker tables and chairs that were perfect for quiet conversation. The silks and satins of the ladies' gowns and trains swished and swirled as they strolled past, whispering with their companions, smiling mysteriously.

Alex wished she could be like them, sophisticated and mysterious. That she could be the right sort of woman for a companion like Malcolm. But she feared, fairy folk or not, she never would be.

She went to the balustrade and stared out into the night. The gardens had a wonderful view of the city and it was indeed a city of sparkling lights. A city of secrets and magic, beauty, where a person could hide. Could become anything they wanted to be.

'Isn't it glorious?' she said softly, afraid to break the spell of Paris.

He leaned his hands on the balustrade next to her, standing so close she could smell his summer scent, feel the heat of him. 'I could never have imagined anything like it, until I saw it for myself.'

'When I was a child, I found a book of engravings in our library, images of Paris and some of the chateaus, like Versailles,' Alex said. She remembered all the hours she was lost in that book, in that world that seemed like a fairy tale. 'I didn't believe such beauty existed outside a book, until I came here.'

'When I was a lad, I only knew the countryside. The cold, grey sky, the scrubby hillsides, all purple and green. Very different.'

'And now you are here. In Paris. More than that, you are the master of the city!'

He glanced down at her, his eyes shadowed in the half-light, unreadable. 'Yes. Here we are.'

And it was just as much a dream to her as that book had once been. He held out his hand and she reached out to take it, dazed and dizzy from looking into his eyes. They strolled slowly towards the far edge of the terrace where the light was even dimmer, the voices quieter. She could smell the damp greenness from the garden, the trace of the ladies' perfumes on the breeze.

'Have you been to Versailles, then?' he asked. 'Was it like you imagined from your book?'

Alex shook her head. 'I fear I've never visited the palace. I have to work at my teaching now and haven't had the time. Though I suppose I ought to take my little charges, once our historical lessons reach the eighteenth century. I haven't even had time to return to Eiffel's Tower since the Prince and Princess visited so long ago! I've been longing to see it again, not just glimpsed over the roofs.'

'Then perhaps you would let me buy you luncheon at one of the Tower's cafés soon?' he said, his voice soft yet intense, as if he was unsure of her answer.

'I...' Alex hesitated, then reminded herself to

be bold. To do what she liked sometimes. To let herself feel whatever it was she was feeling when she saw him. 'I think I would like that. I usually do have two half-days free.'

'Alexandra,' she heard her father say and she turned to see him waiting in the doorway. She wondered if she should feel embarrassed to be there with Malcolm. Suddenly, she realised she did not care. She liked being with Malcolm; with him, she felt free, like herself. Honest. It was a delirious feeling.

'Coming, Papa,' she called. She smiled up at Malcolm. 'I will look forward to the Tower, Mr Gordston, thank you.'

And even as she walked away, she couldn't stop smiling. Or wondering if he watched her, if he, too, looked forward to seeing her again. It was a heady thought indeed.

Malcolm watched Lady Alexandra walk back into the restaurant, her shoulders as straight and regal as any lady's should be, her golden hair shimmering in the light. She glanced back just as she stepped through the door, her eyes shining, and she even gave him a small wave.

Her father didn't look nearly as happy.

Malcolm laughed and took a cigar out of his pocket to light up in the fine night air. Of course the Duke, the man who had ruled his estate like an iron-fisted maharajah, who tossed people out when he had no use for them, wouldn't want a shopkeeper with his lovely daughter. Even a rich one. Malcolm knew he should feel triumphant at getting one over on the man and he did indeed. The taste of comeuppance was no less sweet when it was cold. That would fade soon enough, he was afraid, and leave the old feelings of not being good enough. Not quite right.

Yet there was something else there, too, something he didn't want to look at too closely. A feeling of—of excitement at seeing Alexandra again. Of something fizzy and light and bright, like champagne. She was an intriguing woman, a pretty girl grown into a delicate beauty, whose every move spoke of high breeding and yet she was making her way alone in the world.

What had happened to her since they last met? Had she come to see the universe as he had, something full of dangers and pitfalls to be conquered? He did hope not. She had always been so sweet, so happy and innocent, and if he could he would have made her whole life that way for her.

He frowned as he stared down at the bright glow at the tip of his cigar, a spot of light in the Parisian night. Nothing in life ever went like that, even for someone like Lady Alexandra, and there were hard lessons around every corner. A person had to seize what they wanted. And he found he wanted *her*. Wanted all she represented.

But he wanted that on his own terms. He was his own man now, he had created his own destiny and he would never be weak like his own father. He would always be in control of his heart, of what happened to his life from now on, even with a lady like Alex. *Especially* with a lady like her. Fairies were unpredictable creatures, always elusive.

He just had to figure out how to get her and pin her wings to his own life.

Chapter Nine

❦

Alex couldn't believe she had waited so long to come back to the Champ de Mars, to Monsieur Eiffel's Tower. It was stunning, overwhelming, like something out of the mundane world and up into the sky with that lacy, impossibly light-looking iron spire.

She held on to her hat and tipped her head back, staring up and up, absorbed in the elaborate scrolls and swirls. It was a beautiful warm day, the French azure sky without a cloud to mar it, the sun soft and shimmering. With most of the pavilions of the Exposition cleared away, the park was reclaiming its cool sweep of green grass. Trees cut into perfect topiary shapes were being tended and repaired by bustling teams of blue-smocked gardeners, red and yellow and white flowers reappearing in the triangular beds, people hurrying along the paths. The rush and excitement of the Exposition was over, but Paris was as elegant, as full of life, as usual.

It almost made her forget the nervousness of why she was there—to meet with Malcolm Gordston.

Alex turned away from the Tower, a shiver flowing over her. She had barely slept at all last night, once she was tucked up safely in her little room at the Bullards'. All she could do was wonder what boldness had overcome her at Véfour, what had made her accept his invitation. She'd tossed and turned for hours, going over every instant she'd spent in his company. Every moment of the dance, every step on the terrace, every smile, every word. It wasn't like her to leap into something like walking in the park with a man.

And not just any man. Malcolm Gordston, surely the most handsome man she had ever seen. He had such a masculine confidence about him, a graceful, panther-like ease that was dangerously attractive. She remembered her girlish infatuation with him in Scotland, how he had possessed that quality of assurance even as a boy and it had always drawn her in. Was she quite wise to meet him that day?

Yet she knew why she had agreed to see him. Why she *had* to see him. It was the way she felt when he kissed her hand. She had never known anything like that sensation before. The heat and excitement of his touch.

She made her way past a cluster of children rolling their hoops along the pathway and sat down on one of the wrought-iron benches in the shade of a fragrant chestnut tree. She smoothed the skirt of her gown, one of her afternoon dresses left from her old life, of pale blue muslin and creamy lace with a darker blue jacket, and straightened her hat. She fiddled with the ivory handle of her parasol and wished she could sit still. Could smile serenely and mysteriously, as a woman of the world like Lady Smythe-Tomas would do. But she was just too nervous.

Don't be silly, she scolded herself. It was just an afternoon stroll, two people who had known each other as children. But what if it was, just maybe—something a little more? He had been attracted to her that day in Hyde Park, when he didn't know who she was. Maybe he still thought her pretty?

She didn't quite know if the thought intrigued her, or terrified her. And what did she think of him?

She thought he was terribly fascinating. And terribly bad for her equilibrium.

Alex twisted at the carved parasol handle. Maybe her father's talk of marriage was affecting her more than it should. She hadn't thought of romance in such a long time and never with a man like Malcolm.

She stood up and turned to leave, to run away. But she was too late. He stood there on the pathway, just a few feet away. The brim of his hat cast mysterious shadows on his elegantly carved face and the sun shimmered on his bright hair.

He tilted the hat to her and smiled, a flash of white that drew her closer. 'Lady Alexandra. It's a lovely day for a stroll, isn't it?'

And any urge to flee was gone, like a vanishing cloud in that perfect blue sky over their heads. Alex smiled back at him. 'So it is.'

'My secretary told me to give you her thanks for getting me out of the office. She thinks I'm looking peaked from lack of fresh air.'

Alex thought his secretary must be blind. Malcolm was the most healthy specimen she had ever seen, tall and vigorous, his skin golden from the sun. She laughed. 'She is quite welcome, then. You must be very busy, with the grand opening party coming up soon.'

'Will you be attending?'

'Oh, yes, along with my friend Miss Fortescue.'

'I'm glad to hear it. It should be quite the show, with singers, *tableaux vivants*, a buffet supper.'

Alex laughed and took his offered arm as they turned towards the Tower. 'I fear I would have nothing grand enough to wear to such a thing. But I do always love a nice buffet.'

He glanced down at her, his expression hidden by his hat. 'You would outshine everyone there no matter what you wore.'

Alex felt her cheeks turn warm. Could he mean it—or was it mere flattery, of the sort she had heard too much? She thought of Lady S.-T., her fashionable gowns, and knew she could never compete with that. 'It's kind of you to say so. But we are in Paris, the land of Paquin and Worth…' Her eyes widened when she glimpsed the hat of a lady passing them on the path. As wide as a carriage wheel, trimmed with sweeping peacock feathers. 'Of things like that. Oh, my.'

Malcolm studied the chapeau, his blue eyes narrowed in professional appraisal. 'Would you like to wear something like that? Is it to your taste? Your *true* taste, not what the fashion papers say.'

He sounded as if he really wanted to know the answer, as if her opinion mattered. Alex couldn't remember the last time someone had done that. 'No, not really. I'm sure I would topple over if I tried to wear it! I'm not tall enough.' She touched the brim of the hat she wore. It was seasons out of date, a straw creation with blue streamers and creamy silk roses, but it was one of her favourites. It reminded her of a country morning, fresh and bright and pretty. 'I guess I feel more comfortable in something simpler. I'm afraid it doesn't make me very à la mode.'

'You, Lady Alexandra, could set the fashions if you chose. People would follow you, not the other way around. They would all want to look like you.'

Alex felt flustered at his words. 'Oh, surely not. I have never been of much interest. My tastes are surely too—girlish.'

'Trust me, Lady Alexandra, fashion and learning to lead the way has made me my fortune. You are exactly the sort of lady most likely to lead fashion—one who doesn't care for its dictates in the least.'

Alex laughed. 'But that doesn't make sense. Surely someone must think about fashion a great deal to know how to lead it.'

'Not at all. Nothing is more attractive than indifference, originality. You know what suits you and you wear it, no matter what everyone else is doing. That is real style.'

'I think it's necessity. I live on a governess's wages now.'

'If you had the fortune of a queen, would you dress differently?'

Alex considered this. 'I would have *more* clothes, certainly, for I do like them. But I'm not sure they would look terribly different.'

They stepped into the shadow of the Tower, waiting in line at the ticket office as the crowds swirled around them.

'And your employers?' he asked. 'Do they dictate your clothes?'

'Oh, no, not at all. I am most fortunate, the Bullards are kind and the girls quite adorable, if sometimes high-spirited! They are at their dance lessons today, which will leave them mercifully worn out this evening. They have several outside lessons and Lady Bullard doesn't care what I do with this free time.'

'Then what do you usually do? Not shopping, I think. We haven't seen you in Gordston's lately.'

Alex hesitated. She hadn't really told anyone what she did on those long Paris afternoons. 'Sometimes I go to a museum. But mostly I am at my charity work.'

'Your charity?' he asked, his tone curious.

'Yes. I suppose most ladies do have their work of that sort, but I teach at a school run by Mademoiselle Gardinier. She helps young women

who have fallen into unfortunate circumstances
train for new employment.'

'I know of Mademoiselle Gardinier and her
work.'

Alex was surprised. The school was most discreet. 'You do?'

'Yes. Gordston's sometimes employs her graduates. A Mademoiselle Elise has just been taken
on as an embroiderer.'

'Elise!' Alex said happily. 'Oh, I am glad.'

'You taught her?'

'Her sewing skills are far beyond my meagre
efforts, but we did a bit of writing, some English.
And you have employed her?'

'Indeed. She seems quite promising.'

Alex had the suspicion that he was much
kinder than he wanted people to believe. Before she could say more, ask him about his own
charitable efforts, they reached the front of the
line and Malcolm purchased their tickets. 'Lift
or stairs?' he asked.

'Oh, stairs! I love to watch the view changing
slowly as we go higher and higher.'

He gave her a doubtful glance. 'Are you sure?'

'Of course. I am stronger than I look, Mr
Gordston! Shall I race you?'

He smiled, a wide grin that made him look
irresistibly like Thor about to plunge into battle.

She grabbed a handful of her skirts and they both took off running up the winding iron stairs, past startled-looking dawdlers. His legs were much longer than hers, but she was used to dashing after the energetic Bullard girls and she could dodge and feint. By the time they reached the first platform, she was steps ahead of him.

'I cede the victory, Lady Alexandra,' he said, slightly out of breath.

Alex laughed, pressing her hand to her side as she tried to breathe deeply past her corset. 'I think it was more of a dead heat.'

'Not at all. You were ahead of me fair and square. I think I owe the winner a glass of champagne. I remember you liked it at Véfour?'

Alex glanced at the little bar tucked near the railing, the maids hurrying past the tall mirrors to pour wine, round tables and wicker chairs scattered about. She worried about the effect champagne *and* Malcolm together might have on her, making her feel even more giddy and silly. But suddenly she really wanted to be silly, just once. 'Oh, it's true, I do love champagne. Very well, I accept the laurels of victory.'

She sat down at one of the chairs near the railing, watching him as he fetched their glasses at the bar. The maids giggled as he talked to them and she was glad she wasn't the only one who felt ridiculous when he was near. She smiled as he came back and sipped at her fizzy drink.

She turned to gaze over the railing at the city far below, giving herself time to compose her feelings a little. 'Do you think Paris is more beautiful by day than night? I can never decide.'

'I think Paris is always beautiful. The loveliest place I have ever seen.'

'And do you ever miss the countryside in Scotland?' she asked, remembering how when they were young he seemed to belong to those wild hills. Yet he also seemed to belong to this glamorous city. He was a chameleon and she found she longed to know every side of him. 'I know you said you left when you were still young to become an apprentice. But do you think of how it was when you were a child?'

Malcolm frowned a bit and took a drink from his own glass. 'Of course. Once Scotland is in your blood, it won't be out again.'

'I do think I should like to go back there one day, though I doubt my brother would want me bursting in on his solitude at our old lodge.'

'Your brother?'

'Yes, Charles. Perhaps you remember him? But back then he thought himself quite grown up and wanted nothing to do with his little sister. He lives there now, he's become quite the recluse. I haven't seen the place in ages and ages. I wonder what it all looks like now.'

'Not as it is in our memories, I'm sure,' he said in a strangely hard voice.

Alex wondered if she had said something wrong. 'Probably not.'

He smiled at her again and she wondered if she had imagined that sudden distance. He looked utterly transformed. Which was the real Malcolm? she wondered. 'Another glass of champagne, then?'

She laughed. 'Oh, it is much too tempting! I shouldn't.'

'Look at this afternoon as a holiday. A chance to pretend to be real Parisians.'

'I would like that, to be Parisian. Thank you.'

He fetched two more glasses and, as the bubbles went giddily to her head, they basked in the warm day, tried to identify landmarks of the city from their dizzying height, chatted about the wonders of the Exposition they had seen. She found herself laughing, feeling herself float in the lightness of the day, the city, the sun, the champagne, the man beside her.

'Gordston! I want a word with you,' a man suddenly shouted, bursting the shimmering, delicate bubble of the bright afternoon, attracting the attention of the people around them.

Startled, Alex twisted around in her chair to see a man striding towards them. He wore no hat, his thinning brown hair tousled, his face red above a beard, his eyes glowing like something unworldly. She found herself frightened against her will and reached for her parasol.

Malcolm took Alex's arm and drew her up from her chair, his hand firm on her sleeve, sliding her slightly behind him as they made their way towards the stairs. The man followed.

'Not now, Nixson,' Malcolm said quietly. 'This is obviously not a place of business. There is a lady present.'

The man drew a scathing glance over Alex, making her fist tighten on the handle of her parasol in anger. 'Lady, is it? With *you*? I doubt it.'

Malcolm pushed Alex gently away, standing in front of her. She wondered suddenly if there really was some danger there, something she knew nothing about.

'If you persist in insulting her,' Malcolm said, 'I will answer you in kind. If you have something of a professional nature to say to me, call at my office. But my answer will still stand. I have told you that and I am sure Lady Smythe-Tomas has done the same.'

'You bastard!' the man growled. 'You don't

know what you have done, what you have turned away. Listen to me, I beg you…'

'I said no, Nixson, and that is final,' Malcolm said firmly, just as two of the Tower's blue-suited guards arrived and dragged the man away. Everyone around them gaped as if they were watching a show at the Comédie-Française.

'Whatever was that all about?' she gasped as Malcolm took her arm and led her towards the stairs. Behind them, the man was still shouting, but the guards had subdued him. 'Who is he?'

'A business matter,' Malcolm growled, his brogue thick. 'Nothing to be concerned about.'

'Nothing?' Alex glanced at him, remembering the man's face, bright scarlet with anger. 'But he was so furious!'

Malcolm stopped on the stairs and turned to look at her. His face seemed to be carved of granite, her charming, laughing companion of only moments before vanished. 'In business, Lady Alexandra, there are times a man must be ruthless. Surely your family understands that very well.'

'My family?' she said, puzzled. 'I don't understand.'

He strode ahead of her and she was moving too quickly to catch up with him, bewildered by all that had just happened, when the heel of her shoe caught in a metal grating of the stairs. It sent her pitching head-first towards the banister.

Cold fear rushed through her, like ice in her veins. Her foot caught in her heavy skirts and sent her twirling even more wildly. Her ankle gave a painful wrench. But what felt like an hour of falling was really only an instant.

Malcolm caught her around her waist, swinging her off her feet. 'Are you hurt?' he cried, his face a mask of horror.

'My—my ankle,' Alex gasped as pain shot up her leg.

He set her down on the step, ignoring the curious passers-by as he knelt in front of her. 'Let me see.'

Alex felt herself blush, felt foolish for making such a fuss. 'Oh, no...'

'It might be broken. And it's all my blasted fault, rushing you like that. My temper— I'm so sorry. May I look?'

She swallowed hard and nodded. She slowly lifted her hem a few inches and held out her foot in its soft leather shoe.

Malcolm slid his hand around her ankle, just above the scalloped edge of the leather. His fingers were strong, warm, gentle through her white-knit stocking. She couldn't help but shiver just a bit as his touch slid against her, checking for an injury. She quite forgot the wrenching pain of the fall.

She reached out to balance her hands on his shoulders, but the feel of those muscles under layers of fine wool and linen only made her feel dizzier.

'I don't think it's broken, but it's starting to swell a bit,' he said softly. 'Let me take you to the store so we can get it bandaged as soon as possible.'

Alex wasn't sure she could trust herself to be alone with him. 'I'm sure that's not necessary. It's probably nothing at all.'

'It was my fault you were hurt,' he said firmly. 'Please, let me help you now. Let me make amends for spoiling our lovely afternoon.'

Alex slowly nodded. 'Very well, then. To Gordston's we go.'

'I'm afraid my secretary, Miss Mersey, is gone for the day, so you'll have to put up with my clumsy nursing,' Malcolm said, setting Alex down gently on a *chaise* in the corner of his office. He found a cushion and carefully propped it under her foot.

'I'm sure you'll be a perfect Florence Nightingale,' she said. In truth, her foot felt rather better now, a mere dull ache, and her nerves had settled once they were in the quiet of the Gordston's building and away from the clamour on the Tower. But she was guiltily enjoying a little moment of pampering from him. She doubted it happened often.

'I don't know about that,' he said ruefully. 'For one thing, I don't have a lamp. But I'll do my best.' He poured out a tumbler of dark amber brandy from the sideboard and pressed it into her hand. 'Here, sip this and I'll go try to find some bandages.'

As he hurried out of the room, Alex studied his office with great curiosity, sure she would never have the chance to see it again. It was an elegant space, spare compared to the marble-and-velvet opulence of the rest of the store. Dark panelled walls, along with a thick forest-green carpet and the green upholstered chairs and *chaise*, made it feel cosy and quiet, surely a haven on busy days.

The desk was neatly organised, but covered with papers and folders, very businesslike. Two shelves were filled with ledgers and several paintings in dull gilt frames hung on the walls.

Alex carefully stood up and hobbled over to examine them. A person's taste in art said so much about them, she thought. The family portraits and dull landscapes her parents liked, which had been in their home for generations and could not be moved; the bright, modern Impressionists Emily collected. What would Malcolm have? Any portraits of lost loves? Wistful memories of Scottish hillsides?

It turned out he had Old Masters. Views of Dutch cities under pearl-grey skies, saints and war heroes, still lifes that looked glowingly real. She could tell all were quite authentic and of the best quality, thanks to Miss Grantley's education. And nothing that seemed to tell her anything about the enigmatic Malcolm Gordston himself, except that he had good taste. She felt overwhelmed by it all, almost closed in.

Except for one on an easel near his desk. It was a smallish Raphael, a Madonna and child, all glowing jewel tones of red, blue and gold. But what was so lovely, so fascinating, was the great tenderness between the mother and her baby. Their golden heads were bent close together, the child's hand on her cheek. So filled with love and protective care. Surely the kind of mother any child would want. The kind Alex wished she herself had.

She wondered what Malcolm's own childhood had been like. She couldn't remember his mother at all and she knew he had gone away to work

when he was young. Did he long for such tenderness, such love?

She turned away, unable to look into the Madonna's painted blue eyes without crying. She
took a deep, steadying sip of the brandy.

Malcolm came back into the office, a basin of
water and a small box in his hands, a towel over
his arm. He scowled when he saw her standing
there.

'You shouldn't be walking,' he said sternly. He
put down his burden and took off his coat, his
shoulders broad beneath the thin, fine linen of
his shirt. Alex couldn't quite look away.

'I wanted to see your paintings,' she said, low-
ering herself on to the nearest chair. 'They are
quite beautiful. Especially this one. Raphael, is
it?'

'Yes.' He glanced at the painting, his blue eyes
shadowed. 'I had a devil of a time getting it. An
auction in Dusseldorf, five others bidding for it.'

'But you had to have it,' she murmured. She
wondered why he loved it so.

'When there is something I really want, I am
willing to work very hard to obtain it.' He knelt
down beside her, his hair brushing her arm, and
reached for her shoe to carefully slide it off.
Slowly, so slowly she dared not breathe, he rolled

away her torn stocking and lowered her toes into the warm water of the basin.

Alex knew she had to distract herself or she would faint. 'Does she—the Madonna, I mean—look like your own mother?'

Malcolm looked up at her, his brows raised in surprise. 'My mother? I hardly know. I barely remember her. She did have blue eyes like that, though. And she would smile like that as she tucked me in at night.'

'Is that why you bought it, then?'

'To remind me of my mother?' He was quiet for a long moment, a thoughtful frown on his face. 'I don't know. I think it was just a bit of sweetness, softness. I don't get much of that around here.'

Alex felt so sad at his words. She longed to reach out, to touch his hair, to comfort him somehow. But even though they were so close physically at that moment, she still felt shy, distant. She curled her hand into a fist.

He carefully dried her foot and examined the swollen ankle. She longed to pull back, for no one had ever seen her bare skin like that before. But his touch felt so good, so warm, so—strangely exciting. As much as she longed to hide, she wanted more for the moment to go on and on.

'It looks swollen still,' he said. 'You'll have

to be careful on it for a few days. Nothing broken, though.'

'It already feels better.'

He opened the box and took out a silk scarf, a length of the most beautiful peacock-blue-and-green colours she had ever seen. It glowed in the darkened room.

He started to wrap it around her ankle and Alex cried out in protest. 'You can't use such a beautiful thing like that as a bandage!'

'I couldn't find any real bandages,' he said. 'Surely this will work instead. Is the colour wrong? I could fetch a pink one, or green maybe.'

Alex laughed. She couldn't help it. His baffled expression as he studied the makeshift bandage was too adorable. 'No, blue is perfectly acceptable. But it's much too pretty, too expensive.'

'Not at all. You can't hobble around with this ankle unbound all day, it will make it feel much worse.' He tied the scarf around her ankle tightly, finishing in a neat knot, before she could protest again. He was most careful and gentle, treating her as if she was made of porcelain.

Alex thought he must be two different people, the one who argued so fiercely with the man at the Tower and the gentle one who took care of her now. He was always changing, right in front of her eyes. Would she ever know the real Malcolm?

'There,' he said. 'That should do until you can see a doctor.'

Alex examined the very stylish bandage. 'I don't think a doctor could possibly do a better job. Where did you learn first aid like that?'

He shrugged. 'I was a farmer's son and now I run a store with a shipping dock. Accidents happen.'

'Then I'm lucky I took a fall near *you*, Mr Nightingale,' she teased.

He shook his head. 'You wouldn't have been in such a rush if I hadn't let my temper get the better of me. Mr Nixson is a fool, but I never should have lost my temper like that.'

Alex longed to ask what their feud was about, but she was sure Malcolm wouldn't tell her. Instead she held out her foot and thought she had no shoes that could possibly look more elegant.

Malcolm sat back on his heels, his hands braced to the arms of the chair beside her, so close she could smell the warm summer scent of him, feel his arm against hers. If she leaned forward, just the tiniest amount, she could press her lips to his cheek and taste his skin at last. Slide her lips just a little tiny bit to the side and then...

His eyes met hers for a long moment, the blue darkening like a stormy sky. For a breathless, endless instant, she was sure he could read her thoughts, her desires. That he would kiss her. But then he looked away, drew back, and Alex slumped back with a cold rush of disappointment.

He rose to his feet and turned away, reaching for his coat. Alex twisted her fingers in her skirt, wishing she was more sophisticated, more elegant. That she knew how to get him to kiss her.

'Let me fetch a carriage to take you home,' he said.

'Oh, it's not far…' she began.

'*Bawheed*, woman, you can't walk about and ruin my good work! I will send for my driver and that's the end of it.' He spun around and stalked out of the room.

Alex pressed her hand to her mouth, trying not to laugh.

Chapter Ten

He couldn't go on like this. It was blatherskite. Madness.

Malcolm threw down his pen and pushed the papers across his desk. The store was closed as darkness fell over the Parisian streets beyond the windows and everyone else had long gone home. It was usually the time he liked best, when quiet descended over the office and it was just him and the work. He usually lost himself in it, so absorbed that the world outside didn't exist.

Not tonight. Tonight, Alexandra kept invading his inner sanctum, as real as if she had floated in and perched on the edge of the desk. She was there on the *chaise*, in his precious painting. He could almost smell her perfume, hear her laughter, her soft voice. The rules that governed his life, put into such careful place and always adhered to after the chaos of his youth, had been overturned.

He had to regain control over his life.

Malcolm gave up on work and sat back in his chair. Behind his closed eyes, he saw Alex at the Tower, the iron-dappled sun on her face as she sipped her champagne and laughed at the outrageous fashions around them. The light, fleeting fairy touch of her hand on his arm, the way she leaned into him as they danced at the Véfour. The shy way she peeked up at him through her lashes. The delight she took in the world around her. The way everything about her spoke of delicate refinement, but without a hint of snobbery or artifice. It was just—who she was.

And the way he wanted to know more and more about her. Wanted to know everything. Wanted to see her again so much she even invaded his work.

Who would have ever thought he could be so enchanted with the daughter of the Duke of Waverton? The man who had ruined Malcolm's own father's life?

Malcolm opened his eyes and stared out into the shadows of his office beyond the lamplit desk. With Alex, there had been none of that silence, those shadows.

He remembered what Miss Mersey said—he

needed a wife. Someone to give him a home, help him in society. He had scoffed, but was she really right? And was Alexandra what he needed, what he had waited for so long without even knowing he was missing it?

The thought was startling. Since Mairie, he had been a solitary soul and he had found he liked the privacy of relying only on himself. He'd been certain it would be that way for the rest of his life. But now that didn't feel as right as it once had.

Perhaps he did want a home, someone waiting for him after a day's work. Alexandra's smile at the door, her laughter at his dinner table, her beauty on his arm at parties. A real, true home, not rented lodgings. He was sure she *would* make a fine home, elegant, warm, welcoming, and the invitations to exclusive gatherings where a store owner had not previously been welcomed would pile up. And Alex would be his, in his bed every night, his longing to touch her fulfilled at last. He could definitely see the advantages of marriage there.

And there was one more advantage, too, one he was not entirely proud of himself for considering. The Duke of Waverton, disgraced as he was now, would surely feel even more ashamed to have a tradesman as a son-in-law, even a tradesman who could buy and sell him three times over. To see the son of one of his former employees, a man the Duke had treated so shamefully, raise his fine, delicate daughter back to security and luxury where he could not. It would be satisfying indeed. More than satisfying.

And Alex would be so grateful she would surely not interfere in his carefully built life too much.

Was he truly thinking about this? Marrying? *Him?* He almost laughed at how little he recognised himself in that moment. Yet it was a tempting thought, like a glistening, forbidden apple that was somehow suddenly within his reach.

But was it really? What would the apple itself, Alexandra, think if he suddenly presented her with a ring?

Malcolm scowled into the darkness. How could he entice her? She didn't seem to yearn after expensive gowns, furs, jewels, carriages, though he would happily shower all of those things at her feet. Diamonds every day if she would let him, emeralds and pearls worthy of her beauty. Maybe she wanted to rule society, as other ladies did, but he doubted it. Grand homes? Travel to all corners of the world?

He shook his head as he realised how very little her sweet smile gave away of her true thoughts, her desires, her longings. For just one moment, one unguarded, still instant in time, he had thought she might want him to kiss her. To touch her, as he so longed for. But then it had vanished.

He suddenly remembered her face when she spoke of her work at Mademoiselle Gardinier's school, the charity for young women fallen on hard times. Her enthusiasm for the work, her yearning to help. That he could certainly give her. She could support all the charities in Paris if she liked, even start her own.

But was it enough?

Restless with his thoughts, Malcolm pushed back from the desk and stalked out of the office. The lifts were silent at that hour, so he took the stairs, moving from the narrow, carpeted treads of the office floors to the marble of the third storey, where the jewellery department resided.

The store at night, emptied of the bright rush of customers, was a strange, haunted place, his own best domain. At that hour, it was his alone.

He went to the counter that held trays of rings behind its thick glass walls, covered and locked after hours. He opened the top tray, where the finest jewels were carefully arranged on purple velvet, and stared down at them. A pink diamond surrounded by a halo of smaller white diamonds.

A sapphire the size of a baby's thumb. A cluster of blood-red rubies.

Somehow he could picture none of them on Alexandra's finger. Couldn't imagine any of them making her eyes light up with pleasure. He scanned the other case, yet nothing there seemed right, either.

For the first time in a very long time, Malcolm Gordston, master of the business world, had no idea how to finalise a deal.

Alex watched as the girls read over their lessons, their little faces scrunched in concentration. Charlotte, the elder, never glanced up, but little Amelia fidgeted in her seat. Alex's heart ached at how adorable they were.

It was a golden morning outside the schoolroom window, the sun streaming warmly over the polished floors. The street below was busy with cooks headed to market with their baskets over their arms, nannies taking their charges to the park, carriages dashing to the shops, but inside the Bullard house all was quiet serenity.

Alex couldn't help but think about Malcolm, about the energy that seemed to vibrate from his very being all the time, the confidence and passion. How she had longed for him to kiss her there in his office! How she still wanted it. She couldn't quite stop thinking about him, even as she did her work.

She sighed. Her father had left for England that morning and Emily was off on some business in Lyon. Maybe she was just feeling a bit lonely, at a loose end, and that was why she kept daydreaming. But she knew that wasn't it. It was just Malcolm himself. She reached up and touched the hem of the soft blue scarf she wore around her neck and remembered how it felt when *he* had touched her.

'What are you thinking about, Miss Mannerly?' she heard Charlotte ask. She glanced up and found the girl watching her with a frown.

Alex smiled ruefully. 'I'm sorry, my dears. I'm afraid I was wool-gathering. Are you finished with your reading?'

'Were you thinking about a suitor?' Amelia asked, her little face very serious.

'Why would you think that, Amelia darling?' Alex said, wondering with alarm if she had given her thoughts away even to the children.

The girls exchanged a glance. 'We were looking at one of Mama's books. There was a governess in it and she received a—a...' Amelia stumbled.

'A *billet-doux*,' Charlotte said. 'From a gentleman. She fainted directly.'

Alex bit her lip to keep from laughing. 'First of all, I have never received a *billet-doux*, nor do I faint. And your mother's books are not for you to read. Not for several years.' She remembered her own purloined romance novels at Miss Grantley's, when she and Diana and Emily were students, and shook her head.

'But they're so much more interesting than our books,' Charlotte said. '*Do* you have a suitor, even if he doesn't send you letters?'

Alex thought of Malcolm, his icy-blue eyes, the way they crinkled when he gave one of his rare smiles. The feel of his touch on her skin. Was he a suitor? Surely not. He had far more sophisticated, elegant ladies to claim his attentions. A dance, a glass of champagne—they didn't make a courtship.

But would she like him to be a suitor? She had never thought about it in that way, and the notion made her feel a strange tingle of—excitement. What would that be like?

'I'm sorry to disappoint you girls, but I don't,' she said.

'Oh,' Amelia whispered. 'We should so like to be bridesmaids. With flower crowns and blue sashes.'

Alex laughed. 'Well, if I ever do have a suitor,

I will remember that. Now, show me how far you have come in your reading.'

After another half-hour of lessons, there was a knock at the schoolroom door and Lady Bullard hurried in, tugging on her gloves, the small train of her stylish blue-satin-and-velvet carriage dress swirling. 'Come, my dears, the music teacher is here and I have my appointment at Monsieur Worth's! Time to leave Miss Mannerly alone for a while.'

When the girls dashed out, Lady Bullard helped Alex put away the books and push the chairs back into their places.

'I'm rather afraid the girls have been peeking at novels,' Alex said. She knew most governesses would be afraid to admit such a thing, for fear they would be blamed for not properly supervising their charges. But Lady Bullard just laughed. 'It was about fainting governesses.'

'Oh, no!' Lady Bullard said, shaking her head. 'My sister sent me some of the latest romances from London. I'll be sure to put them away next time the girls come to my sitting room. We don't need any little Gothic nightmares waking us all up if they find the more lurid novels. Castles in storms, shipwrecks, things like that.'

'They have been secretly planning my wedding after seeing the governess with love letters story,' Alex said.

'Those scamps!' She gave Alex a speculative glance. 'I haven't seen any letters come for you except from your mother and from Lady Blakely in Vienna, but—well, if you *had* a suitor...'

'I don't,' Alex said, pushing away thoughts of Malcolm. 'At least I don't think so.'

'Don't think so?' Lady Bullard sat down on one of the little chairs, her appointment seemingly forgotten. 'Miss Mannerly, I know I'm not really a great deal older than you, but I *am* married and I know your mother is far away. You've done me a great favour coming to Paris to help with the girls. If I can assist in any way, give any advice...'

Alex longed to ask *someone* what her feelings meant, but she hated to impose on Lady Bullard's kindness. 'There—well, there is a man I find interesting, I suppose. But he isn't a suitor. I'm sure he would never look at a woman such as myself seriously.'

Lady Bullard looked most astonished. 'Yes, why would he? You are only pretty, kind and well connected,' she said wryly.

But Malcolm had built his fortune all on his own and was a man of the wider world. 'I don't think such things matter to him.'

'Pretty always matters. The important thing is to know his intentions. A lady can never be too careful in such matters.'

'Yes, I know,' Alex said, thinking of her own precarious position in the world.

Lady Bullard nodded. 'Of course you do. Well, are you going to Mademoiselle Gardinier's this afternoon? I have a box of books for them.'

Half an hour later, Alex was on her way to the school, box in hand. The street was busy at that time of day, full of bustle and movement, but her thoughts were far away, in the quiet office at Gordston's Department Store. With Malcolm.

Can't be too careful. She knew Lady Bullard was absolutely right. She saw it every day, with the poor girls at the school. Her own place was quite uncertain now. But she feared that when it came to Malcolm, she didn't feel careful at all.

Chapter Eleven

Alex turned to wave at the girls in their second-storey window as she left Mademoiselle Gardinier's after the afternoon lessons. As always after her work, she felt tired yet bolstered. The girls always made her laugh, made her appreciate everything in a new light. Despite the trials they had faced in their lives, they were always merry and curious, and always full of funny, sad and educational stories.

Alex wished she could ask for their advice. They knew much more of men than she did. Surely they could help her sort out all the feelings she had been having. The thoughts about Malcolm that kept her up at night.

She sighed as she turned away from the school, her textbooks balanced in her arms. There was really no shortage of people she *could* ask for advice, even with her family far away. Mademoiselle Gardinier's girls, Lady Bullard, Emily, even Miss Grantley wouldn't mind a letter. But they all thought her far more mature and level-headed than she currently felt herself to be. She didn't want to reveal herself to be the unsure, silly romantic she felt lately.

She turned the corner of Mademoiselle Gardinier's quiet lane to the busier *rue* leading down to the river and felt the books she held start to slip. She frantically tried to catch them before they all tumbled to the cobblestones.

'Here, let me help you,' a deep voice said and an arm in a fine blue-wool sleeve reached out.

A *familiar* voice. Startled, Alex looked up into Malcolm's blue eyes. He smiled and the day turned even brighter.

She let him take the books, her breath caught in her throat. 'How lucky you happened to be passing by, Mr Gordston!' Then she remembered what he had said in his office—she should call him Malcolm.

His smile widened. 'I do have a confession to make. I was waiting for you here.'

'Waiting for me?' Alex asked, startled.

'Yes. I called at the Bullards' and the butler said you were at Mademoiselle Gardinier's.'

'You wanted to see me about something?'

'Yes, I—well, I don't think we could talk long

here. Shall we go to that café over there? Or are you expected back by Lady Bullard?'

'No, my work is done for the day. I'd be happy to sit with you for a while.' In truth, she was wildly excited at the chance to be with him for a while, to be near him. She wondered what he wanted to say to her so urgently.

He led her to one of the small outdoor tables under the café's red awning and a waiter quickly brought a ewer of wine. Alex studied Malcolm carefully over the edge of her glass, not knowing what to say. He looked—different somehow. Just as handsome as ever, his hair golden in the sun, but maybe unsure.

Yet why would that be? Malcolm Gordston was never unsure. His confidence was always a palpable thing, a glowing aura about him. She felt a touch of disquiet deep inside.

Something was definitely different. He drained his glass, looked as if he was about to say something, shook his head and fell back into silence again.

Alex touched the edge of her blue scarf tucked into her tweed jacket and tried desperately to think of something to say. She remembered the warm intimacy of those moments in his office, the breathless instant she thought he would kiss her.

'Malcolm—Mr Gordston...' she began. 'If I have done something that concerns you...'

'Not at all.' He gave her a strange, strained smile and reached out to touch her hand. His fingers were warm through her glove. 'I just have something I want to say to you and I'm not sure how to do it.'

Alex felt flustered, flushed. 'Surely I am not so difficult to talk to?'

'Of course not. In fact, I feel as if I could say almost anything to you.'

'Except right now?'

'Except for this. You see, Lady Alexandra...'

'Just Alex. Remember?'

He smiled. 'Just Alex. Yes. You see—it's been brought to my attention lately, several times, that I might be in need of a wife.'

The moment seemed to freeze around Alex, something bizarre and unreal. 'A wife?'

'Yes. Someone to make a real home, to be a partner in life. I never thought of such a thing before, or at least not in a long time. But I admit it begins to make sense to me. I'm not getting any younger, and...what is it?'

A strange, strangled laugh escaped from Alex and she pressed her hand to her lips. 'Nothing, it's just—so odd. I was recently told the same. That I should marry.'

He frowned. 'Maybe it is fate, then?'

'Fate?'

He reached into his coat and took out a small velvet box. He opened it to reveal a beautiful ring, an antique cameo in a delicate setting of pearls. 'I have the honour to beg for your hand in marriage, Lady Alexandra.'

Now Alex was quite sure she *was* dreaming. She stared down at the ring, stunned at the suddenness of the moment, by a flash of hope and fear all tangled into one. 'But we don't know each other very well, do we?'

He watched her intently with those uncanny blue eyes and she found she didn't want to break away. 'Do we not? I feel as if I know *you*. You are kind and cultured, beautiful, unreadable. I think we like each other. We could do well together. Don't you think so?'

Liked each other—could do well. It wasn't exactly the grand, passionate declaration Alex read about in novels, but somehow it sounded even better. More like something that could be made good in the real world. Something she could build on.

She studied him carefully, longing to know what he really thought, felt, what was really happening between them. What she should do.

'I know I am not what you must have hoped

for,' he said quietly, as if he misread her dumb-struck silence for hesitation. 'But I want to try to make you happy. To make your life comfortable.'

'Comfortable?' she whispered. Comfort was always the last thing she felt around him—unsure, off balance, fluttery, all those things, yes. But despite the hard lessons she had learned about the real world, she wanted something more. Something special.

'What about Mademoiselle Gardinier's? You could spend more time working there and as many funds for your charities as you would like.'

'You don't need to bribe me, Malcolm,' she said, even as his words did have real appeal. If he had offered her jewels, furs, she would have been able to turn them away. She had learned riches could hold a person down, turn their souls. Just as it had done with him, that sweet boy she knew so long ago. The one she wanted to know again. But to help the school...

He laughed. 'You have to forgive me. I've been a businessman too long. Negotiations are part of my nature. But I do truly think we could make a good life together. And I want to see you happy. I'm just not sure how to do that. You're quite un-like any other woman I've ever met.'

'Telling me I could give my charities unlim-ited funds for their projects is very tempting indeed. I would say you know me rather well,' Alex said. Even more tempting, though she couldn't say it aloud, was the thought of having such a man as her husband. So handsome, with so much vitality and energy, so many interests. Surely she *could* help him, knowing society as she did. And there might be children…

She felt her cheeks turn warm at the thought of having a family with him. *Making* that family.

'Then you will consider it?' he asked, his voice taut.

Alex stared down at the ring, the delicately carved flowers on the coral background. 'What if I did accept you? What would you think?'

'I would think I was the most fortunate man in Paris.' He laid his hand gently over hers. 'Are you saying yes?'

'I—I don't know.' She shook her head, wishing everything would stop spinning in such a confusing way, that she knew clearly what she should do to make them both happy. 'You have rather caught me by surprise.' To say the least. She ran her fingertip gently over the pearls of the ring.

'Is the ring not right? I looked at grander ones, but they didn't seem to fit. I saw this one in an antique dealer's window and somehow it reminded me of you,' he said. 'You can have your pick of any ring at Gordston's, of course. Diamonds, emeralds...'

'Oh, no!' Alex cried. She didn't want to exchange the pretty cameo for any jewel in the world. 'This one is truly lovely. I just don't know what to say. May I have time to think about what you have said?'

'As much time as you like. Perhaps we could have dinner later this week? Give me some time for a proper courtship.'

Alex nodded. 'Yes, dinner. I would like that.'

Dinner—but would it be more than that? Her head was spinning too much to know what was up and what was down yet, but she did know one thing. His proposal was very tempting indeed.

Chapter Twelve

This could be it. After tonight's dinner, he could be an engaged man—or all his plans could be in ruins.

Malcolm studied his reflection in the mirror as he fastened his pearl cravat pin. He wore his finest evening suit, the softest, blackest wool cashmere, a rich gold-brocade waistcoat, his hair trimmed. Did he look enough like a respectable husband? Was he wearing the right thing for a lady like her, or should he change?

He laughed at himself. He had to keep control. 'Och, man, calm down,' he muttered. 'You've done more difficult things in your life than gone to dinner with a lady.' Yet complicated business deals felt like a mere snap of the fingers compared to trying to get a wife.

Not just any wife. Lady Alexandra.

Malcolm remembered how it felt to kiss her hand at the café. Just that tiny touch had made a burning desire roar through him. He had never felt anything like it, that sudden rush of intense need for one particular woman. The startled look in her eyes had held him back from taking her in his arms as he longed to do. He knew she was different, his fairy girl; he had to move softly, cautiously, if he wanted to win her over.

And he found he did. Very much. Too much. When Miss Mersey had suggested he should find a wife, the thought seemed absurd. Now it was something he couldn't imagine being without. Not just any wife, though. Only Alex.

He wanted her, in his bed, at his dinner table, by his side, and he wanted to do so much for her, too. To make her life happy. To see her laugh. It was amazing, strange, unfathomable.

Malcolm reached for the box with the antique ring. He still felt as if something grander would be more appropriate for a duke's daughter, but the look on Alex's face when she stared down at the cameo had told him his instincts were correct. The quiet elegance of the ring suited her.

He only hoped that by the end of the evening he would have closed the deal and the ring would be on Alex's slender finger.

Alex twisted in front of the mirror, taking in her reflection from each side. She wished she had something new to wear, something up to the minute in fashion, but the apple-green taffeta gown trimmed with creamy lace was still lovely. The colour made her think of summer and the bows at the neckline were pertly pretty. She wore a strand of pearls that had once been her grandmother's, and Amelia and Charlotte had insisted on helping her pin up her hair and tie it with white ribbons. The girls had even declared she looked 'just like a princess'.

But did she look like a lady about to be engaged to one of the most important businessmen in the city?

Was she about to be engaged? Alex wished she knew the right thing to do. She'd thought of nothing else all night and day. She still half-believed Malcolm's proposal was only a dream. Why would he want to marry her, when there were far more sophisticated beauties in Paris, elegant, wealthy, wise ladies he could have?

She remembered all those years ago in Scotland, the sweet boy who had taught her to fish, had walked on the moors with her, how she had idolised him. Was that boy still there, deep inside the man? And what about the girl she had seen with him back then, the tender looks between them, the hands entwined? Did he still think of her?

When he proposed, her first instinct had been to throw herself into his arms and shout 'Yes!' Yet something had held her back there at the café. Marriage was the most serious step. She'd never met anyone who made her feel even a sliver of what Malcolm did with only one look. But how did he really feel about her? What could she bring him as his wife?

She wished she knew more, that she had seen more of the world. A duke's daughter was so hidden from so many truths of life and she hadn't been walking her own path long enough to discover all she had missed. She just had to stumble forward the best she could, listen to her own instincts.

And her instincts told her she wanted Malcolm Gordston and that it was no use trying to be sensible about it. She reached for her gloves and turned to leave.

'Miss Mannerly, a carriage is here!' she heard Charlotte shout, just before the girls burst into her room, their eyes shining eagerly. 'And it's ever so grand.'

Alex peeked out the window to the street below and saw the girls were right. It was very grand, all glossy black, drawn by matched greys.

The moment of decision was rushing towards

her. No matter which way she turned, her life would be very different.

What would she do?

The Alibert Bistro was very elegant, but not grand like the Véfour, not meant for showing off and making noise. In fact, it rather reminded Alex of Malcolm's own office, all dark wood and plush velvet, red banquettes behind polished tables, thick carpet underfoot to muffle footsteps. The air smelled of fine wine, faint cigar smoke, rich beefsteaks and dark chocolate.

The maître d' led them to a quiet table in the corner, cosy and comfortable with red-velvet cushions and crisp white table linens, half-screened off from the rest of the dining room. He and Malcolm had a quiet, serious conversation about the wine list, then he bowed and left, and Alex was alone with Malcolm.

How handsome he looked in the candlelight, she thought, his bright hair neatly trimmed, the brocade of his fine waistcoat gleaming, his eyes so very blue, so intense as he smiled at her. She felt nervous, yet more sure than ever that she was where she ought to be.

'Is your store ready for its grand party?' she asked, pleating her napkin under her nervous fingers as the waiter poured the wine.

'Nothing is ever entirely ready as far as I'm concerned, at least not one of my stores,' he said with a smile.

Alex laughed. 'You mean it is not *perfect*.'

'No, and it should be.'

'Nothing can ever be absolutely perfect, but your stores are surely as near to it as possible. I've never seen anything so luxurious, so elegant, and yet so...'

'So?'

'Well, comfortable, I suppose. Welcoming. Surely everyone, from a princess to a café girl, loves to shop there. The warmth, the way it smells, the sparkle, it must be a haven from the world. A place out of time.'

He looked startled. 'Yes. That is exactly what I wish to create. A haven for ladies.'

'And the party will be just the same! Tell me what you have arranged. You said there will be actors performing tableaux?'

'From the Comédie-Française, yes. As well as an orchestra and possibly a bicycle racer to explain the contraption so ladies will rush off to buy sporting costumes.'

As they were served the soup course, they chatted about the party plans and Alex made a few suggestions. As they talked, her nervousness faded and she was only there in the moment with him, laughing, at ease, enjoying the visions he created of his fine store.

She looked at him across the table as they were served the fish course. He looked even more like a golden Norse god there in the candlelight, his hair and skin burnished like a summer's day, his smile wide as he talked about his pride in his work. And suddenly she knew what she had to do. Caution was all very well, but she had no use for it now. She wanted to marry Malcolm Gordston. That was all. She wanted to help him in his work, create that cosy home for them both, see what the future held for them.

Mostly she just wanted to be with *him*. To learn more about him, to spend more time with him. To help him, if she could. To feel his touch on her again, to know what his kiss was like.

As soon as she recognised that, she saw the way forward and a tingling sense of excitement came over her. Surely this was right? Surely a grand adventure lay in wait.

She smiled at Malcolm and he went very still.

'Have you thought about what I asked, then?' he said, his voice quiet, tense.

'Of course. I've thought about little else, I admit,' she said. She took a deep gulp of wine to help steady her. 'And I think—well, I *know*. I accept your kind offer, Malcolm.'

A tentative smile touched his lips. 'You will be my wife?'

Alex nodded. It felt as if a great weight flew off her, leaving her so light, so free. 'I will.' She laughed, more a nervous giggle she couldn't hold back. She *did* wish she was more sophisticated, more like Lady Smythe-Tomas or her friends, but she couldn't hide her delight in the moment. Her fear, her hope.

Malcolm reached for her, his lips coming down to meet hers. His kiss was passionate, demanding, hot and consuming, his hands on her bare skin seeking. She was suddenly overwhelmed, filled with longing she had no idea what to do with.

Alex drew back, not sure where to look or what to do. Her cheeks felt as if they were on fire and she cursed her ridiculously pale skin that revealed too much when she was flustered or unsure. She'd never been kissed before, but she had read about kissing many times and she was sure she had done it all wrong. Every inch of her being screamed at her to grab him in her arms and kiss him again! To create that wondrous feeling over and over, and show him she knew what to do.

But she knew she could not. The propriety she had lived with all her life was too strong a bond and she knew it wasn't the lady's place to kiss the man. She didn't want to do anything wrong yet again. She slid back on the banquette and looked away, feeling more silly with every moment.

Malcolm also turned away and she couldn't read his expression at all. His jaw looked tight, almost angry, and she cursed herself again.

'I—I'm sorry, what a silly I am…' she whispered.

Malcolm shook his head fiercely. 'No, Lady Alexandra, it's my fault. I promise I will control myself in the future.'

Alex did hope he wouldn't. 'No, I—that is, I just—' He interrupted her by taking her hand and sliding the antique cameo on to her finger. It fit perfectly, shimmering delicately in the light, a bond between them.

She studied it carefully, turning it this way and that. She knew she should be wildly happy in that moment. But her clumsiness in the kiss seemed to have altered something between them, disrupted something, and she had no idea how to even begin to fix it.

Chapter Thirteen

He had been an unconscionable brute. He had done what he always promised he never would: he had lost control, let things spin beyond him, and that would never do.

Malcolm paced the mezzanine of his store, glancing at his watch and then at the floor below for the hundredth time. Alexandra was due to arrive any moment at Gordston's to choose a gown for the opening party, but she wasn't there yet. It would be the first time they had seen each other since their engagement. He longed for it—and dreaded it.

He should never have let his desire for her overpower him like that. She had been right to draw away from his kiss. He wasn't used to not being in absolute iron control at all times, but when he touched her, tasted her, that need roared through him. Even kissing her hand when he left her at the Bullards' door had filled him with raw need.

He had to be careful with her, control himself, not let his animal need take over. Alex was different, delicate, special. He couldn't drive her away. Not now, when having her was so close within his grasp. He couldn't let emotions get in the way of a good business deal. He wouldn't.

'Mr Gordston, can you look at these papers…?' Miss Mersey began saying, hurrying towards him with a pile of documents in her arms. She paused when he practically gave her a bearish growl. 'Oh, I see. Lady Alexandra hasn't yet arrived?'

Miss Mersey had been the first he told about his engagement and she had informed the rest of the staff. They had all immediately insisted on decorating the store with flower bells and white bunting to celebrate and his secretary had been insufferably smiley ever since.

'No, not yet,' he said shortly. He hoped when she did arrive, it was not to break the engagement. To run away from him. If she arrived at all.

'The girls in evening wear are beside themselves with excitement,' Miss Mersey said. 'Every gown in the department has been brought out for Lady Alexandra's approval! She will look lovely at the party and what a grand advertisement for the store.'

'She's not a blasted advertisement! She's going to be my wife,' he snapped.

Miss Mersey blinked. 'Of course she is not. She is your bride and we all couldn't be happier about it. The question is, Mr, Gordston, are *you* happy about it? Really?'

Happy? Malcolm stared at her blankly for a moment. He hardly knew what that meant, happiness. He had never really known it. There was the satisfaction of work in his life and that always seemed like enough. Alexandra was a prize any man could be proud to win.

But he realised that when she was near, he felt—different. Lighter, calmer. Free. Was that happiness? It was a strange, almost frightening thought. He pulled himself back, took back his control.

'Of course I am happy,' he said to Miss Mersey and she beamed. How could he tell her that Lady Alexandra might very well back out of their engagement? That he had driven her away?

He remembered how she looked when she pulled away from his kiss, her face so pale, her hands shaking, and he felt sick all over again.

'That is very good,' Miss Mersey said. 'Now, should you sign these papers before your beautiful bride arrives?'

* * *

Alex fidgeted on the plush velvet seat of the carriage Malcolm had sent for her, the glossy black equipage with the matched greys she had so admired when she last saw it. She had never imagined she would ride in it again so soon, co-cooned in the luxury of its plush seats, its glass-smooth path easing her along the lane towards the store.

She took off her glove and stared down at the ring, then put her glove back on. She glanced out the window at the fine shops flashing by. She straightened her hat and wished she had been able to walk. That blasted shyness, nervousness, had come back over her again and she wished it would go away. She had to show a confident, happy face to the world, to Malcolm's world.

She had become accustomed in the last few months to moving quietly through the world, observing rather than observed. After a lifetime of being under scrutiny, the Duke's daughter whose appearance and behaviour had to be perfect, it was nice. Now that would all be changed.

As Malcolm Gordston's fiancée, she would be watched again and she didn't want to disappoint Malcolm, especially as her father's scandal still hung over her. She didn't want to ruin their bargain before it even began. He had a glittering job, one he obviously loved; he deserved a glittering, fashionable wife. One who would make him proud.

She cringed as she remembered their kiss, the way he'd looked at her when she had pulled away, so flustered. He had looked appalled, completely taken aback by her silly behaviour. How ridiculous she felt, how naive, to be so overcome by emotions at a simple kiss! Now wonder he had seemed baffled by her, almost angry. She wished so much that she knew what to do. The heroines in novels were no help, they were usually so missish, always fainting when kissed.

Alex closed her eyes and wished she was a different kind of woman. One sophisticated, elegant. Long ago, Malcolm had humiliated her so when he threw her naive friendship, her care, back into her face. Now he courted her and she wanted so much to believe things had changed. To think it was a new future. She just wished she could be sure.

Alex sighed. She did wish she could ask her mother, but even when the Duchess was near she would never dare talk to her about such things. And she didn't want to write to her parents and tell them Malcolm had withdrawn his proposal because she was a silly goose, either, not when her father had just given his written approval.

Maybe if Diana was there? She was a married lady now, she was sure to know.

Alex straightened her hat again and tried to take a deep breath. That day felt so important, a second chance to show Malcolm she could make him a good wife. If he didn't take back the ring and toss her out of his store first. If she didn't run away in fear, chased by old memories.

'Stop being so silly,' she told herself. Malcolm would not do such a thing. Despite his origins, he was more a gentleman than anyone she had ever met. He wouldn't make a scene.

He would just ask her into his office for a conversation about their lack of compatibility or something of the sort. Which sounded even worse than a scene.

She stiffened her shoulders. She just would not let that happen. She couldn't. Not now she realised how much she truly, deeply wanted to marry Malcolm Gordston.

The carriage rolled to a halt at the bottom of the Gordston's glowing marble steps and the doorman hurried to help her alight. Alex took a moment to steady herself before she went inside, staring up at the store's beautiful façade, the classical statues at each corner, the myriad of jewel-like windows. The fashionable ladies hurrying in and out, the feathers on their hats floating, their skirts all filmy and swishing. This might be her world now.

She adjusted her velvet muff on her arm, decorated with two snow-white gardenias Malcolm had sent her, and sailed through the revolving doors.

He waited for her in the lobby, along with a stern-looking, bespectacled lady in navy-blue silk. Alex swallowed hard and gathered her courage before she looked up into Malcolm's eyes, but his expression was perfectly unreadable. As handsome and still as one of the statues on the façade.

'Alexandra,' he said and kissed her cheek with cool lips. 'Welcome back to Gordston's. May I introduce my secretary, Miss Mersey? She can help you with any wedding arrangements that are needed.'

'How do you do, Miss Mersey,' Alex said and held out her hand shyly.

Miss Mersey beamed at her, no longer so stern. 'My lady. May I say, on behalf of all the staff at Gordston's, that we offer our deepest best wishes? It's about time he brought us a bride. We began to think it would never happen.'

Much to Alex's astonishment, a deep red flush spread over Malcolm's cut-glass cheekbones. 'Miss Mersey…' he muttered.

'You know it is true, Mr Gordston,' Miss Mersey said. 'Now, my lady, I know we haven't much time to put together a grand wedding, but all of Gordston's is at your disposal. You need only ask for anything you might require. I have taken the liberty of drawing up a few plans, which I can show you after the tour for your approval.'

'Thank you very much, Miss Mersey,' Alex answered, confused. She hadn't yet spoken to Malcolm about the wedding itself, but she had assumed something quite small and quiet, given her family's situation. Given their past together. Why was he giving her all this now? 'I am sure a simple ceremony can't be too complicated to plan. I don't want to disrupt anyone's work.'

Miss Mersey laughed. 'Oh, my lady. I am sure "simple" is a different thing to a duke's daughter. But you must never hesitate to ask us for anything. We are pleased to help, indeed eager to do so.'

Alex nodded, and Malcolm took her arm to lead her into the store. The black-and-white marble floor was lined with potted palms and soft velvet sofas where ladies could wait for their carriages, until they moved into the main hall, where the hat and glove counters waited, sparkling with their luxurious wares.

'I really don't want to put more work on to anyone,' she whispered to him. 'I should be able to do all that is needed for a small ceremony.'

'Nonsense,' he answered gruffly. 'I don't want anyone saying you did not receive all that you deserve. A proper wedding is necessary. I have an appointment to speak to the British consul about using the chapel at the embassy. I'm sure there will be no problem. As soon as you know when your parents can arrive, a date can be set and Miss Mersey can write up the invitation cards. She is already arranging a list and will want your names.'

Alex bit her lip, but she realised he was truly not going to break things off because she was a terrible kisser, not if he was planning a wedding. But a large ceremony at the embassy, with lists and lists of guests? It made her feel terribly shy all over again.

'Malcolm, you must not…' she said. But she could say no more, as they stopped to meet the staff arrayed in front of their counters, waiting to greet her. She could only smile, nod and accept their good wishes, filing away their names in her memory. At least her training and education had been good for that.

On the second floor, they came to ladies' ready-to-wear, where a flock of eager girls in their crisp dark dresses with white collars held up a rainbow of evening gowns for her to examine.

'For the opening party here at the store, my lady,' the head of the department said. She displayed a creation of lavender satin, sewn with sparkling silver beads in a pattern of ivy and tulips. Two other girls stepped forward with gowns of dark blue velvet and pale silver tulle. 'Whichever you choose, of course, but these are our newest designs. The lavender is inspired by Princess Alexandra herself.'

Alex gently touched the lace on the cap sleeves of the satin. It had been a long time since she had something so new, so lovely. 'It is beautiful indeed, but...'

'You must go to Worth to order your wedding gown, of course,' Malcolm said quickly, as if he misunderstood her hesitation. 'And whatever else you may need. But as the party is very soon, I doubt there will be time for couturier.'

Alex blushed to realise she had so given the wrong impression. If only she could persuade him she didn't want this, she just wanted him! The two of them together, simple and kind. 'Oh, no! I am sure everything I need is right here. The lavender will be perfect for the party. And perhaps I could order the blue velvet and one of those white tea gowns? And perhaps a new suit. I can't resist, they are all so lovely.'

The assistants beamed as they hurried to fetch more garments for her examination. 'The alterations can be finished by the end of the day, my lady,' the department head said.

After she had ordered a few more pieces, Malcolm led her up to the jewellery department, where more gorgeous items were laid out for her perusal. The rich, quiet sheen of a pearl necklace, a sapphire-and-diamond bracelet, diamond-star hair ornaments, all of which the jeweller said would go well with a lavender evening gown.

Alex's head was spinning with all that luxury. She had never seen so much of it at once, all hers for the asking, not even when her father had held his place in society. It was quite overwhelming. She smiled and exclaimed over it all, determined that her shyness would not again be taken for snobbery, making the sales assistants look quite pleased. But when they started boxing up the diamond stars, the pearls and even a pair of ruby earrings, she grew rather alarmed.

'Malcolm,' she whispered. 'You cannot give me these now, it is too much! Surely I can just borrow them for the evening of the party?'

'Of course they are yours. And are you quite sure you're happy with your ring?' he said, ges-

turing to a tray of rings sparkling with more emeralds and diamonds, grander than Aladdin's
cave. 'We have a new ruby from Siam...'

'No!' Alex cried. She was willing to do whatever she had to in order to be a good chatelaine
for the store, but she wouldn't give up her precious cameo. She curled her hand into a fist over
it. 'My ring is perfect, Malcolm. I never want to
change it.'

He frowned doubtfully, but finally nodded. He
took her arm again and led her through a doorway at the end of the room, into a long, narrow
chamber with high windows, filled with sewing
machines, tables spread with a vivid array of
fabrics, ribbons, laces. Girls in blue smocks all
stood up and curtsied, and she smiled and nodded in return.

'This is our alterations department,' Malcolm
said, 'and soon we will be doing our own original line of fashions here, if all goes as planned.'

'How fascinating,' Alex said, reaching out to
touch a gossamer length of white linen. At the
end of the row, she glimpsed a familiar face beneath a sweep of dark blonde hair, neatly tucked
into a white cap.

'Elise!' she cried happily, overjoyed to see the
young woman she had met at Mademoiselle Gardinier's school looking so happy and healthy. She

rushed to hug her, as Malcolm stayed back to talk to the head seamstress. 'I heard that you found a place here. How are you faring?'

'Very well, *mademoiselle*—that is, my lady,' Elise said with a smile. 'The work is most interesting and my new neighbour stays with my boy during the day. I must say congratulations to you on your engagement, I could hardly imagine it was my Mademoiselle Mannerly who was the bride! They make you sound so grand, the daughter of Monsieur le Duc.'

'I suppose I will be Madame Gordston soon,' Alex said, trying to laugh.

'He may look gruff, my lady, but really he is most kind,' Elise whispered. 'Everyone here would do anything for him. We all work hard, but for excellent pay and in such fine surroundings. And no one works harder than Monsieur Gordston himself. We are all so happy he found such a pretty wife.'

Alex nodded, smiling. Elise's words just confirmed what she thought herself—Malcolm was indeed a gentleman, with a soft heart he didn't seem to want anyone to see. 'I think you are quite right, Elise. I am a fortunate lady indeed.'

After Elise and the others eagerly showed her the blue-silk cloth they were cutting for her after-wedding, going-away costume, the embroidery patterns and sketches for new coats and suits and tea gowns, Alex's head was whirling. She was quite sure she would need a whole separate room in their house, wherever they would live, to hold all the new clothes!

It was quite a relief when the efficient Miss Mersey appeared, and said, 'I am sure you would like a restorative cup of tea now, my lady. I fear all we have until the Fortescues' café opens is our own canteen, but it is acceptable. I have had a tray sent up to Mr Gordston's office for when you are finished here. I have also left some more notes for the wedding plans on the desk.'

'Oh, thank you, Miss Mersey,' Alex answered gratefully, for she did indeed long for a cup of tea. 'You are a jewel indeed.'

After she thanked Elise and the others for their excellent work, she took Malcolm's arm and let him lead her back upstairs to his office. It looked much the same as it had when he took her there to tend her ankle, the dark wood walls, the shelves of books, except for perhaps even more paperwork piled on the desk. She was sure it never ceased for him, but perhaps he would let her help him with it all.

Alex sighed. She had so much to learn about the man she was about to marry, so much she longed to know.

As one of the sales assistants brought in a silver tray of tea things and set it up by the window, Alex studied the Madonna and child on their easel, the jewelled colours glowing, the mother's face full of tenderness as she stared down at the baby.

'Some tea?' Malcolm asked and she nodded.

They sat down across from each other at the table and she reached for the heavy Wedgwood teapot. She suddenly realised she didn't even know one basic thing about him—how he took his tea. 'Milk or lemon?' she asked.

He smiled at her. 'Just lemon, thank you.' He watched her closely as she poured. 'You do that very gracefully.'

Alex laughed. 'It was one of the primary elements of my education, pouring tea properly. Before I went to Miss Grantley's, that is.' She took a sip of the strong Indian tea and looked at his crowded desk with a sigh. 'I suppose we should take a look at Miss Mersey's wedding plans?'

'If anything isn't to your liking, it can be changed immediately.'

'I'm sure it is all quite lovely. In truth, I have such little idea of how to go about planning a wedding, especially in Paris. I want it all to be most suitably elegant.'

'How can it help but be, with you as the bride?

Alexandra, I—' he uttered hoarsely, his teacup rattling into its saucer. He broke off and shook his head. 'I suppose what I mean to say is, if you have changed your mind about any of it, it is not too late to break off. I will take full responsibility.'

Alex was utterly bewildered. How had they come from wedding plans to breaking things off? 'Breaking the engagement?'

'After—well, after my behaviour, when I kissed you at the café.' His brogue had grown thick again and he wouldn't quite look at her. 'I am not so accustomed to the company of fine ladies like yourself and I fear I rather lost control. You looked so beautiful in that moment. If you can no longer bear to be in my company...'

Alex felt her cheeks flame and she looked down at the napkin in her lap, the window, the desk, anywhere but him, afraid he would find her naive. 'Oh, Malcolm. I fear I am the one who must apologise. I am such a silly. You see, I had never really been kissed before and I was so sure I was doing it wrong, it happened so suddenly. I thought you would laugh at me. My heart was pounding so and I just—why are you laughing *now*?'

For Malcolm was indeed laughing, his face alight. 'Oh, Alexandra. My fairy queen. I am not laughing at *you*. I am laughing at *us*. I think we both have so much to learn.'

'Yes. I suppose we do,' she murmured, confused, but tempted to giggle all at the same time.

He held out his hand to her and said gently, 'Will you let me try again?'

She nodded wordlessly, unable to breathe, and took his hand to let him draw her to her feet. His arms came around her and his lips sought hers, softly at first, tenderly, carefully. She drew back a bit to reach up and touch the curve of his lower lip, wondering at his beauty. She was surprised at how soft it was, how rough his cheek was when she caressed it. She went up on tiptoe and they kissed again, harder, eagerly.

In all the world, she knew only him in that moment. How he looked, how he smelled like a warm summer's day, how he felt in her arms. He had to be a dream; surely she would wake and find herself alone again in her room at Miss Grantley's, or in her parents' home, waiting for her life to begin.

Yet he was real. This was her life now. Lips on lips, his hands warm on her waist, the way he tasted of tea and something darker, sweeter, that was only him. She wrapped her arms tightly around his neck as if she would never let him go.

His hands slid over her hips, up her back, as if he craved her just as much as she did him.

How alive she felt in that moment! How desirable and real, for the very first time. This time she was not frightened at all.

After what felt like an eternity, and yet also only an instant too quickly gone, he stepped back, his breath ragged. He still held her close.

'So,' he whispered against her hair. 'Shall we go ahead with the wedding plans?'

'Oh, yes,' she whispered back. There was no way she was letting him get away from her now.

Chapter Fourteen

Alex had thought the store was a palace during the day, but she was utterly astonished to see it by night. It was transformed to something utterly magical for the party and she couldn't believe she was to be a part of it all.

As she stepped through the doors, she came to a sudden, astonished halt, almost making Lord and Lady Bullard bump into her. Mr Edison's new electric lights, installed throughout the floors, glowed on the gleaming glass counters, the polished marble floors, the brilliant array of merchandise on display everywhere a person could turn. Music from a string quartet on the mezzanine above, a swooping, swirly waltz, floated down on the gathering and on a stage at the far end of the lobby the troupe from the Comédie-Française created a tableau of Jupiter and his daughters in a blue-satin sea. Bicycle racers demonstrated the equipage at the other end, next to a display of ladies' sportswear. Waiters circulated with trays of canapés and glasses of champagne.

It was all astonishing, modern, luxurious, something in a dream. And Malcolm, the man she was to marry, had created it all.

Alex couldn't help but laugh at the sudden burst of joy in the moment, the vision she had of the future opening before her in ways she had never imagined.

'How beautiful it all is,' Lady Bullard exclaimed, examining a display of bright silk scarves. 'I can't believe I have never been in here before. I've been missing so much! Oh, look at those hats.'

Lord Bullard, a gentleman several years older than his wife, but handsome and distinguished, devoted to Lady Bullard and their daughters, gave a deep groan. 'Lady Alexandra, I must protest that you have led my wife here to this insidious place. My bank balance will never recover.'

'And look at these hair ornaments! They must be Lalique. Oh, the girls would love them,' Lady Bullard said and hurried off towards another counter, her husband trailing ruefully behind her.

For just a moment, Alex found herself alone in the midst of the crowd. She caught a glimpse of her reflection in one of the floor-to-ceiling, silver-framed mirrors. She wore the lavender gown, shimmering in the lights with its silver beads, the diamond-star ornaments in her hair, an ostrich feather fan clutched in her gloved hands. She looked like Lady Alexandra again, her old self, and yet inside—inside she felt like something entirely new. Something she didn't quite recognise yet.

She curled her hand tight around the ivory handle of her fan and felt the press of her new ring under her glove. The ring Malcolm had given her. That was what she was now—the future Lady Alexandra Gordston. The thought made her want to laugh and shiver all at the same time.

'Alex! There you are. Don't you look lovely! Is that a new gown?' she heard Emily call.

She spun around to see her friend rushing towards her through the crowd. Relieved to see a familiar face, she hurried to kiss Emily's cheek and exclaim over her green-velvet-and-gold-satin gown.

'Yes, mine is quite new,' Alex said, twirling a bit in her satin skirt. 'From right here at Gordston's. Am I fashionable enough? They did say it's inspired by the Princess.'

'Most beautiful. Everyone who sees you will be rushing upstairs to put in their orders.' Emily took two wineglasses from the waiter and handed one to Alex. 'Oh, my dear, I was quite astonished to find your message waiting when I returned from Lyon. Engaged, and to Malcolm Gordston himself!'

'I know. It was terribly sudden, I admit.'

Emily studied her over the edge of her glass, looking a bit doubtful. 'I can quite see why he would be able to sweep a lady off her feet, he is entirely overwhelming. But are you sure?'

Of course Alex was not sure. It felt like stepping off a cliff into something unseen, ocean waves below her that would either sweep her away, or buoy her up. But something deep inside her somehow told her that she was doing the right thing. 'I think so. He is most fascinating. Not like anyone I have ever known.'

'I would imagine not. He doesn't exactly mix with the ducal sorts. Father says he is quite the most ruthless business rival he has ever seen, but also one of the most honest. He didn't build all this on dirty dealings. But are *you* sure? You can't have known him long.'

'I have known him long enough to be sure he is the one I should marry,' Alex answered, trying to sound perfectly confident. Perfectly certain of the future.

'He is rich, of course, and has a certain—fascination,' Emily said. 'But you are my dearest, sweetest friend. I can't help but worry.'

'There is no need to worry!' Alex exclaimed. She saw Malcolm coming towards them now, towering over everyone around them, her handsome Norse god. He was with her cousin Chris, the two of them laughing over some joke, and her heart seemed to skip a beat just to know he would soon be her own husband.

'Alexandra, how lovely you look,' Malcolm said and bent to kiss her cheek. The brush of his lips on her skin made her shiver.

She laughed nervously, trying not to blush like a silly goose just because he kissed her cheek. 'Entirely due to the efforts of your fine staff. I feel like a princess today! Cinderella, maybe.'

He smiled, the corners of his eyes crinkling most delightfully. 'Or queen of the fairies?'

'It is that. The whole store looks like fairyland tonight.' She gestured to the sparkling lights, the laughing crowds, the luscious displays. It was a magical place—and he had created it all. The man she had promised to marry.

'Come and meet some of my acquaintances,' he said, offering her his arm. 'They are a few of the store's best patrons.'

Alex took his arm and walked with him up the stone stairs, studying the people around them. Grand, elegant people, dressed in the latest fashions, the prettiest jewels. She glimpsed Emily and Chris walking away below and waved at them. 'How could anyone *not* be a patron of Gordston's? It's wondrous!'

Malcolm laughed. 'See, that is why I need you to be my unofficial head of publicity. To convince people to come into the store…'

'And once they are in, they're caught!' she said with a smile. 'How marvellous.'

She took a glass of wine from one of the waiters and glanced down at the main floor, where a group of newcomers had just arrived. She recognised the Duc d'Aumeuil, who she had met at a party with the Prince and Princess of Wales during the Exposition; Viscountess Rippon, a leader of style in London; and she knew both the Duc and the Viscountess were great patrons of the arts. But she knew no one else with them and studied the group curiously. Whoever they were, they were quite fashionable, which could only be good for the store.

A lady took the Duc's arm and whispered in his ear, catching Alex's attention. She'd never seen the woman before and Alex was sure she would have remembered her for the woman was quite astonishingly beautiful. Tall and slender, dark, glossy hair piled high atop her head and bound with a rope of rubies that went with her red-satin gown trimmed with ruffles of black lace and ropes of beaded jet, she was as vivid and eye-catching as a portrait of a Spanish dancer.

Yet even as Alex knew she had never met the woman before, there was something startlingly familiar about her. Was she an actress, or maybe foreign nobility? Alex tried to place her, but remembered nothing specifically. She was distracted from her thoughts by the Viscountess, who climbed up the stairs and struck up an animated conversation with her.

After the Viscountess had moved away, Malcolm came to her side and smiled down at her. He looked so perfectly at ease, so happy, that he made her smile, too. 'Are you having a good time?' he asked. 'I know the Viscountess can talk a person's ear off, but she was utterly charmed by you.'

Alex smiled back. 'She does seem very kind. I'm glad she likes me.' She gestured with her glass to the Duc's party below. 'Monsieur le Duc has arrived and brought quite a crowd.'

'Has he indeed? I'm sure the newspapers will love that.' Malcolm studied the newcomers, his eyes narrowed. 'But it is a surprise.'

'Do you know him?'

'Only vaguely. We have been to some of the

same clubs lately. He seems far more interested in his American railroad investments than in shops.'

'I'm sure he knows a good investment when he sees it. Or maybe he wants to please his lady companion. She's very beautiful, I'm sure she would be a very good advertisement for Gordston's wares.'

'His companion?'

'The woman in the gorgeous red gown.' Alex pointed her out. 'I thought she might be someone famous, but I'm not sure. I'm not good at keeping track of such things, as Emily is.'

Malcolm looked down—and he froze beside her. His face, smiling and relaxed only an instant before, seemed to turn to granite. His hand curled into a fist on the balustrade and Alex felt a cold touch of disquiet.

'Do you know her?' she asked softly, fearful of his answer. Malcolm was a very handsome man indeed; she herself had been dangerously fascinated by him ever since they'd met. Of course he had not lived as a monk, despite his devotion to his work. But that lady was so astonishingly beautiful, holding the rapt attention of all the men around her. Alex knew she could never compete.

'I am not sure,' he said tonelessly. Someone

from behind them called him away and he left after giving Alex a quick, tight smile.

Feeling unsettled, Alex looked back down at the woman in red. Suddenly, she was sure she *had* seen the woman before. She had a fleeting memory of Malcolm kissing a girl in a red shawl, her long, dark hair streaming down her back.

Was it the same lady, grown up now as they all were, so beautiful and elegant? Alex studied her again, those laughing, painted red lips, those large, slightly slanting dark eyes, the airy wave of her lace fan. Surely it was the same girl. But what did it mean? Why was she here, now? And who was she?

The woman vanished in the crowd on the Duc's arm and Alex slowly returned to Malcolm's side. His earlier relaxed, lazy pleasure had gone and, even though he smiled as the Viscountess told him her thoughts about the millinery department, there was an edge to it, a tightness that wasn't there before.

She wondered then if the past, whatever horrors and secrets it held, would ever truly be gone.

Chapter Fifteen

Alex was so excited she could barely sit still, even on the plush seats of Malcolm's carriage. As they waited to alight at the opera, she stared at the spectacle before her in astonishment.

'It's like a grand wedding cake,' she gasped and indeed it was. A cake, glowing with thousands of lights, sparkling like something alive. Garnier's opera house, built only in the eighteen-seventies, was astonishing. Three levels of pale stone carved with flourishes of columns, statues, balconies and towers that soared above the Paris street. The bronze sculptures of Harmony, Poetry, Drama and Dance gleamed amid the busts of great composers, looking down at the city they had once conquered, Apollo reigning over all.

She had seen it during the day, wondered what lay behind that glorious, riotous façade, what treasures were concealed in its circuitous halls, but she had never been inside until tonight. When he heard she had never been, he immediately procured tickets to the ballet as a surprise. She had not been able to resist the chance to see it, even as she felt the cold touch of trepidation. Malcolm had no need to buy her; if only she could make him see that.

He would spoil her, she thought, until she didn't recognise herself any more. He had given her gowns, jewels, roomfuls of flowers, so many chocolates she had to share them with the delighted Bullard children until they were all three ill. She wouldn't be human if she didn't truly enjoy it, but it worried her, too. Was he showering her with so many things because he feared she would leave their agreement otherwise? Was it a substitute for giving of himself? What would their future be like?

'Shall I order a cake made to look like the opera house, then, for the wedding?' he said. 'Sugar-icing statues, spun-sugar glass windows? I'm sure the caterers would be up for the challenge and it would only cost a few hundred francs to change...'

'Don't you dare!' Alex cried. The wedding plans were already absurdly expensive and she didn't have her appointment at Worth until the next day, which would surely be the most expensive of all. She spun around to face him—and dissolved in laughter. He was grinning at her unrepentantly. 'You are teasing me.'

'Maybe a bit. You do look so adorable when you're excited about something, like a night at the ballet. I couldn't resist.'

Alex settled back on the carriage seat and looped her arm through Malcolm's. She couldn't quite believe she could do that whenever she wanted, touch him, be close to him. She could get used to that, even more than the gowns and flowers.

But even in her contentment, she felt that spark of uncertainty deep inside that she couldn't quite extinguish. She'd seen so little of the world, really, knew so little. Everything she experienced now, the parties with Malcolm and no chaperons watching her every move with him, the kisses, the embraces, made her feel so overwhelmed and, yes, excited that she couldn't contain it.

She thought of women like Lady Smythe-Tomas, like the woman in red at the party. How stylish they were, how cool and controlled and full of sophistication. So—so *knowing* about everything. How could she ever compare to them, learn to be more like them?

'I will try to contain myself,' she said. 'Surely one day, very soon, things like this will be commonplace to me and I won't notice them at all. Ho-hum, another day at the opera.'

'Never do that,' he said, his tone so fierce she looked up at him in surprise. He was frowning out the window, his eyes very dark. 'Always be yourself, Alexandra, I beg you. The way you see the world, as if it's all new and bright and good—it's amazing.'

He was amazing, she thought. 'There is always something new and astounding to be seen, if we look for it.'

'But I seem to have forgotten that, if I ever knew it at all. Work has been all I can see, for such a long time.'

She squeezed his arm and smiled. 'Well, now you have me! I will make you look beyond the stores and you will teach me more about business. I want to learn all about how Gordston's runs!'

He shook his head. 'You would find it dull.'

'I am sure I never would. Just from what Emily has told me about her own work, it sounds fascinating. The styles one must follow, the merchants you meet—I want to learn it, so I can help you all I can.' She remembered that Emily had also said he was most ruthless in business and she wondered what that meant. She had not seen it in him, except in flashes like glimpses of lightning.

'You already help me. The party at the store was a great success and the department heads tell me they have seen many prominent ladies of society shopping in the last few days. English, French and German. The receipts are definitely up.'

'So these society ladies have been buying from the assistants?'

'They have. Anything lavender has been flying from the counters, as well as that blue scarf you wear. I told you that you could lead fashion if you wished.'

'They buy my foot bandage, you mean?' she said, laughing with a little glow of satisfaction. She *had* done something! A small something, but it was a beginning. Surely she could show him that she could be of help, if he let her. 'If they will make a list of who shops with them, I will call on those ladies after the wedding, maybe with some new style of hat or brooch on so they can see it. And once we find a house, I can plan a proper reception.'

'After the honeymoon, you mean.'

Alex glanced at him curiously. It was the first she had heard of any wedding trip. 'Honeymoon?'

'Of course. Every bride deserves one.'

'But can you take the time away? Where are we going?'

He smiled like the cat that got the cream. 'It is a surprise. It can't be a long honeymoon, you're right, for the new store still needs too much close attention. But I think you will like it. It's a special place.'

She had no time to cajole him for more information, as their carriage at last arrived at the head of the long line of theatregoers. A footman opened the door and lowered the steps.

After they left their cloaks and Alex smoothed the skirt of her new midnight-blue-velvet theatre gown and straightened the diamond stars in her hair, Malcolm led her into the grand foyer amid the stream of bejewelled, silken, perfumed guests.

Alex gasped at the sight of the grand double staircase that suddenly soared upwards before her. She had seen engravings of the scene in the newspapers, but no image could have captured fully its grandeur. One flight of marble steps, laid out in varied colours, divided into two at a grand landing and led up to arched walkways, all of it illuminated by crystal chandeliers and gilded classical statues holding aloft electric torches. High above their heads were painted scenes of gods playing music, all blue and white and gold.

And the crowds that flowed up and down the stairs, that peered down from between the arches, were just as glittering. Trains bedecked in bouquets of silk flowers, lace ruffles, velvet bows, trailed over the marble and feathers and jewels glittered in upswept hair.

She was a part of it, Alex realised, startled. After Malcolm's party, she knew these people and they knew her. It was different from the way she had been part of things in the past, a young girl, the unmarried debutante daughter. She was nearly a married woman of fortune. A lady of style, if she could figure out how.

'Lady Alexandra, Mr Gordston,' she heard someone say and turned to see Princess Ingrid of the kingdom of Anhalt-Hesse, a lady of expensive taste and impressive red curls whom they had met at the party. 'How lovely to see you again! I have worn my new aigrette from Gordston's, you see, *ja*?'

'Indeed, your Highness. It does look lovely,' Alex answered. The Princess introduced them to her husband and a few other friends, who all promised to come to Gordston's soon and invited Alex to tea.

As they finished and strolled away, moving slowly up the staircase, Alex noticed that Malcolm looked almost—smug. He smiled down at her.

'They never would have spoken to me in public before,' he said. 'Even though the Princess runs quite a large charge account.'

'Indeed?' Alex glanced back at the German party and caught a few other high-born eyes watching her. She nodded and smiled at them, and tightened her clasp on Malcolm's arm, feeling strangely protective of him.

'Of course they would not. But now that I have you…'

Now he had her. To help him move up the society staircase? Alex kept smiling, but now she didn't feel quite so very confident.

They made their way down a corridor, their footsteps buried in deep, crimson carpet, their reflection flashing past in floor-to-ceiling antique mirrors, and past a row of closed doors. Each one was guarded by a footman in eighteenth-century scarlet livery and powdered wigs. At the end of the row, Malcolm opened a door and ushered her inside.

'This is ours?' she whispered, spinning around in an actual dining room. The polished mahogany table was laid with silver, heavy crystal and flower-painted china, matching the arrangements in tall silver urns along the red-velvet walls.

'For the whole season, if you wish it,' he said proudly, sweeping aside a heavy red curtain and showing her their seats, gilded and cushioned with satin, looking out over the jewel box of the house. 'Supper will be brought in at the long interval and I've invited a few people to join us, including Miss Fortescue.'

'Emily? Oh, how lovely!' Alex said, glad she would see a familiar face. Surely Em would save her from being quite so overwhelmed.

She made her way past the curtain into the front section of their box, the rows of chairs behind the railing. Beyond was the great theatre itself and for a long time she could do nothing but clasp at the railing of their box and stare and stare. It was magnificent, glorious, so sparkling and ornate she barely knew where to look next. The enormous bronze chandelier sparkling overhead? The crowd in their boxes? The dome of the ceiling high overhead? The swags of red-and-gold velvet that cloaked the stage?

'Oh, yes,' she murmured. 'I think I will indeed want it for the whole season.'

Malcolm laughed. 'You haven't even seen the performance yet.'

Alex whirled around to find him holding out her chair, a boyish smile of delight on his face that he could give her such a gift. 'I am sure I will love it, but it almost doesn't matter. This alone is too fine a show to miss.' She sat down and took her opera glasses from her reticule. 'Do you come often to the theatre?'

He sat down beside her, the fine wool sleeve of his black coat brushing her arm. 'Not often. I am always working.'

'Even at night?'

'Of course. During the day there are always emergencies to be dealt with, people to meet. At night, it's quiet and I can go over accounts, examine the displays.'

Alex was sure she would change all that, now that she was there to build them a social life. To give him a home to come to after he worked. 'But you have said yourself that mixing in society is also good for business. That it's essential to know people.'

'You have a good memory.'

'Of course I do. I was educated at Miss Grantley's. Yet surely there is always time, even for a man of business like yourself, to enjoy something. Life is too short and when you have something like a box at the opera house at your disposal…'

His smile widened. 'It would be a crime to waste it.'

'Exactly.'

'I do come here once in a while. I know little of things like opera and ballet, but I can always appreciate a craftsman or artist at the top of their game, as they are here.'

She remembered hearing married friends whisper of what their husbands really liked at the theatre—the ballet dancers. She wondered if Malcolm came to the theatre to look at the pretty women on the stage as they did, but then she realised that he was different from other men. His reactions, his emotions, they were not like those of others. And she wondered if she would ever really know him at all.

Flustered by the thought, Alex raised her glass and studied the crowd in the stalls below, in the other boxes around them. It was indeed like a gilded jewel box and they were the gems scattered in its velvet interior, a show in themselves.

Her attention was caught by a movement in the box across from theirs. Without her glass, the newcomers were a mere blur, a flash of bright colours among a kaleidoscope of so many others, but up close she could see the details.

At first, Alex was caught in admiration of the lady's gown. Emerald-green satin trimmed in black velvet, she was sure it must be Worth. No one else draped a skirt like that. She also wore an emerald-and-diamond collar necklace above a rope of pearls, blindingly sparkly.

Alex's glass moved up—and she gasped. It was the dark-haired woman from the party, laughing vivaciously, waving her fan, even more beautiful than the last time Alex saw her.

The woman reached out to lay her gloved hand on her escort's sleeve, whispered to him from behind her black-lace fan. Alex aimed her glass at him and frowned. Surely it was Mr Nixson, the man who had quarrelled with Malcolm that day on Eiffel's Tower! Yes, it had to be. She would remember that nose, that greyish pallor, anywhere.

She lowered the glass, puzzled. The woman looked very familiar, as well.

'What is it?' Malcolm asked. 'You look upset about something.' He reached for the glass.

Alex tucked it under her reticule and looked towards the stage. 'Nothing at all, of course. I just thought someone had a prettier gown than mine.'

'Impossible! Let me see.'

'I will not. You'll think her lovelier than me, I'm sure, and I will be terribly jealous.' She leaned towards him and kissed his cheek, hoping to distract him, to keep his attention on their happy night.

He smiled at her, but his eyes were narrowed, as if she did indeed puzzle him.

The red-and-gold curtain swung open on a scene of a bucolic village as the orchestra launched into the prelude and Malcolm glanced away. Alex quickly peeked at the other box through her glass.

The lady in emerald-green was watching her in return, her painted lips pursed.

Alex felt her cheeks turn warm and swung her attention back to the stage where a line of dancers in fluffy blue 'peasant' tutus fluttered like butterflies. She soon forgot the woman, Nixson, everything else in the beautiful dancing, the magical world before her, Malcolm's hand on hers.

When the curtain came down on the first interval, she looked once more to the other box. It was empty.

'I think I should like a lemonade,' she said.

'I'll send the footman,' Malcolm answered, rising to his feet.

'Oh, no, I'd like to fetch it myself,' she said. 'Then I can see more of this astonishing place. Do you think they would let us go behind the stage, see the rehearsal spaces? I think I'd like to pretend I was a dancer myself, soaring across the stage on my tippy-toes in a lovely tulle skirt!'

He gave her an indulgent smile. 'Maybe they

won't let us backstage tonight, but I am sure I could get you a tour very soon. They say the director is always trying to raise funds for something. But we can see the Grand Foyer now and find a drink.'

Alex took his arm and followed him up the stairs to the Grand Foyer. For a moment, her eyes were so dazzled that she could barely believe it was real. 'It's astonishing,' she whispered. So long and sparkling, all gold and mirrors, with tall windows leading out to the night and an open loggia. She knew it was modelled on the Hall of Mirrors at Versailles, which surely could be not so grand. She tilted her head back and stared at the paintings high overhead, allegories of the history of music that seemed to draw her up and up into their sky-bound world.

'Should we build a house that looks like this?' Malcolm asked teasingly.

'Don't you dare,' Alex gasped. 'I could never live in such a fantasy. It's much too fine for every day and you know it!'

She spun around—and suddenly stopped, her skirts swaying. A woman was walking towards them, a dark-haired, exotic beauty, a small smile on her rouged lips. The woman from the box, the one in the beautiful emerald gown.

'Malcolm. We meet again at last. It must be

fate,' she said, her voice deep and rich, like velvet, and full of some intimate amusement Alex could only guess at.

Malcolm gave her a small bow, his face made of stone, his eyes very pale. 'Indeed. Mademoiselle Fleurie, is it now?'

She smiled, a smile full of knowledge and even hope. 'Oh, come now. It has not been so very long as all that. Surely you can call me Mairie again.'

Mairie? Alex glanced between them, startled. So she was the girl from Scotland, the one who once wore a red shawl and whose hand was kissed by Malcolm. The one Alex had envied so much. Now they stared at each other, the two of them, as if the crowded foyer had vanished.

Of course she should have recognised her. But the bejewelled, rouged lady before her was so very different from the girl with the loose, long dark hair and the red shawl. As different as Malcolm had been back then.

'It has been a long time,' Malcolm said. 'Too long for such things. We are different people now than we were then.'

Mairie stepped closer, staring up at him with her large, dark, velvety eyes. It was as if Alex was no longer there at all, as if she watched a drama on the stage. 'I do not feel so very different. Not now.'

Malcolm reached out and took Alex's hand. 'I am sure you remember my fiancée. I think you met at the store. Lady Alexandra Mannerly.'

Mairie's dark eyes flickered over Alex before turning back to Malcolm. 'Of course. The Duke of Waverton's daughter. Things *have* changed, I suppose, for you anyway. I am surprised you could even stand to look at a Waverton. But we all do have our price.'

Alex was confused, frightened. Was she a 'price' for Malcolm, something to compensate for the past? But she refused to show any uncertainty in front of this woman, any weakness. 'And some of our prices are Mr Nixson, I suppose,' she said, surprising herself at her own sharp tone.

Mairie turned back to her, her lips parted in astonishment. Then she smiled. 'So the Duke's daughter speaks.'

'Nixson?' Malcolm said sharply.

Mairie waved her lace fan. 'Oh, yes, your little misunderstanding at Monsieur Eiffel's Tower, I did hear about that. Such children you men can be. If you would only talk to him…'

Malcolm scowled. 'You know that won't hap-

pen. Your judgement in friends has been slipping, Mairie.'

She sighed and tapped Malcolm's sleeve with
her fan. 'I suppose it has, that's true enough. I
often wish I could go back to those days in Scotland, don't you, Malcolm dearest? But when my
father wanted me to marry some dreary grocer,
I knew I could not do that. It would be too dull.
I made my own way in the world. But once those
days were lovely, how perfect in every way, until
they were spoiled.'

'We must all grow up. And everything has
come out as it should.'

'Has it? For you, I suppose. Riches *and* Waverton's daughter. How appalled he must be!
And how it must give you such satisfaction, Malcolm.' She smiled again, sly, cat-like and gone in
a flash. 'Well. I am sure we will meet again soon
and can talk more about such matters.'

She gave Malcolm one more smile, one more
touch on his hand with her closed fan, then spun
away and disappeared into the crowd, her emerald gown melting into the bright swirl. She left
a trace of her heavy jasmine perfume behind
like a ghost.

Malcolm's arm was stiff beneath Alex's hand.
She peeked up at him and found that he stared

at the spot where Mairie had just stood, his face hard.

'You saw her with Nixson?' he asked softly.

'Yes, in their box. Only for a moment. I hope he will not appear here.'

'And they seemed—close?'

Alex remembered how Mairie whispered into the man's ear, how she smiled at him. 'I think so. I know little of these things. Who is this Mr Nixson, really, Malcolm? I know you had a business deal go sour with him, but was there something else? And this Mademoiselle Fleurie—you knew her before, didn't you? I am sure of it.'

His jaw tightened. 'A long time ago, in Scotland.'

Alex nodded. 'You were in love with her?'

'What a ridiculous thing to ask. I was too young to know what love was.'

Alex drew away from him, stung by his abrupt tone. She knew there was more to the tale of Mairie, more to his life in Scotland, but she also knew he would never tell her more that night. Maybe he would never tell her more at all. Maybe he would never truly see her as the partner and wife she wanted to be.

'And Nixson?' she asked.

'I am sure you remember him,' Malcolm said,

staring straight ahead. 'The scene at the Eiffel Tower would be hard to forget.'

'Yes,' Alex agreed, feeling a twinge in her ankle at the memory.

'He had brought me a business proposition, but anyone with any reputation to maintain in the business world knows better than to get involved with him. Especially when it has to do with the Far East trade—and rumours of smuggling.'

'Smuggling?' she whispered.

'Opium. A department store would be a perfect front for such a thing, though Nixson believes I am too foolish to know that is what is going on. I turned him away and you remember he was not happy about it. Rumour has it he is bankrupt.'

And Malcolm's old love was somehow mixed up with such a man. She was astonished and a little frightened. 'Should we go home, then?' she asked.

'Of course not. You wouldn't want to miss the next act and we have guests coming to the box for supper.'

'You could tell them I was taken ill,' she said, even as she knew she wanted to see Emily very much. Having her friends nearby was always such a soothing thing.

'This is part of our job, remember? To socialise, see and be seen.'

Alex nodded. She wondered if that was truly all he wanted, to see and be seen with her. Waverton's *daughter*, as Mairie had said.

But she just smiled and nodded, and took his arm again as she knew she should. They strolled to the end of the Grand Foyer, which was just as sparkling, just as regal as before. Yet some of the magic had gone out of the night for her. She felt tired and cold, and confused.

Only the sight of Emily made her feel steady again, back in a world she knew. She glimpsed her friend at the table near the terrace doors and rushed over to greet her with a hug, her peach-and-tawny-satin skirts gleaming. As they chatted about their upcoming trip to Worth to order the wedding gown, Malcolm strolled away to speak to the Viscountess Rippon, who waved at him from across the room.

'Em,' Alex whispered quickly, 'what do you know about people named Mr Nixson and a Mademoiselle Fleurie? I don't think she is actually French, though.'

Emily frowned in thought. 'Nixson owns an import business, ivory and silk from the East mostly, but Father would never deal with him. There are rumours opium finds its way into his shipments far more often than it should and possibly even worse. He seems to have a great deal of money, grand houses and such, but no respectable man with a business like the one he purports to have could afford such things. His legal company has been on the verge of collapse more than once. Why do you ask? Your Malcolm is not involved with the likes of Nixson, is he?'

'Oh, no. Quite the opposite. He warned me about the same thing, the smuggling, that is. I thought they would come to blows when they met.' She hoped they would not come face to face with the man that night. Especially not with Mairie in the mix.

'And Mademoiselle Fleurie?' Emily tapped her gloved finger to her chin. 'I think I have heard the name, though I don't know a great deal about her. I think she used to be something of an actress, though now she just seems to be a member of the professional demi-monde. She has accounts at many of the fashion houses, but I don't know about her protectors or where she came from before Paris. I can find out more gossip, I'm sure. Why do you want to know? Are you going to start writing salacious novels?'

Alex glanced at Malcolm, who was still deep in conversation with the Viscountess. 'I'm not sure yet why I need to know.'

'Most intriguing,' Emily whispered, her eyes alight. She did like a chance to make mischief, Alex remembered, and she had a mind like a steel trap for any scrap of gossip. She had been one of the greatest mischief-makers at Miss Grantley's, though she was never caught.

'Shall we return to the box?' Malcolm asked, holding out his hand to Alex as the interval bell tolled.

'I'll see you at supper,' Emily said and added in a whisper, 'Let me see what lovely dirt I can dig up in the meantime!'

Alex took Malcolm's hand and followed him back along the corridor to their waiting box. The footmen were laying out the supper things for the next interval, silver-covered dishes that emanated delicious, spicy scents, and crystal vases of more roses and carnations. The perfect setting for a perfect evening, a perfect life. But what did it all mean? Where would it all lead?

'I am sorry for being such a growly bear,' Malcolm said with a rueful smile. 'Miss Mersey often tells me I need to find an etiquette school.'

'I think you could join us in Amelia and Charlotte's classes,' Alex said, though she couldn't shake off the cold disquiet she had felt at seeing Mr Nixson and Mademoiselle Fleurie together. 'We are all certainly entitled to our moods, Malcolm, or for being caught by surprise when the past comes into the present.'

'But I don't have only myself to think of now in these moods. I have you, my future wife. You deserve a husband you can rely on.'

Alex studied him carefully in the golden light, his smile, his eyes that were no longer like ice, as they had been when they met Mairie. He was indeed changeable. And yet she knew the man she cared for was in there, always. How could she ever keep up? How could she ever let go of the past? 'I am certain I can rely on you, Malcolm. I would not marry you otherwise, not for all the opera boxes in the world. But I do hope you know you can tell me anything you wish to. I am good at keeping secrets.'

'I don't think I have any interesting secrets. None worth keeping, anyway.' He paused outside the curtain to their seats and gave her an uncertain glance. 'Mairie and I, we were a sort of childhood sweethearts, I suppose. Her father was a shopkeeper and I always knew she was beyond my reach. After my father died and I left for my apprenticeship, we wrote each other for a time. I had—hopes. Foolish hopes. But then she vanished. I could hardly blame her; I always knew she wanted a better life than I could provide then. I never saw her again until Paris. I didn't know she was Mademoiselle Fleurie, what she had become.'

Alex looked at him. She knew there was more to know somewhere in there, but she could also see how hard it was for him to confide anything at all about the past. About secrets he had kept locked up inside for so long. She was satisfied with that—for now. She went up on tiptoe to softly kiss his lips, feeling their warmth yielding beneath her touch. That connection between them. Surely she did not imagine that. Surely it would grow, if she was patient and careful. Surely it could?

She pushed away painful doubts and slowly nodded.

'It was a very long time ago,' he said roughly.

'And this is the present,' she said. '*We* are the present. But I am sure it must be worrying that someone you cared for is now mixed up with the likes of Mr Nixson.'

'Yes,' he said shortly.

Alex heard the first strains of music from beyond the curtain, the soft patter of toe shoes on the stage. 'Shall we sit down? You're quite right, I would hate to miss any of the dancing.'

He nodded and hand in hand they returned to their seats, to the glittering world that was theirs if they could just reach out and pick it up. The box across the way remained empty.

Malcolm tossed his cravat to the floor and tore open his starched shirt, sure it was strangling him. He paced to the end of his chamber and pushed open the window, letting in a flood of cool night air, the sounds of the city.

Despite the late hour, Paris was still alive. Music, the clatter of horses' hooves on the streets, laughter. The constant motion, the reminder of the wide outside world, steadied him even as he wanted to battle the past back into its place. Banish it, as he had done for so long, by sheer force of will and the power of hard work.

But the past had come roaring back, bursting out of the box where he had locked it. Mairie had returned. No, she was Mademoiselle Fleurie now and she associated with men like Nixson. And in her eyes, those dark eyes he would have given anything to have look at him and only him once upon a time, he saw the reflection of what he, too, had become. Hard, cynical. Selfish even. He didn't want to be that way, but the world had forced it on him. She was right, a boy like him could never in a million years have dreamed of a duke's daughter, yet here they were.

Yet Alex was none of those things. Malcolm

closed his eyes and remembered her as she peered out the carriage window at the spectacle of the grand opera house. Her fairy face glowed with excitement at the moment, with the anticipation of the glories life might hold. Her enthusiasm had reached out and taken hold of him in a way nothing had in so very long and made him feel excited, too. Nothing mattered in that moment but her, not the past, not revenge, not ambition.

Alexandra made him feel alive, truly alive, once more. When he was with her, he forgot the hardness of his world, the coldness. She made him want to laugh again, to be free, to catch her in his arms and feel all her summer-sun warmth in his own heart again.

He had never known anything like her, had never dared hope any lady like her could be his. Yet she was to be his wife. If he could hold on to her, hide his secrets from her until she couldn't escape.

Malcolm curled his fists on to the windowsill, feeling the wood dig into his skin, grounding him. He wouldn't let the past take away the present. For a moment, Mairie had held out the lure of the boy he had once been. Alex was the man he *was*, or the man he wanted to be. The fulfilment of all he had worked for so hard for so long. He wasn't going to let that go.

No matter what it took.

Chapter Sixteen

Mairie McGregor Fleurie poured out a generous measure of brandy and gulped it down, letting its sharpness catch her at the back of her throat as she prayed for its warm forgetfulness. She closed her eyes. It didn't work. So she poured out some more.

Thankfully, that fool Nixson had gone home after the ballet instead of staying to pester her. She had only reeled him in because she'd heard he was a business associate of Malcolm's. She hadn't realised business *enemies* was more like it, or that Nixson didn't have nearly as much money as he liked to claim.

But the man had served his purpose. She had seen Malcolm again, caught his attention. What happened next was up to her.

She hadn't expected the *milquetoast* fiancée,

though. The daughter of the Duke of Waverton, of all people. That had indeed been a surprise.

Mairie closed her eyes and for a moment she let herself do something she seldom allowed herself to indulge in—remembering the past. Before Mademoiselle Fleurie, the men like Nixson, the villas and diamonds and satin gowns. When she was just Mairie, a Scottish girl wandering the fields with a handsome boy, laughing, holding hands, kissing. Dreaming. Until it all came crashing down. Her father lost his money and she knew she had to make her own way in the world. Find her own fortune and it lay in her beautiful face. She had done many things she was not proud of, but she had survived.

She opened her eyes and, rather than a field of heather, saw her pink-velvet-and-gilt drawing room. Malcolm was even more handsome than he had been when they were young, harder, more intriguing. What game was he playing with the Duke's girl? Surely it was some kind of revenge. The Duke had been cruel to the Gordstons and his daughter was surely just as haughty. What kind of scheme was it? And yet the way he looked at the pale little mouse…

Mairie shook her head. She'd thought once she found him again it would be so easy. She could reel him in, get what she wanted from him at last. Yet when she looked into his eyes, she saw only blue, hard ice. This was not going to be as easy as she thought.

Mairie dropped down on to her satin *chaise*, kicking off her silk evening shoes to dig her toes into her thick fur rug. She tilted back her head and studied the fine view from her windows. The apartment was paid for not by that fool Nixson, but by another admirer, long departed. The place was her great pride. Yet today its luxurious lustre seemed dimmed, tawdry even. The memory of those heather fields had eclipsed the paintings, the gold clocks, the marble fireplace. Yet it was irretrievable. Except in Malcolm.

She could not give up now, not when he was so close.

She thought of that Duke's daughter. Lady Alexandra, so pale, so perfect. Maybe she was the key.

Chapter Seventeen

It was her wedding day.

Alex could hardly believe the truth of those words, even as she repeated them to herself over and over. She had never really been one of those young girls who planned every detail of their future day, even though she did like studying engravings of satin and orange blossoms in the fashion papers. But no matter what she might have imagined back then, it couldn't have been this. A grand day in Paris.

As Lady Bullard and Emily fussed over her hair, Alex glanced out the window. It had been a grey morning earlier, threatening rain, yet now the sun was peeking out of a pale sky, shining on the white stone of the buildings and turning the flowers on the cart at the corner to jewels. Even though her mother had not been able to leave her spa cure in time for the wedding, her friends were all the help and support she needed.

'There! What do you think?' Emily said.

Alex turned to the full-length mirror. 'I hardly know myself,' she whispered. It was like looking at something that had stepped from a book. Her hair was curled and piled atop her head by the most fashionable coiffeur in Paris, anchored with pearl pins and covered by the Brussels lace veil held by a wreath of white rosebuds. Pearl and diamond earrings glittered beneath the haze of the lace.

The gown from Worth was quite beyond anything she had ever dreamed of wearing before. Heavy white satin, as lustrous as a new fall of snow, spread out from a narrow skirt in the newest fashion into a long train, embroidered with cascades of seed pearls. They also gleamed at the high neck and on the long sleeves.

'You look like the snow queen in our book,' Charlotte said, pausing from racing around the room with her sister in their white bridesmaids' dresses with blue sashes to stare up at Alex.

A winter fairy, Alex thought. Would Malcolm think so when he saw her? Would he think her beautiful, be proud she was to be his wife? Would he forget Mairie and the past? She did hope so, with all her might.

But what if he could not forget, what if all he could see was the beautiful, dark-haired love of his youth as Alex walked towards him down the aisle? Emily had said she could find out nothing about Mademoiselle Fleurie except that the woman was once from Scotland, said she was descended from Robert the Bruce and liked to dance the Highland fling at racy parties, but that was all. No tragic past loves.

Was Alex making a mistake? No matter how she tried to banish them, worries plagued her mind. In the days since their night at the opera, she had only seen Malcolm briefly, though he sent flowers every day. She wished she could talk to him alone once more, reassure herself that this step was the right one.

But there was no more time to worry now. No time to turn back. She hoped so fervently for the best, for future happiness for them both. For the past to be forgotten. She had to hold that thought, those wishes, close.

'Now, my dear,' Lady Bullard whispered as she arranged Alex's lace veil. 'I know your mother is far away, but I am sure she would want me to tell you what happens on the night after the wedding…'

Alex felt her cheeks turn hot. 'I—well, I think I know.'

Lady Bullard pursed her lips. 'I am sure you know *what* happens. What bits go where. Miss Grantley would never let her girls leave school ignorant of *that*. At first it might feel—odd. Uncomfortable, even. But if you relax and close your eyes, it can be quite nice, really. Just don't be afraid.'

Afraid of Malcolm? Alex was sure she could not be. But the thought of what might happen in the dark, after she became his wife—it made her blush even harder. 'I will not.'

Lady Bullard gave a satisfied nod, as if her duty was done, and Emily handed Alex the bouquet of white roses and sweetly scented orange blossoms. Lady Bullard straightened her wide-brimmed pink hat and gathered up the girls, making sure they had their baskets of rose petals. The maid straightened Alex's train and draped it over her arm, and they all made their way down the stairs of the Bullards' house to where the Duke waited in the hall with Lord Bullard.

Her father took her hand and looked down at her, solemn as if they were headed to funeral. He kissed her cheek and said quietly, 'I cannot thank you enough, my dear, for the sacrifice you make today, Flower. I knew you would do your duty. You have always been a good child, unlike your unfathomable brother. He would never marry, no matter how dire our situation would be. I knew I could count on you.'

Alex stared up at him in astonishment. She couldn't even think what to answer. Her wedding was hardly a sacrifice, a virgin chained to a rock waiting for a sea monster—it was a dream. But, yes, she knew the pressure her father had always put on her to do her duty and she always did it.

She just shook her head and took his arm to let him lead her out to the waiting carriages. They were just as festive as everyone's new Worth fashions, bedecked in wreaths of flowers, all white and gleaming. Neighbours leaned out of their windows to wave them off. Alex and her father climbed into the first carriage, Emily and the Bullards in the other, and they set off in their small, festive caravan.

The short drive to the palatial British embassy on the Rue de Faubourg Saint-Honoré was made mostly in silence. Alex did not know what to say to her father, did not know how to feel about the approaching ceremony. Happy? Excited? Scared? Unsure? She was all that and more. She fiddled with her bouquet and watched the city roll past. It was gone much too fast.

As they drew to a halt, she stared up at the embassy, trying to remember to breathe. It was a stark yet elegant place, all grey stone, gilded balconies, a black-painted door with the British flag snapping in the breeze above its portal. A footman opened the door. Alex drew her lace veil down and stepped out, moving towards a new life she could barely imagine.

Her father took her arm and they went up the steps into the cool cream-and-blue marble hall, where the ambassador and his wife waited below the statue of Pauline Borghese, who had once owned the house. Alex stared at her marble smile, her bare breasts and elegant hands, and thought surely Princess Pauline had never felt nervous at all. Especially not when it came to romance.

'How lovely it is to have a wedding today!' the ambassador's wife said as she and her husband led Alex and the Duke up the winding staircase. 'It makes a nice change from dull business, does it not, my dear?'

The chapel doors on the second storey were closed, but Alex could hear the strains of music, the hushed chatter of guests. Emily and Lady Bullard arranged her veil and train, told the girls to stop fidgeting and the doors suddenly swung open.

For an instant, Alex was quite overwhelmed. The room, long and soaring, lit by tall stained-glass windows, was crowded with morning suits and feathered hats, every eye on her. She took a step on the plush red carpet towards the waiting gilded altar and sucked in a breath, trying not to faint. The music swelled from the organ, a stately march, the girls stepped forward to scatter their rose petals and the Duke gave Alex's arm a sharp tug. He looked down at her with alarm, as if he feared she might flee.

As if she would ever back out now.

Alex tilted up her chin and glided ahead, trying to remember to smile even as she trembled all over.

Then she saw Malcolm waiting for her at the steps to the altar, his hair gleaming gold in the light, his shoulders broad and strong under his grey-and-black suit, his face so solemn as he looked only at her. Her fear flew away and she knew she was exactly where she should be.

They reached the front of the chapel and she heard the vicar speak, though the exact words were hazy through the pounding of her heart. Her father stiffly gave her hand to Malcolm and stepped away, and she was alone with the only person who truly mattered.

She smiled up at him through her veil, trying to reassure him, too, hoping he might feel the same way she did. Hoping he was happy to be there. Finally, finally, he smiled back.

'We are gathered together today in the sight of God to join this man and this woman in holy matrimony…' the vicar began and she knew it was done. She and Malcolm were as one now, come what may.

'To the bride!'

Glasses filled with effervescent golden champagne were raised again, sparkling against the white-rose-and-carnation arrangements on the embassy dining room's damask-draped tables. It was the fifth toast and everyone seemed ever merrier as the champagne flowed and the wedding breakfast of delicacies was consumed, but Alex was sure she could never tire of it all. She hadn't had so much fun in—well, *ever*. Her cheeks ached from smiling.

She barely even noticed her father's stern, silent presence to her left. The Duke barely spoke to anyone except Lady Bullard, who sat on his other side, and he never laughed or smiled. Yet she could only see Malcolm, her husband now. He smiled at her, squeezed her hand, made sure her glass was full, laughed at the jests of the other guests.

The whole marriage idea, which had been so hasty, so strange, now seemed so very right. She seemed to have stumbled into a fairyland, a sparkling, magical place of happiness and beauty. He was surely her Malcolm, the boy she once knew, deep down inside, and she would find him again beneath the hard Mr Gordston.

Malcolm laid his hand on her satin sleeve and leaned closer. She smiled up at him and saw that his blue eyes no longer looked like ice, but like a summer sky. Could he be feeling as she did? Happy at their day, at what they had done?

'I think they'll bring in the cake soon,' he said. 'It's meant to be a surprise. The chef has been working on a special design.'

Alex laughed. 'This whole wedding has been a surprise.' And it had. Despite Miss Mersey consulting Alex on some decisions, showing her drawings of flower arrangements and lists of musical selections, Malcolm had arranged most of it. And it had all ended up perfect. A beautiful society wedding.

She glanced at her father, who still frowned as he looked at the elegant blue-and-gold room, all bedecked in flowers and swaths of tulle. She knew he had met with Malcolm and the lawyers a couple of times and she couldn't help but wonder what Malcolm had arranged *there*. What 'sacrifices' her father had talked about.

But she wouldn't let grey clouds mar that perfect day. Her wedding day.

'Cake!' Amelia and Charlotte cried, bouncing in excitement. They had been dashing around the reception for an hour, their blue sashes coming untied and the flowers in their hair askew, never seeming to tire of it all. Alex thought them quite adorable.

'I think you monkeys have had quite enough treats today,' Lady Bullard said, hugging her daughters close. 'You will have stomach aches tomorrow and it will be beef tea for a week. You should go to nanny now.'

'No, Mama!' Amelia cried.

'It's bad luck not to eat the cake at a wedding,' Charlotte declared.

Alex smiled at them tenderly. 'I shall miss you two very much.'

Lady Bullard grinned at her over Amelia's rumpled curls. 'But you will surely have your own monkeys soon!'

'Playmates for us,' Charlotte said.

Her own children. How strange that sounded—how wonderful. It made her feel warm and shivery all at once to think of that, little ones with Malcolm's bright hair and blue eyes, playing at her feet. Making a real family.

She glanced at Malcolm, wondering if he had heard, but he was talking to Emily and Chris, who sat across from them, deep in conversation about some business matter. Did he want a family, too? Look forward to cosy evenings by the fire, watching children arrange their dolls, reading stories together? She couldn't yet envision such a thing. But it did fill her with a sweet, aching hope.

The cake was brought, wheeled on a satin-draped cart, and it was indeed an impressive edifice. White icing moulded into the shape of a medieval castle, all turrets and battlements, blue icing forming a moat around it.

'Oh, how lovely,' Alex gasped. She rose from her chair for a better look and Emily hurried to arrange her train before she could crush it. Alex smiled her thanks and had a sudden thought—now that she was a married lady, surely she should find a match for Em! Her friend deserved someone wonderful, someone to help her in her work. But who would be spectacular enough?

Malcolm took her hand, his fingers warm and strong curled around hers. 'Do you like the cake? Really?' he asked, his voice almost boyishly eager in a way she had never heard from him before.

'Oh, yes. It's all so perfect today,' she said. And it was, every single moment of it. Especially his touch on her hand. Floating on such a cloud of happiness, Alex was sure the future suddenly looked bright and promising indeed.

Before they went to cut the cake, she impulsively turned and handed her bouquet to Emily. 'For you,' she whispered. 'I'm sure it will be soon.' But Emily frowned, not nearly as happy at such a prospect as Alex was herself.

Chapter Eighteen

$\mathcal{A}$lex brushed her hair, again and again, until
the fine, slippery, silvery strands crackled. She
had already brushed it twice, but she didn't know
what else to do. She couldn't just sit still. She
couldn't pace the floor like some caged tiger.
The clock on the marble fireplace mantel ticked
away the moments of the night, later and later.

The hotel chamber where they had retired
after the wedding party was lavish, beautiful,
all pale blue and gold silk, the lights of Paris
sparkling outside the windows, beyond the elaborate swags of the velvet curtains. Tall vases of
white roses and lilies perfumed the air, perfect
for a wedding. And the snowy sheets and blue-
satin blankets of the bed were turned back, the
cushions plumped up invitingly.

Alex had sent the maid away hours before and

now wondered if she should have kept her there. Would chatter be better than the silent waiting?

She reached for a pot of rose-scented cream and rubbed it absently on her trembling fingers. The lamplight flashed on her cameo engagement ring, her new, shiny gold wedding band. What would happen next?

Oh, she knew *what* would happen. She'd heard the whispers of the girls at Miss Grantley's, read the novels. She remembered what Lady Bullard said. *'If you relax and close your eyes, it can be quite nice.'*

But knowing *what* happened didn't tell her how it would *feel*. She closed her eyes and re-membered Malcolm's kisses, the delight and wonder of them. If it felt half as nice as that…

She opened her eyes and studied her reflection in the mirror. Why did she have to be so ridicu-lously pale? So wide-eyed and nervous-looking? She smoothed the satin bows that tied the neck of her new, cobweb-thin muslin gown and shook her hair over her shoulders. She thought of women like Mairie Fleurie and Lady Smythe-Tomas, their confidence and elegance, and tried to put on that kind of mask. It didn't quite work.

She glanced again at the clock, a confection of shepherds and their maids cavorting around the ivory face, the gold numbers. Still ticking away.

Then, at last, the knock at the door that connected her room to Malcolm's. It sounded so loud in the silence.

'C-come in,' she called, standing up, smoothing the skirt of her nightgown.

He stepped into the room, the light from the fire gleaming on his gold-brocade dressing gown, his bright hair. Her husband, her beautiful husband. For an instant, she couldn't breathe.

'Alexandra,' he said simply and yet there was so much in that, in just the sound of her name. He held out his hand to her and she reached out and accepted it. Accepted *him*.

She held on to his hand, feeling the warm safety of him envelop her until all her nervousness, her fears, vanished and the two of them, alone, was all there could be in the whole world. His arms came around her and drew her close, and she felt a spark of something deep inside, growing warm and vital, like coming awake to life itself after a very long sleep. The pain of the past, the anger and hurt, surely it could all be gone. They were just the two of them now.

She didn't want to lose that feeling, ever. That sense that the story was just beginning.

She went up on tiptoe and wound her arms tightly around his neck so he couldn't fly away from her. His hair curled around her fingertips, so soft, his body so warm and solid and delicious against hers.

'How beautiful you are,' she whispered before she could stop herself.

He gave a surprised laugh and Alex stopped him with a kiss, pressing one quick, shy caress to his lips, then another and another, teasing him, tasting him, until he groaned and roughly pulled her even closer. There was not even a breath between them they were so close.

She felt his wordless moan against her lips, the sound echoing inside her heart, and he deepened the kiss. His tongue sought hers and she answered with a caress of her own, lost in him. She needed so desperately to be just that close to him, always, to be surrounded by his taste, his green summery scent, pull all that he was into her until he was truly hers.

It was nothing like their first frightening, nervous kiss so long ago when he proposed to her. It was desperate, hungry, filled with wild yearning. The need to know that this was real.

For once in her life, Alex did not feel nervous, frightened. She knew what she wanted—Malcolm, her husband.

He drew back slowly, pressing tiny, soft kisses to her cheek, her temple, the sensitive spot behind her ear. She shivered and heard the rush of his breath in her ear. Surely he wanted her, too, just as much as she wanted him. What an astonishing thought. She shuddered and clung to him, afraid she might fall.

'Alex,' he said roughly. He stepped back and took her hand. He led her towards the waiting bed, the lacy sheets drawn back invitingly, the scattered rose petals. They sat down together, so close, and Alex could hardly breathe as he slowly untied the ribbons of her gown. His fingers suddenly fumbled, as if he, too, was overcome by the moment. Alex drew down the edge of the thin muslin, revealing her shoulders, her breasts.

Was she doing this right? She felt another burst of fear, but she pushed it away. *No.* She wouldn't be afraid any longer, not with him. This was right. This was where she was meant to be.

She shook the fall of her hair back from her shoulders, leaving herself bare, and reached out for him. She kissed his roughened cheek, his throat, the golden skin where his dressing gown fell away. How golden he was all over, glowing with vibrant, powerful life.

'Alexandra,' he moaned and tore off his clothes, revealing the beautiful strength of him. Her Thor, rippling with muscles, a pale silver scar on his hip. Malcolm always held so tightly to his emotions, burying them under layers of reserve and careful thought, but now that seemed tossed aside. He was unleashed, like a tiger, all for her. And it was beyond thrilling.

His mouth met hers again and they fell together to the bed, the gathered silk canopy whirling dizzily over her head. As he rose above her, she reached out with trembling fingers to trace the light, coarse golden hair on his broad chest. She dared not go lower, not yet. His stomach muscles tightened and his breath was harsh, uneven.

Shyly, she peeked lower at last. She had seen so many ancient statues in galleries and museums, and yet to see him, living, vibrant—it was, well, different. Fascinating. She lightly touched him and felt the warm, satin skin lengthen under her hand.

'You will drive me insane, Alex,' he growled and they fell back into each other's arms, their kiss frantic. It was all sun-hot, desperate, urgent, needful. This, she knew, was true connection, true freedom, all at the same time.

She closed her eyes to shut out everything but his touch, the press of his mouth on her breast, his hand on her hip. Her own hand sliding down his back. Lost in another person. She spread her legs to welcome him.

'I don't want to hurt you,' he gasped.

'Oh, Malcolm. You never could,' she said and pulled him closer.

He slid inside her and for an instant it *did* hurt, just as Lady Bullard had tried to warn her. How could it not? A burn, but it was nothing to the feeling of being with him at last. She arched her back against the pain, wrapping her legs around him so he wouldn't leave her. He went very still, his cheek pressed to her hair.

Then slowly, slowly, he moved again within her, drawing back, plunging closer, just a little deeper, a little more intimate each time until she moved with him. Alex gasped as the ache ebbed away and there was only pleasure. A glorious delight that grew inside of her, a burst of light like fireworks. She had never imagined such a thing before, even in books.

She gasped at the wonder of it all, the flames that shot through her. How could anyone not be consumed by it all?

Above her, all around her, she heard Malcolm gasp, his shoulders tense under her touch.

'Alexandra!' he shouted. *'M'eudail.'*

And she exploded among those flashing lights.

After long moments, hearing only their mingled breath, she slowly opened her eyes, sure she had fallen into some new world. Yet the room still looked the same, all opulent blue and gold and flowers.

The same—yet so utterly different. Everything in life was different now.

Collapsed beside her on the pillows, his arms tight around her, was Malcolm. Her husband now in truth. His eyes were closed, his limbs loose and sprawled in exhaustion. The god after battle, or after love.

Alex smiled and snuggled close beside him, letting the tiredness overwhelm her mind. She had never been so exhausted, or quite so very happy. Surely it was all going to be well now. Her Malcolm was returning to her.

Chapter Nineteen

Alex leaned on Malcolm's shoulder as their carriage dashed away from the streets of Paris into the green serenity of the countryside. She couldn't seem to stop smiling after last night, after their breakfast together that morning, even as she tried to maintain a suitably serious expression for a respectable matron. But that grin kept breaking through.

It was getting late in the afternoon, the light turning to a pale amber-pink that gave a glow to everything around them. The fields and hedges that replaced the crowds of the city, the glimpses of roofs and chimneys in the distance, seemed bathed in heavenly, serene gold light, embroidered with flashes of bright flowers popping up here and there, all silent but for the swoosh of their wheels on the road, the softness of her husband's breath.

Her *husband.* Alex giggled at that word. She couldn't help it, it seemed so strange, so wondrous. Her *husband* was asleep and she raised her head to study him closely while he could not look back and make her feel shy.

The evening light turned him to gold just as it did the world outside, bathing him in its glow just as if he was a Norse god in truth, her Thor. His bright hair was tousled over his brow, the velvet collar of his travel coat, his skin gilded, and in sleep he looked so much younger. Lighter, free.

Alex reached out to touch a loose, silken strand of his hair, but her fingers hesitated. Last night they had been so close, as close as two people could be, and she had felt as if her soul truly met his. But that had been in the darkness of their bedroom. Here, in the light of day, it felt so different.

He was her husband; surely she had the right to touch him. And yet she hesitated. She thought she knew him. The kindness he showed his employees, his strength and anger when wronged by the likes of Mr Nixson, his joy when he gave her a gift like her castle wedding cake. Surely those things were real. Surely the boy she once knew in Scotland was still there somewhere beneath Malcolm's grown-up armour? Surely she knew her own husband, the man who had made such passionate love to her, had held her so tenderly.

Yet she also knew that in many ways she couldn't see into him at all. He was still a stranger to her and she sensed there were parts of himself he carefully hid from her. Hid from everyone. Would she ever truly know him? What would their future be like?

Alex folded her hands in the lap of her new purple-velvet travel suit and tried to peer into the years ahead. She could see some of it: the parties they would give and attend, making business connections for Gordston's. Perhaps even making real friends. That was little different from the life she had always seen mapped out for her. She had never pictured it with a husband like Malcolm, though. That part had her mystified, confused, hopeful and scared.

She thought of their wedding night, the surprise and wonder of it all. Could it always be like that between them, that consuming flame? Or would it fade? Would he turn from her, back to exotic, fascinating women like Mademoiselle Fleurie?

Alex shivered, but she also felt a new determination. She was Malcolm's wife now. They were together; she could make him see *her*, make him find the young man she had once known again, the one she knew was underneath there still. She had pictured a life for them, a life of children and home, and she would do all she could to make and keep it. She promised herself that. No matter what, he was *her* husband. She would fight for their future.

She finally reached up to touch him, running her fingertips over his cheek, feeling the warmth of his skin, the roughness of his afternoon beard.

His eyes opened, darker blue from his dreams, and he stretched lazily. He looked even more like a golden god, languid yet powerful.

'Did you have a good rest?' Alex said softly.

He wrapped his arms around her and drew her close, so close she was nearly in his lap. The brim of her hat hit him on the forehead, making him laugh, and she tossed it to the opposite seat so she could rest her head on his shoulder.

'Very good indeed,' he said roughly. 'Someone quite depleted my energy last night.'

'And she intends to do it again tonight,' Alex said, giggling at her own boldness.

'I knew there must be a good reason everyone kept urging me to marry,' he growled and bowed his head to kiss her. Alex clung to him, kissing him back with everything in her, every desire that had been brought to life on their wedding night—until the carriage hit a bump in the road, jolting Malcolm's head against the tufted wall and making them laugh.

Alex was utterly breathless when he let her go, flushed and laughing and feeling utterly unlike her proper self. She tried to force her curls back into their pins, but finally gave up and rested her head on Malcolm's shoulder again to watch the scenery fly past the window.

It had grown darker while they were absorbed in each other, the light turning coral and rose, violet at the edges. The countryside had given way to a few white-and-old-gold country villas, set back behind iron gates and towering lanes of trees.

'I do wish you would tell me where we're going,' she sighed. 'Is it very far away?'

'I told you, it's a surprise. And not far now.'

Alex smiled and closed her eyes, snuggling close to Malcolm. How warm he felt, how secure and safe and exciting all at the same time. She must have dozed off a little, for she was jolted awake when the carriage slowed and turned.

She opened her eyes to see the grandest pair of gates she could ever have imagined gleaming in the twilight. Gilded at the tips, crowned with a fleur-de-lys. Beyond she saw a palace, ghostly in the shadows, a thousand windows gleaming.

'Are we going to Versailles?' she gasped.

Surely not even Malcolm, who seemed able to accomplish anything, could procure Versailles for their honeymoon?

He laughed, a wonderful, light sound. 'Not exactly. I have heard it is really run down inside, anyway, not at all fit for a fairy princess. We aren't far, though.'

Intrigued, Alex watched avidly as they turned down a narrow lane, lined with chestnut trees. The gates of Versailles faded behind them and soon a new dwelling came into view, like a pale apparition appearing out of the twilight.

It was a chateau, but in exquisite miniature, all white stone and tall windows, grey-brick chimneys curling inviting silvery smoke. A perfect, simple treasure set in an enchanted garden of flowerbeds, groves of trees and a tiny temple of white marble columns.

The carriage circled a fountain at the centre of the drive, Artemis poised with her bow. The emerging moonlight gleamed on her arrow and water tumbled around her.

'How beautiful,' Alex whispered. It was not like what she had almost expected, feared, not a grand place, overwhelming. It was like something that could really be a home.

'Do you really like it?' Malcolm asked, his tone taut, even anxious.

She glanced up at him, and found he watched her solemnly. 'It looks like the most perfect home I could have ever imagined.'

He smiled, and it was like the sun breaking through grey clouds. 'Good. Because it is yours.'

'Mine?' Alex gasped. Surely he had not just given her a whole house, the house she would have wanted above all others if she could have imagined the perfect abode?

'For a wedding present. We'll have to find a house in London, of course, and an apartment in Paris, but you will always have your own place to come to in France.'

Before she could say any more, a footman opened the carriage door and a butler, house-keeper and flock of maids in their white aprons appeared on the marble front steps. Alex quickly put her hat back on, straightened her jacket and stepped down to the white gravel drive.

'My lady,' the butler said with a low bow, his voice English. 'I am Smithson, the butler, and this is Mrs Andrews, the housekeeper, and Made-moiselle LeClerc, who will be your lady's maid, if it pleases you. We have the Chateau d'Or all in preparation, but you must never hesitate to ask for anything you need right away. Dinner will be ready soon.'

'How do you do,' Alex greeted them all shyly,

her own household. She was quite delighted to see that Mademoiselle LeClerc was from Mademoiselle Gardinier's school.

Malcolm suddenly reached down and swept Alex into his arms, lifting her high and making her laugh as he carried her through the doors into the warmth of their waiting home. 'Malcolm!' she cried.

'Every bride must be carried across the threshold,' he insisted. 'For luck!'

She had a whirling glimpse of a flowered Aubusson carpet on a warm parquet floor, tapestries on silk-papered walls, tall vases of fresh pink-and-white flowers, before he carried her up the curve of marble stairs. 'Oh, promise me that some day you and I, will take our love together to some sky! Where we can be alone and faith renew, and find the hollows where those flowers grew...' he sang, making Alex laugh even harder.

She had never seen him like that, so light-hearted, so—silly. It made her feel silly, too, gloriously so. She realised she'd been quite right when she thought she didn't know everything about her husband yet. She would surely always be discovering new things about him and that thrilled her. Their life would always be an adventure!

He carried her through a doorway into a bedchamber that had already been prepared to welcome her. A white four-poster bed, carved with vines and flowers and draped in pink silk, sat on a small dais, near a dressing table skirted in pink tulle and already laid with her brushes and bottles. Windows looked down at the gardens, curtained in white satin tied with pink bows, and Boucher paintings of court ladies in pink satin hung on the silk walls. It looked like something Marie Antoinette would have slept in, perfect and dreamlike.

Malcolm put her down on the tufted-velvet bench in front of the dressing table and knelt at her feet. Alex ran her fingers through the rough silk of his hair, smiling down at him. 'Are you sure you like it?' he said. 'We can change anything you want.'

'It's perfect. A fairy palace,' she answered and tossed her hat on to the dressing table. 'I think we'll have many fine days here, don't you?'

He took her hand tightly in his and kissed her fingers. 'I only want you to be happy, no matter what. This house is yours, in your own name, as well as a large share in the stores. If something should happen...'

Alex was alarmed by his sudden seriousness. 'What can happen, Malcolm? We are only beginning. There's so much ahead.' She had pushed away so many of her worries, tried to forget Mairie and the past. Had she been mistaken?

He gave her a crooked smile. 'I know. That's what I'm afraid of.'

Alex leaned down and kissed him, putting all her fear, all her desire, all the fire of her feelings into that caress. Malcolm drew her closer, his mouth opening against hers, whispering her name.

Her own fierce desire roared awake and rose up to meet his. With a moan, she slid her arms tightly around him as he picked her up and they tumbled on to the bed. His weight, so familiar to her now, was so heavy and sweet, their bodies fitting perfectly together as if always meant to be just that way.

She needed him, craved him, in a way she could never have imagined possible. Couldn't live without.

She shoved his coat from his shoulders with impatient hands, fumbled with his cravat, his shirt, as he tossed back her skirts—all the ridiculous barriers between them, until they were bare to each other's touch. She scraped her nails lightly over the groove of his spine, over his taut buttocks, pulling him close to her. Her husband, her own.

Malcolm growled, low and hoarse, his tongue

seeking hers in a kiss not soft, seductive, but full of hunger. She wrapped her legs around him, skin to skin, their bodies fitted together. 'Malcolm,' she whispered. And then she could say no more, think no more, she could only feel.

The light from the windows was hazy when Alex opened her eyes; it was almost evening outside, the golden hour. Yet she felt so heavy and lazy she couldn't move.

Their clothes were scattered on the flowered carpet, Malcolm's arm draped over her waist, the sheets tangled around them. She glanced at him to find his eyes closed, a half-smile on his lips. How beautiful he was in that amber light, her bright god.

His eyes opened and he smiled down at her lazily, his arms closing around her.

'Tell me a story,' she said, snuggling closer to him. 'A fairy story from Scotland.'

He laughed and kissed the top of her head. 'My nanna used to tell me one every night before I went to sleep, when I was a bairn. I have too many.'

'Well—what was one of your favourites?'

He thought for a moment. 'Well, there was the queen who sought a drink from a sacred well.'

'Why did she do that?'

'Because she was very ill and this well was said to have healing powers. She also had three beautiful daughters and she sent them to fetch the water to her.'

'And did they do it?' Alex asked.

'They tried, but you see, the well was guarded by a hideous *losgann*, a toad, and he demanded each one marry him in exchange for a drink of the water.'

'A toad! That doesn't sound so fearsome.'

'He was a magical toad, obviously. But the daughters refused, all but the youngest. The prettiest and the bravest. She agreed and took the water to her mother, who recovered. Then one day the *losgann* showed up and reminded her of her promise. She tried to hide him behind a door, under a bucket, because he was not a suitable bridegroom for a princess.'

Alex frowned, thinking that once her own parents would have said the same about Malcolm. 'What happened then?'

'He told the Princess to cut off his head with a rusty sword.'

'Cut off his head!' she cried.

'Yes, so she did. And he turned into a handsome prince and they lived happily ever after.'

'Without his head?'

'Hush,' Malcolm said, giving her arm a light,

teasing pinch. 'It's a magical story. I'm sure his head grew back.'

'Well, it makes no sense to me. My nanny used to tell me things like Cinderella, with ballgowns and lost shoes.'

'There was a Scots Cinderella, too.'

'Did she lose her shoe?'

'No, but she lived with a cruel stepmother who made her do all the housework. One day, she sent the poor girl with a sieve to fetch water from the well at the end of the world and told her not to come back without it. The girl, your Cinderella, searched and searched for it.'

'Hmm,' Alex said. 'Even if she found it, how would she get the water to stay in the sieve?'

'Because a magical toad told her how to do it, in exchange for marrying him.'

'And did it work?'

'Aye.'

'And she cut off his head?'

'Yes, and he turned into a handsome prince and they lived happily ever after.'

Alex shook her head. 'Why are you Scots so obsessed with toads and beheadings? It's very silly.'

She glanced up at him and to her surprise he looked very solemn, older than his years as he frowned into the light. 'The toad knew the dangers of caring for another person, of the evils that can lurk out in the world when people are unwary. He knew he had to hold on to control, at every moment. That he could rely only on himself. A magical toad he might have been, but he was wise.' Malcolm gave a thoughtful frown. 'Even a toad can be clever and able to get what he wants, when he's willing to do whatever it takes. Willing to keep control of his own heart at all times.'

Alex felt suddenly cold, as if she was glimpsing a tiny piece of Malcolm's soul he usually kept hidden. 'Control is the most vital thing in life?'

'Aye, of course. We are all on our own in the end, my fairy, and have to rely on ourselves. To always know what we are about at every moment.'

Alex closed her eyes against his words. Did he really think that? Would he never give away even a part of his control, his heart, to her? Or was she merely deluding herself all along? She wished she knew the truth, all of it. She wished she had some of his control.

He pulled her even closer, tucking the blankets around them until they were closed into their own warm little world. She only wished she knew it was real. 'Hush. I've told you all the tales I remember. I think we should sleep for a while before you make me talk my head off.'

Alex yawned. 'Sleep does sound lovely. Though I am sure now I will have nightmares about hideous toads with swords marrying fair princesses...' And of husbands who guarded their hearts with iron.

Chapter Twenty

Alex was sure she had never seen a more beautiful day. The sky stretched over the vast, pale, sparkling edifice of the palace at Versailles, not a single cloud to break the rippling, azure-satin expanse. A light breeze danced through the trees over her head, making them ripple and whisper, and carrying the heady scent of flowers from Marie Antoinette's little Trianon garden nearby.

Alex lay on the picnic blanket she and Malcolm had spread in a little grove, within sight of the canal where other couples drifted past in rowboats. The ladies' parasols were like flowers themselves, all ruffled pastel petals, and the wind carried echoes of their flirtatious laughter over the water. Yet everyone else seemed far away; Alex revelled in the sense of being alone with Malcolm, wrapped around in their own green bower. The worries of their first night here, the glimpse she had had of his essential aloneness, seemed so far away. She could only hope it was a dark dream.

She glanced down at her husband, who seemed to be asleep in a patch of warm, golden sun. He had discarded his coat, which he used as a pillow under his rumpled golden head, and loosened his cravat and rolled up his white shirtsleeves.

She sighed when she thought over the last few blissful days in their Chateau d'Or. The long dinners, reading by the fire, playing Blind Man's Buff in the garden, tea by the fountain—making love in the still darkness of the night. Whoever came up with the old term 'honeymoon' had been quite right. It was sweet indeed.

She knew it wouldn't last for ever. They would have to return soon to Paris, and then to London, for Malcolm's business waited for him and she could tell he was anxious for it even when he laughed and played with her in their tiny new palace. What would life be like then, when they had to find a real, day-to-day existence together? She intended to hold on to the honeymoon magic as long as she could. She had never felt so free, so full of hope before, and she longed for it to last.

She hoped with all her heart that *this* was the reality. That Malcolm would come to love her and their loneliness would be over.

Alex opened her own parasol and turned it towards the brightest light, casting their little island of blanket into shadow. The remains of their luncheon—pâté and ham, strawberry tarts and lemon meringues, bottles of wine—were scattered about the basket. As well as being beautiful beyond words, their little chateau boasted the finest chef and housekeeping staff she had ever seen, even in her mother's meticulously run households.

They hardly needed her supervision at all and she had only to grow fat, lazy and disgustingly content in those perfect rooms. Yet she so *wanted* to be useful, even as she revelled in the hours of laughter and lovemaking with her new husband, in the time to read every novel on the overflowing library shelves, wear the beautiful clothes Mademoiselle LeClerc produced and eat the delicious confections the chef produced. She had married Malcolm partly because she was sure she could help him, be of use to him in his work, his life. But how?

Alex slid off her kid shoes and wriggled her stockinged toes in the soft, lush grass as she smiled at Malcolm's deep, even breathing, the way he kept his fingers curled in the linen folds of her skirt even in sleep. The palace rose just beyond her view, just as much a magical mirage as the rest of her golden days. Vast and white, float-ing like a cloud above its terraces. The rooms that had been turned into a museum after the palace was vacated as a royal residence were closed that day for cleaning, but she wasn't too disappointed. The day was too warm for dry history, perfect for a lazy picnic, and now that she had a house nearby she could come back whenever she liked. The days with Malcolm and his golden touch that made everything so spellbinding seemed to stretch ahead and ahead.

She closed her eyes and tried to picture it, tried to envision that family she dreamed of.

She heard Malcolm stretch beside her and opened her eyes to see he had woken. He stared up at her, his eyes as blue as the French sky above, his expression serious. Surely too seri-ous for such a lovely day.

'How long was I asleep?' he said, sitting up. 'You should have woken me.'

'Certainly not! It's a day absolutely made for perfect laziness. Besides, you look too handsome when you sleep, a god in repose, and I can stare at you as much as I like without one of my hor-rid blushes.'

He smiled up at her. 'But I adore your blushes. You look like a little pink rose.' His lips covered hers for a long kiss, sweet and heated all at once. 'So you think I'm handsome, then?'

Alex laughed. 'You know you are, you conceited thing. I've never seen anyone like you in real life, outside of paintings. Even when we were young, in Scotland, you were too beautiful. I had quite the childish pash on you then.'

He sat back on the blanket, smiling too smugly. 'Did you indeed?'

'Of course. Every girl on the estate did, all of the housemaids.' Alex remembered the girl in the red shawl, Mairie who was now Mademoiselle Fleurie and so very beautiful, and she frowned. She wanted nothing to mar their day, especially not old memories.

Malcolm snorted. 'They did not.'

'They did! There weren't very many young men on the estate and none who looked like you. Like—like Thor among trolls! But even if there were scads of men about, you would have stood out. You still do.'

'I don't remember anything like that.'

'You were probably only thinking of your future ambitions back then. How to leave the croft behind and make your fortune.'

His jaw tightened. 'I was that, aye.'

Alex laid back on the blanket, staring up at the lacy pattern of trees. Maybe she could get him to open his heart to her a bit, to tell her the truth she wanted to see there. Or feared to see. 'Tell me more about that time. About a secret of your childhood.'

'I don't have any secrets from then, not any more,' he said. 'Mr Boyne, the bookseller in the village, used to loan me volumes. I would hide them in a hole in my mattress and memorise them at night. Even my nan didn't know that.'

'Why hide them?'

'So my father wouldn't find them. He could barely read and write himself and he couldn't imagine why anyone else would want to do so. My ambition threatened the way he lived, the only way he knew how to be. After my mother died, he started drinking more and it grew worse. The slightest spark could set off a conflagration of fury.'

Malcolm spoke steadily, matter of factly, but Alex could see more just beneath the surface. A tightness, a buried anger, even a sadness. She knew because she felt that way herself about the past. About the need to perform an act all the time that grew heavier and heavier, grown over with scar tissue. 'So you hid your books? That sounds terrible.'

He shrugged. 'He only found one once. Worst hiding I ever got from him. That scar on my hip?'

Alex nodded, horrified as she remembered the pale, jagged mark on his gilded skin.

'From his belt buckle. But he never had the chance to do that again,' Malcolm said quietly. 'I made sure of that.'

'You—you said it was the worst hiding he gave you,' she said. He nodded. 'There were others.'

'Oh, aye, a lot. After my mother, everything I did seemed to set him off. He didn't like the vicar giving me lessons, or having me do anything at all. Everything but working in the fields with him, or *for* him if he was off with the whisky.'

'Like wanting to leave?'

'Yes. I could never talk about that.'

'And maybe girls?' She thought of the beautiful Mairie and how they were parted. Maybe that was why he guarded his heart now.

Malcolm laughed roughly. 'Almost worse than books. Girls were alluring witches, he thought, good only for luring men off the path and into heartache.'

'What would he think of me?'

'That you were the greatest witch of all, the queen of the fairy folk,' he said, seizing her around the waist and rolling across the blanket with her until she giggled. 'I am under your terrible bewitchment!'

Alex stared up into his eyes, so blue, so full

of laughter now where a moment before there had been such sadness. *I love you*, she suddenly thought, the words horrifyingly loud and clear in her mind. She loved him. Of course she did.

She opened her mouth to say them, but something held her back. Something made her feel just as scared as she was giddy. She sat up and apart from him a bit, and he smiled at her wryly. He would not say it to her, not now, she knew that. She had to be patient.

'You know all about my misspent reading youth, then,' he said. 'What's a secret from *your* childhood?'

She looked down, brushing bits of grass from white skirt. 'I don't have any secrets. It was a perfectly ordinary childhood and there were too many nannies and tutors around to leave much space for mischief.'

'An ordinary childhood for a duke's daughter? I am sure most children would disagree,' he teased.

'I was fortunate, true. I was never beaten or starved. I could have as many books as I liked and read them right out in the open. But...'

'But?'

'But I was sometimes, well, rather lonely.'

He didn't laugh at her or dismiss her sadness.

He reached out and took her hand gently in his. 'In what way?'

'My parents were very busy, of course. My father had estates to run and my mother was a leader of society. My brother and I only saw them once in a while at tea and the rest of the time we had those nannies and teachers. I never had friends of my own age until I went to Miss Grantley's and I had to beg and cry to be allowed to go to school. My parents thought it would cure my shyness. But at home, it was all so terribly quiet and I still often feel timid of other people.'

'I think you underestimate your attraction. Other people always want to be around *you*. I want to be around you, all the time.'

He did? Alex felt herself flush with pleasure at his words. 'That was why I liked Scotland so much, you see. My parents didn't care so much what we did, we weren't always in the nursery like in London. I could roam the fields, fish in the river—talk to you.' Until he was gone and she could no longer see him at all. It felt like a cloud passed over their golden palace at the memory.

But he smiled at her, banishing the grey shadow. 'And now we're both free to do whatever we like.'

'So we are!' Alex cried. 'How marvellous.'

'What would you like to do, then? Right now?'

Alex studied the vast garden around them, the lawns and flowerbeds, the trees, the marble statues that watched over it all. 'I want to go for a row on the canal.'

'Are you sure?'

'Positive!' Alex put her shoes back on and reached for her wide-brimmed straw hat. She leaped to her feet and dashed towards the water, Malcolm hurrying after her as he laughed at her eagerness. Soon they were gliding out into the silvery waves among the other couples, Malcolm pulling at the oars.

'I haven't done such a thing in years,' he said. 'Not since the fishing on the lochs. I'm quite out of condition. If I collapse here like a galley slave, it will be all your fault, Wife.'

Alex laughed merrily. He was surely the *least* out-of-condition person she had ever seen, the muscles of his shoulders and back straining against his shirt, his skin gleaming. She opened her parasol and sat back on the cushioned seat, enjoying the sun, the soft splash of the water, the other laughing couples around them, the sight of her handsome husband. For a few minutes, they were just like any other pair of sweethearts, revelling in being together in the perfect bright spring day.

She was quite sure her heart would burst with

happiness. Maybe she couldn't yet say 'I love you'. Maybe he wouldn't say it back. But one say, surely, it would come true.

Wouldn't it? For the moment, she had only hope and that would have to be enough.

'We have an invitation to Viscountess Rippon's garden party,' Malcolm said as he lazily sorted through the post after dinner.

Alex glanced up from the book she was reading, her hair a glimmering silver in the firelight. After the warm day the breeze had turned brisk and she had a cashmere shawl wrapped over her white-tulle dinner gown, the diamonds from their wedding sparkling in her ears. Her cheeks were flushed pink from their afternoon rowing on the canal and she looked happy and tired and absolutely beautiful. 'A garden party?'

'Yes. There are a few invitations here already, despite the fact that everyone knows we're on our honeymoon. Everyone wants to meet the charming daughter of Monsieur le Duc Anglais.'

Alex laughed. 'You mean they want to meet Lady Alexandra Gordston. And most of them surely want to meet the handsome *monsieur* and satisfy their curiosity.'

Malcolm grinned. 'Curiosity is quite right. But I say it's definitely you they want to meet. The

Viscountess would never have invited me otherwise.' And wasn't that why he had told himself he married Alexandra in the first place? That she could open doors to him he could not unlock himself? And yet now it seemed so much more. So different.

He had to be very careful and not let her any closer.

'I remember the Viscountess. She seems quite formidable,' she said.

'They say she's one of the most fashionable ladies in Parisian society, since she prefers to leave the Viscount back home in Derbyshire and live in the Seventh *Arrondissement* instead. But I don't think she has shopped at Gordston's yet, though she appeared at the opening party. It seems she's bought a little pleasure pavilion near here and wants to have a housewarming fête.'

'Well, if she is one of the most fashionable, she will certainly have many fashionable friends, as well,' Alex said, tapping her fingers on the cover of her book, as she often did when she was deep in thought. 'And that means if she comes to Gordston's, they all will. When is this party?'

Malcolm turned over the stiff white card. 'Monday. It seems there is to be an archery tournament on the lawn.'

Alex clapped her hands. 'Then we must go!

I'm a great shot, I even beat my brother at the target all the time when we were children.'

'Just like our Diana fountain, eh? My wife is ever surprising,' he said, smiling as he imagined her drawing back her bow, that fierce look of concentration on her fairy face. Maybe her white tunic slipping from her pale shoulder...

'I do hope so. Tell the Viscountess we accept. It might be like that garden party where we saw each other again in London. Remember?'

'How could I forget?' he said, thinking of that day. Alex's hand on his arm, the smell of warm greenery and flowers, the buzz of laughter that faded away when he saw her.

'I do have that lovely pink-and-white-striped silk gown from the store, it's so pretty and Emily says it's the latest style. Everyone must see it.'

'They will only see you,' he said softly.

Alex gave him a startled smile. 'Why would they? I would much rather stay here alone with you. But I admit I wouldn't mind letting a few arrows fly for an afternoon.' She put down her book and crossed the room to press a soft kiss to his lips. 'I'm going upstairs. Join me soon?'

He took her hand and kissed her fingertips, smelling her sweet perfume, feeling that softness he had been missing for so long. How he had started to crave her. How dangerous that was.

'Of course. I just need to answer a few of these letters Miss Mersey forwarded.'

'Business never sleeps, does it!' she called as she hurried away, the train of her tulle-and-silk dress coiling behind her, her perfume lingering.

Malcolm went back to the stack of correspondence that had grown ever higher since they came to their chateau. It was the first time in many years he had so neglected his work, distracted by the sunny picnics, the evenings by the fire, laughing, whispering. Kissing. He had forgotten, if he had ever even known before, that business was not all of life.

At the bottom was a letter on thick cream stationery, an unfamiliar looping hand in blue ink. He tore it open, and cursed when he saw the signature at the bottom—Fleurie. Your Mairie.

Mairie. Why was she writing to him now? Why had she come back into his life now, of all times, when his life was so different? When it was finally something like—happy?

He scowled as he remembered her at the opera, her dark eyes so full of old memories, her smile full of secrets and threats.

He glanced at the door; he was quite alone, the house quiet now. The fire still crackled in the grate. He could toss the letter into the flames and pretend it never existed. That the past had never come into the present. Yet he knew that would never work. A man could never run fast enough to escape himself.

He quickly read over the letter, every word like a tiny, sharp pinprick.

M'eudail Malcolm,
Do forgive me for writing to you after so many years of silence. But I could not forget you after we met at the opera, could not cease to think of times so long ago. Do you remember those days, too? How sweet they were, how perfect. I long for them, for the girl I used to be, for the boy I loved then.

Alas for us both, that time has gone. I fear I have done many things I am heartily ashamed of, but for which I had no choice if I wanted to live. And I did, if only for the chance to see you again. Now I have! I have never felt such joy or sorrow.

I must confess something to you, Malcolm, and beg your help. I have become entrapped by the man Nixson, a vile character as I'm sure you're well aware. He has done many unscrupulous things in his business life and he is no different behind closed doors.

He is blackmailing me and I fear I can't

be free of him. Only you are more power-
ful than him. Only you can help me. I beg
of you, for the sake of who we once were!

I have escaped him for a time and am
staying for a few days at the Hôtel du
Charllon in Versailles. If you could meet
me there, just for an hour, I could tell you
all. If you will not, I fear I am lost.
Yours,
Mairie

Malcolm crumpled the letter in his fist. But it
was true—the memories could not be erased so
easily. She belonged to an old life, to a boy who
no longer existed. And now she was under the
power of a drug smuggler like Nixson.

If Malcolm did not help her, set her back on
a steadier course in life, who would? Surely he
could find a place in his heart, a heart Alexandra had only just helped him see was not completely black, to help someone who once meant
something to him?

He cursed again and tossed the letter into
the fire.

Chapter Twenty-One

The Hôtel du Charllon was not the grandest of resort hotels, but nor was it less than respectable. Malcolm stared up at its plain façade, its green awnings, and felt almost as if he was about to step into the mouth of a hellish cave instead of a carpeted hotel.

For an instant, he didn't feel like himself, Malcolm Gordston, builder of mercantile empires. A man whose work was his world, all he needed. He was young Malcolm again, hoping for a world outside the Scottish croft, but not knowing what that could be. The longing to be worthy of someone like Alexandra.

And now she was his wife. He thought of her as he had left her that morning, reading in their garden as she waved at him. Her smile, her pink cheeks, her delicate strength—she was perfect. She was everything he had never thought could exist in the world. He wanted to protect her at all costs from anything tawdry.

He glanced down the street, the row of shops, the people going about their ordinary days, yet he felt utterly changed.

He couldn't turn his back on Mairie. Alex's kindness showed him he had to be worthy of her, had to try to measure up to her. He had cared for Mairie once; she was a part of who he once was, even a part of what made him the man he was now. He remembered that flash of fear behind her bold eyes at the opera. That hidden desperation he understood too well.

She was mixed up with bad people. He had to warn her, help her as she asked him, surely he owed her that. Whatever her life had come to, it could all be changed. He knew that now, he saw it in his own life.

He stepped into the hotel's foyer, taking off his hat and running his hand through his rumpled hair. His new gold ring gleamed. He glimpsed himself in a mirror hanging over a suite of green-velvet furniture and to his surprise he looked just as he had when he left the chateau. Dressed in his dark suit, his pearl tie pin straight. That wedding ring on his finger. He was so sure he would have become a grubby boy in patched corduroy trousers again.

The maître d' directed him to the library, where Mairie waited. The book-lined, darkly lit room was empty except for her, sitting at a table in the corner. She had left behind her bright satins and wore a burgundy-velvet suit, her hair pinned back, her hands folded on the marble table top.

She stood at the sight of him, her skirts rustling. For an instant, just as he had felt himself, she looked like her old self, the girl who ran free in the meadows with her red shawl, her hair loose.

Then she smiled and her new mask was in place, Mademoiselle Fleurie back again, hard and painted and hidden.

'Thank you for coming, Malcolm,' she said. 'I wasn't sure you would.'

'Of course I would,' he answered. 'We're old friends and you said you were in trouble. I want to help you, if I can.' That was one thing Alex had taught him—sometimes helping another person, caring about another person, was what mattered. Alex reminded him of that.

Mairie's smile slipped. 'I knew the Malcolm I once adored would do so. But when I saw you at the opera, I—' She broke off, waving her hand in a small, helpless gesture. Emerald and ruby rings flashed. 'You were no longer my Malcolm at all.'

'I'm sure we've both changed. It's been many years and many things happen in life. I doubt either of us ended up where we thought we might.'

She gave him a strange twist of a grin. 'I am sure *you* have. You were so smart, even when we were so young, always reaching. But me...'

'Your parents said you went away to be married.'

'Obviously it did not work out that way. I ran away from them; I thought I wanted more than their way of life. But *you're* married now. To the Duke of Waverton's daughter, fancy that.'

'Yes,' Malcolm said brusquely, not wanting Alex to be in that room. She was too fine to be mixed up in his past at all.

As he studied Mairie, the hard glow in her eyes, he had the sudden realisation that he, too, could so easily have become like her. Cold, hard, focused on money and the material life. He *had* been like for so long—until Alex.

'How could you do that? After what happened to your father, the Duke's cruel eviction...' Her eyes widened. 'Unless it is some kind of revenge scheme? A way to bring the man even lower?'

Malcolm cringed as he recalled that he had thought that way himself once upon a time. Before he saw the truth. Before he saw Alex herself. 'She has nothing to do with all that. She is quite separate from the past.'

Mairie shook her head. 'Nothing is separate from the past.'

'Including Nixson?'

A noisy party came into the library and sat down nearby, taking out packs of cards. Mairie gave them a wary glance. 'Shall we walk for a while? I will tell you what I know about Nixson.'

'I must return home soon.'

She gave a humourless laugh. 'Domesticated now, are you? I won't keep you long from your fine lady wife. Just let me fetch my parasol. Unless you would like to come up to my chamber?' At his frown, she nodded. 'I thought not. How respectable you have become. Too bad.'

Her hat and parasol located, they left the hotel and found a footpath that ran along a narrow river, shaded by chestnut trees, quieter than the rows of fine shops just beyond. They stopped on an arched bridge, staring at the distant crowds.

'Have you been involved with Nixson long?' Malcolm asked.

Mairie shook her head. She didn't look at him, instead peering out from beneath her black-lace parasol at a group of children floating paper boats on the water below the bridge. 'A few months. My last special friend recently passed away, I was quite alone at the time.'

'I find that hard to believe.'

She laughed. 'Oh, I had, and still have, more casual sorts of friends. The Comte from your party, he is most amusing when he's in town. But when I first met Mr Nixson, I thought he was different. Very generous, indeed, and so full of amusing tales of his travels in the East. But lately I have realised his fortune is not so great as he would like everyone to believe. And when his luck is down, his moods are—changeable.'

Malcolm felt a sudden jolt of anger. 'He has hurt you?'

Mairie shrugged. 'Just shouting, a few broken objects. Except lately.'

'You know of his recent business dealings?'

'He said he took a proposal to you and you refused him. He blames you for his latest failure.'

'I won't be a party to smuggling.'

'I know you would not. At least, the boy I once knew never would. I wasn't sure about the famous Mr Gordston.'

'I have not changed that much.'

'No? I have. Too much.'

'And that is why Nixson is blackmailing you now?'

Mairie looked away. 'I once had a very foolish attachment to someone I should not and I was silly enough to save some letters. It was—well, with a lady. Of good birth. She would never want such a thing to come to light.'

'And Nixson stole these letters?' he said softly, trying to reassure her he could understand.

She nodded. 'He knows you and I were once friends, though not where or how. He wants me to get you to invest in his Chinese scheme after all. If I cannot persuade you…'

Malcolm braced his fists on the bridge railing, silent for a long moment, simmering with fury. Being with Alexandra had showed him life could be different, could be more just. 'Tell him I will help him.'

'Malcolm…' she gasped.

'I will not, of course. But that will give us some time to best decide how to defeat him.'

Mairie looked wary yet hopeful. 'You would do that for me?'

'Certainly. We *were* friends, you're right about that. I won't let such a vile person hurt you. Hurt any woman. And after it's all over, I'm sure I could find you work to do at my stores, work where you would not be beholden to anyone else.'

Mairie laid her hand on his arm, smiling up at him. 'Oh, Malcolm. I always knew you were not like other men. I was such a little fool back then, so silly. To throw away what we had…'

'Mairie, what we had was youthful infatuation. You know that as well as I do.'

'But such things can change, grow. It's why I could never work in your stores, as fine as they might be. I know only this now.' She leaned forward to press her lips to his, cool and dry and expert. When she drew back, she looked up at him, quizzical, sad. 'You do love your little rabbit of a duke's girl, then?'

Loved Alex? Malcolm stared down at Mairie, shocked to his core. Yet he knew she was right. It was like a bolt of sizzling lightning, illuminating what he should have known all along. It was a terrible revelation. 'She doesn't have anything to do with this.'

'Oh, I think she does.' Mairie looked down at her hand on his arm. 'She is very lucky.'

Malcolm shook his head. *He* was the lucky one, he could see that now. The one who had been so foolish. Mairie took his arm and they turned back towards the row of shops beyond the bridge.

'Nixson is to call on me this evening,' she said. 'I will write to you tomorrow about what he says.'

She tried to smile, but Malcolm could hear the

tension in her voice. He pressed his hand over hers in reassurance. 'Don't worry, Mairie. This will all be over very soon and Nixson won't be a worry to you any longer.'

She leaned her head on his shoulder for a moment, smiling, her eyes very dark and soft. For just an instant, they were children again. But they both knew those days were gone.

As Malcolm turned away, he glimpsed a lady standing in the doorway of a bookshop at the end of the lane, her pale hair shining under a tip-tilted tricorn hat. *Alexandra*. Did she see him—him with Mairie? She seemed to have her head bent in their direction, but then she whirled around and hurried into the shop.

Blast it all! he thought. Had he lost everything right at the moment he realised how very much he needed it?

Mairie stared out the window of her hotel room as night gathered closer. She did like the darkness—it hid so many things.

She poured out a glass of cognac and sipped at it as she remembered seeing Malcolm that afternoon. He was certainly more gloriously handsome than ever before, strong, hard, determined.

She had been a fool. She should have run away with Malcolm all those years ago. Look what she could have had. A handsome husband who probably never flew into violent rages and who was probably rather marvellous in bed. Riches. Respect. Instead, she had creatures like Nixson to contend with.

Mairie shuddered to think of the man. How had she ever thought him charming at all?

At least she had persuaded Malcolm to help her be rid of Nixson. Better Malcolm take the risk than her. And maybe soon she could even change Malcolm's mind about other things, too. Surely she knew more about keeping a man happy than the pale rabbit Lady Alexandra did.

She heard Nixson's heavy footsteps in the corridor, and quickly gulped down the last of her cognac. The door banged open and Nixson strode inside, a scowl on his face, a sweaty sheen to his forehead that told her he had been drinking, too, far more than her.

'I saw him,' she said, taking a step back from his reach, from the stench of him. 'He has agreed that perhaps he was too hasty in turning down your proposal. He will reconsider, if the amount is enough.'

Nixson grabbed her wrist, twisting it as he smiled down at her. His eyes were very dark, as if he had been sampling his own opium wares along with wine. 'You're sure of this?'

'Of course I am sure.'

'Good. You know better than to lie to me by now, don't you, my dear?' He dragged her closer, his lips trailing damply over her cheek. She shuddered. No wonder she had found comfort in the soft arms of her own gender, even with the cost in the end. 'You know what happens when I am not happy.'

Mairie closed her eyes tightly, pretending she was far away. In Scotland. With Malcolm, maybe, or with her Alice again. *Oh, yes.* She knew very well what would happen then.

Chapter Twenty-Two

Alex looked down at the book in her lap and realised she had been staring at the same page for nearly an hour. She hadn't deciphered a word. And she would soon have to dress for the Viscountess's garden party. She had to put on her pretty gown, smile, chatter, and here she was frozen to her chair.

She couldn't forget that glimpse she had of her husband with Mairie Fleurie, her hand on his arm, smiling at each other. Looking so lost in each other. Was it real, or a cruel illusion?

He had said nothing about it last night, as they ate dinner, walked in the garden, chatted about the upcoming party, lay beside each other in bed, and she had said nothing, either. She had no idea *what* to say. What to feel.

She knew so well how many marriages worked. Men had mistresses. Women kept the house. They were polite, showed a happy face to the world. She and Malcolm really had nothing else to build upon to make their life together any different.

Yet since her magical wedding day, she had dared to hope for—more. For happiness. She had imagined he had changed, that he saw how life could be when they were together. He didn't need to lavish *things* on her; she just wanted him.

Had that silly, girlish dream already been dashed? Had reading all those romantic novels at Miss Grantley's been a mistake after all?

She tried to be the perfect wife, to do her duty with fashion and parties, but how could she go on doing that if she would never have her husband's heart? His love? She needed those things, not for what she could bring him, but only for herself. But if he couldn't let go of the past, let go of his control, they would never have that. She felt foolish to think she could make it so. It was just like everyone else in the world, all those men and their mistresses and their façades and their lies.

Alex snapped the book shut and tossed it on to the table. Malcolm was *not* like those other men. She had become so sure of that. She *was* sure. The way he was with her, it couldn't all be an act. Could it?

And yet there was the girl he once cared for. The beautiful Mairie.

'Lady Alexandra,' Mademoiselle LeClerc called as she leaned out the window with Alex's pink-and-white silk gown over her arm. 'Shall I help you get ready for the party? We still need to arrange your coiffeur.'

Alex nodded, glad of the distraction. But how could she go to a party, pretend nothing was wrong, that her heart wasn't shattered?

But how could she just stay there, remembering that glimpse of Malcolm with another woman, the thought swirling through her head? She needed to get out, get away. 'Yes, thank you, *mademoiselle*. Do you think the white hat with the pink roses, or maybe the yellow straw?'

She was just pinning on her hat before the mirror when Malcolm appeared in the doorway, his watch in his hand. 'The carriage is waiting, Alex.'

She nodded, not meeting his eyes in the glass, busying herself with her hat pins. She was shaking, not sure what she should, or could, say. 'I am nearly ready. Perhaps someone is waiting for you there?'

He frowned as if puzzled. 'Only the Viscountess and her other guests, I suppose.'

'Not Mairie?' she whispered, wondering why he wouldn't tell her about this meeting. Wouldn't confide in her.

Malcolm froze. 'Alexandra, it is not like that…'

She shook her head. 'Oh, Malcolm. I know our marriage is not some fairy story, not really. You wanted to get back at my father for the past, to have a wife who can help you in society, and I knew that. Really I did. I just…' She had hoped for more. And now she felt so cold, so foolish for doing that. So young and naive to think they could simply be together, the past completely vanished. They had so much; but what about what money could not buy? Would that ever be hers now?

Malcolm came to touch her arm and his fingers seemed to burn through her silk sleeve. How she wanted to throw herself into his arms, to hold on to him and pretend like they were the only people in the world! But that time had vanished, before it even really appeared.

She stepped back and pasted a smile on her lips. 'We should go. You are quite right—it would never do to be improperly late.' And if there was one thing she did know, it was how to be proper.

Alex stepped into Viscountess Rippon's garden on Malcolm's arm, her professional 'Duke's daughter' smile firmly in place, her pink-and-white-striped silk gown swirling around her, her parasol twirling as if she hadn't a worry in the world. The beauty of the flowers helped distract her for a moment, for the Viscountess had left England behind to create a beautifully French space of exquisite topiaries, manicured flower-beds surrounding burbling fountains and a hedge maze in the distance. People in fluttering white linen played lawn tennis in one direction, while servants set up archery targets in the other, the lawns stretching away like lengths of green velvet.

Alex nodded to everyone, smiling, smiling, stopping to greet acquaintances. She was a newlywed wife, after all, no cares in the world. In love, looking at a golden future, walking on a cloud.

Love. She had thought so. Had dared to hope maybe she and Malcolm would have more than they had dreamed about, more than romance novels and impossible dreams and a convenient marriage. But maybe she had been fooling herself about such things, lulled into a romantic haze by their lovely house, by sunshine and rowboats and satin beds.

Maybe he had been in love with someone else all along.

Alex glanced up at her husband. He smiled, too, so handsome in his grey suit and straw hat, so perfect.

How she wished she could just ask him outright! *Are you in love with your old sweetheart? Do you want to be with her?*

Yet that bold confidence she seemed to have found in herself with him was gone now and she was the old, reserved Lady Alexandra who could only really live in books and her own dreams. She was afraid of his answer. Yet how could she now live her whole life not really knowing?

She waved and smiled again as someone called her name. How odd it seemed, she thought, to have such dark doubts in such a lovely place. It was unreal, like a garden in a storybook or in paintings of heaven. Some place where everyone should only be perfectly happy.

She curled her gloved fingers tighter on Malcolm's arm and remembered Lady Cannon's garden party in London. She'd hardly known him then, yet she had felt so drawn to him. Close to him. Now he was her husband, and he seemed further away than ever.

'Do you feel quite well, Alex?' he asked softly.

She looked up at him from under the brim of her white hat. He frowned at her, his eyes crinkled against the sun, dark blue with concern. 'I'm quite fine.'

'You look a bit pale. And you've been so quiet...'

So he had noticed. She had hoped he would not, not until she could arrange her thoughts, stay calm and not turn into a sobbing puddle as she demanded to know the truth. She widened her smile, feeling the awful tension of it.

'Just a bit tired, I suppose,' she said. 'Maybe I should join my mother in Baden-Baden soon. Shall we talk later, at the house? I think I see Mrs Stuyvesant over there, the wealthy American from New York. Does she not shop often at Gordston's in London? I should like to meet her.'

Malcolm looked like he wanted so much to say more, that frown deepening, but he nodded.

'Lady Alexandra! Mr Gordston. How kind you are to attend my little gathering,' Lady Rippon called and Alex turned to see their hostess hurrying towards them, her yellow muslin-and-silk dress from Worth shining like her improbably golden hair.

Alex smiled even more, hoping she wouldn't crack under the mask she knew she had to wear all day. Luckily, she had been raised to wear masks, to always be the perfect Duke's daughter.

The perfect wife.

'You were so good to invite us,' Alex said. 'It's the perfect day for a garden party, Lady Rippon.'

'I am always most careful about my arrangements, with every comfort for my guests,' Lady Rippon said smugly, as if she had ordered the cloudless sky especially and the weather dared not disobey. 'But to interrupt your honeymoon! So kind. I do remember those romantic days when Rippon and I were newlyweds.'

Alex felt the heat of a blush touch her cheeks and hoped everyone would think it was just the sun. 'I understand there is to be archery?'

'Oh, yes! Are you proficient with the bow, Lady Alexandra? There is a diamond-arrow brooch as a prize, I do hope you will try your hand.'

'How could I resist?' Alex said, thinking of how satisfying it might be to let her emotions fly away with the *thunk* of an arrow. To imagine she was destroying her own heart so it never hurt again.

'And you, Mr Gordston?' Lady Rippon asked.

'I fear I have never picked up a bow in my life,' he answered. 'My wife is the athletic one here. I merely push papers around a desk all day.'

Alex thought of the power and ripple of his muscles as he rowed them across the canal, of the way he rose above her in bed, and was sure he protested too much. But she couldn't bear to think of that now.

'Well, there will be none of that today, Mr Gordston,' Lady Rippon said merrily, tapping his arm. She seemed caught in his golden-god allure like every other lady. 'There is croquet, lawn tennis and my husband is in his smoking room if you wish to join him. Lady Alexandra, would you like to come with me? I can show you the archery targets. Have you brought your own bow?'

'Yes, my dear, do get your Artemis armour on,' Malcolm said, pressing a quick kiss to her cheek. 'I will go talk to Mrs Stuyvesant. I want to hear all about New York.'

Alex nodded and followed their hostess across the lawn, glancing back once at Malcolm. He watched her go, that puzzled frown still on his face.

'How is your mother, Lady Alexandra?' Lady Rippon said. 'I met with the dear Duchess several times in London, she was always kindness itself.'

Before the scandal that drove her parents abroad? 'She is at Baden, I believe,' Alex answered, sure *kindness itself* wasn't entirely the way her mother could be described. 'The waters seem to be doing her a great deal of good.'

'I do hope so. How lovely she looked at the

Blakelys' Venetian breakfast the last time we met! And they are your cousins, are they not? Such handsome young men.'

The past seemed to come back to Alex as if it was merely yesterday: family gossip, London talk, light chatter. As they turned the corner of the hedge maze and looked at the bright green archery lawn, there was a sudden rustling of leaves, the crack of branches. Much to Alex's shock, Emily tumbled out, her pale green gown rumpled, her chestnut hair untidy, her hat in her hand.

'Em!' Alex gasped. 'What on earth…?'

'Are you lost, Miss Fortescue?' Lady Rippon asked tightly, her lips pursed.

'Not at all,' Emily said. And then something even more shocking happened—Chris Blakely emerged from the maze right behind Emily, his coat and hair in a similar state of rumpledness. He stared at Alex, his eyes wide, as if he was abashed for the first time in his life.

'Chris!' Alex cried. 'What on earth are you doing here?'

'You know Miss Fortescue?' Lady Rippon gasped.

'She is an old schoolfriend. And Mr Blakely, of course, is my cousin. Nephew of my mother the Duchess,' she said pointedly, trying to remind their hostess of Chris's connections and ward off any gossip.

'I lost my hat,' Emily said with one of her careless smiles. She held up the confection of green straw and net. 'Mr Blakely was kindly helping me look for it.' Em could always get out of any scrape at school; Alex always envied her that. It seemed not much had changed.

But Emily and Chris? It quite made her forget her own romantic quandaries for the moment to think about someone else's. Could they really be together? How delightful that would be! But how improbable. Emily was so energetic, so ambitious, and Chris so—well, he was Chris.

Lady Rippon took Alex's arm and practically marched her away from the maze. No wonder the lady was friends with her mother, they shared such determination about the proprieties.

'I do hope you know I run a most respectable household, Lady Alexandra,' she whispered.

'Of course,' Alex answered. 'And only the finest guests, obviously.'

Lady Rippon's lips tightened. 'Well—if he is your cousin...'

Alex tried not to giggle at the whole absurd situation. 'Yes. My mother the Duchess is most fond of him.'

At the archery lawn, she took up a bow and

let off a few practice shots. It *did* feel good, her fingers tight on the strings, her arrows flying straight and true to land with a shuddering thud in the straw targets. She imagined Mairie Mc-Gregor Fleurie standing there instead and it made her laugh at her silliness.

But perhaps she had imagined it *too* well, for suddenly the real Mairie was standing right beside her, tall, dark, elegant in a burgundy, black-trimmed walking suit, a tiny froth of a burgundy hat on her high-piled curls.

Alex fell back a step, instinctively holding her bow in front of her.

'Please, Lady Alexandra, I mean you no harm,' Mairie said quietly. Unlike at the opera, when her words had been merry, brittle, she now sounded desperate, pleading, her words touched with a soft brogue. She looked different, too, with no rouge on her cheeks, her eyes ringed with dark circles.

'What do you want?' Alex said, glancing around her to see that no one was watching them at all, everyone else was practising their aim with the arrows, chatting and laughing. 'I saw you with Malcolm in the village.'

Mairie shook her head. 'It wasn't what you think, my lady. Malcolm doesn't care for me that way, not now. I can't give him the connections you can, with your father the Duke. I can't help him get his revenge after what happened to his poor father. I needed his help. Just as I'm begging for yours now.'

'My help?' Alex said tightly.

'Please, come with me. Only for a moment,' Mairie said. She reached for Alex's arm with a shaking, black-gloved hand, but then drew back. 'Malcolm is a good man, really, despite all that has happened. I know he could only have married you if you were kind, too, deep in your heart. Please, help me. I promise you will never hear of me again.'

Alex studied the woman carefully. She couldn't resist someone begging for help in any way, no matter who it was. Surely Malcolm had cared about this woman once; he might still. And something about Mairie, despite her fine clothes, her beauty, reminded her of Mademoiselle Gardinier's girls. As Alex studied the woman, the strain around her eyes, the way she wrung her hands together, Alex realised something startling—this was what could happen when a lady did not stand up for herself. Did not ask for what she wanted. Take the life she craved. Mairie had been trapped, even more than Alex was, by the life she was born into. It made her feel rather sorry for the woman.

And maybe she could tell Alex more about Malcolm's dealings with her father. 'Very well,' she said reluctantly. She laid aside her bow and followed Mairie towards the other side of the hedge maze, away from the chatter of the crowd. 'But I cannot stay long at all.'

'I understand,' Mairie said.

'Can't you tell me what this is about? I will help if I can, but if I don't know…'

'It was your father, you know,' Mairie said quickly. 'The Duke evicted Malcolm's family from his home. It was why he went away, why I knew we could not be together. Could not help each other any longer. Your father was not a kind man.'

Alex was shocked, but not surprised. Her father had always believed in his rights as a duke to do as he liked; but surely Malcolm had harboured anger in his heart all these years. Anger towards her own family. Towards her, as well? Was that why he held his heart back from her? 'I am so sorry. I did not know, I…'

Mairie glanced back at her, her face a blank mask. 'I am sorry, Lady Alexandra. You will not believe me, but I truly am.' She shook her head. 'I loved someone once, too. I found out that love, real love, is a weakness as much as a strength, just as it is for Malcolm. We do what we have to in order to protect it. That's all.'

Alex was baffled. 'What...?' But she had no time to say anything else. Mr Nixson stepped out from behind the high thicket of the hedge and his wide smile froze Alex's blood.

As did the knife in his hand. He handed Mairie a packet of letters. 'Thank you, Mademoiselle Fleurie, my dear,' he said, as calm and cool as if they were chatting in a drawing room, not the man overcome with fury she had seen at the Tower. 'Perhaps you would be so kind to fetch Mr Gordston now? I'm sure he would like to join his lovely wife.'

Chapter Twenty-Three

'You didn't say there would be violence!' Mairie cried. 'You said you only wanted to talk to her.'

'Shut up, you silly whore. What did you think would happen?' Nixson growled, some of his jovial mask slipping. He stared at Alex, who felt as if she had turned to ice. She could hear their voices, hear the distant blur of the party, but her ears seemed stopped up, as if she had fallen underwater. She felt trapped, drowning.

She spun around to try to flee, but Mairie had not needed to fetch Malcolm after all. He stood at the corner of the hedge wall, a look of horror on his face. She opened her mouth to shout out his name and Nixson grabbed her arm in a hard, bruising grasp. He yanked her backwards, so hard she felt the soles of her kid boots slip on the grass.

'Stay back, Gordston,' Nixson demanded

and Alex felt the sharp prick of the blade on her shoulder, through the silk of her sleeve. It stung, like a bee's sting. 'I told you that you would be sorry you didn't help me.'

Malcolm held up his hands, taking one slow, measured step towards them, then another. His face seemed carved of the hardest, coldest stone. 'This is no way to settle disputes between businessmen, using ladies like this. Let her go and deal with me.'

'That didn't work, did it? You wouldn't listen. We could have both been rich beyond our wildest dreams. Instead you saw me ruined.' The knife pressed harder to Alex's shoulder, tearing the silk, piercing her skin, and she cried out at the sharp stick of pain.

Malcolm lunged forward, a wild, feral look breaking the stone of his face, her Norse god gone berserker. He had just grabbed her other hand when Alex felt as if someone punched her, hard. She stumbled back, stunned, and the lush green grass rushed up towards her as she slipped beyond both men's grasp. Falling, falling.

Her hat tumbled free, her hair falling from its pins over her eyes, and she landed hard on the ground, staring up at the sky. So very blue, endlessly blue, the sun glowing gold. And yet she felt so very cold.

She could hear shouts, a woman's screams, yet they were so faint. Mostly she just felt confused, numb and that terrible chill. Everything had happened so fast. What was going on?

Malcolm knelt beside her, his coat off, his waistcoat wadded up in his hand. His mouth was pressed into a grim line, his skin ashen beneath his golden tan. He pressed the waistcoat hard to her shoulder and a burning pain roared through her, breaking the icy numbness.

'What are you doing?' she sobbed. 'Malcolm, you are hurting me!'

'My dearest, do lie very still,' she heard Emily say. Her friend knelt at Alex's other side, looking down at her with a gentle smile. 'Don't try to move now, please.'

Alex heard other voices: Chris saying, 'The doctor has been called,' Lady Rippon shouting, 'My party! It's ruined!' And a hoarse shout.

She turned to see Nixson being dragged away, kicking against the grass. Mairie sobbed by the hedge, her dark red gown like a spot of old blood in the beautiful, bright day.

'It's like a scene at the theatre,' Alex whispered, struck by the strangeness of it all. Then the pain grew worse, a growing, living thing. She was sure she was sinking, melting, and she tried to push Malcolm and his bandage away.

'Be still, Alex, please, the doctor is coming,' Emily beseeched. She laid her cool hand on Alex's brow and Alex realised she had never seen her bold, confident friend look like that before. Look—scared.

She twisted her head to look up at Malcolm, who was so pale as he stared down at her. And seeing the fear of the two of them, the bravest people she knew, made her realise how very serious this all was. That this could be the end, right when it was beginning. Right when there were so many things she and Malcolm had to see together.

'I want to go home,' she whispered. Home, to her golden chateau, her garden, her bedroom where she found such joy in Malcolm's arms. Her husband, her love. That was all that mattered now.

'Very soon, my darling,' Malcolm said. 'Just hold on to me. Don't let go.'

'Never.' She squeezed her eyes shut against the pain. 'I need the magical water from the toad's well, I think.'

'The doctor is here,' she heard Chris say and Emily moved away to be replaced by a man with most impressive silver mutton chop whiskers and kind brown eyes.

'Let me see the wound,' he said and eased aside

Malcolm's makeshift bandage. Alex screamed—
and fell down into darkness.

Malcolm stared at Alex's face as he carried
her up the stairs to their bedchamber. Her head
rolled against his shoulder, her skin snow-white,
her lips tinged with a terrifying blue. Her eyes
were closed, yet she murmured in pain. Blood
seeped through the doctor's bandages and her
torn gown.

He had never felt fear like that before. Raw,
fierce, like the world crumbled around him. She
was his world. He saw that now. Nothing mattered but Alex and if he lost her he would be
ended.

He never should have reached for her when
Nixson warned him, Malcolm thought with a
pang of deepest guilt. He never should have met
with Mairie, never kept secrets from Alex. He
had thought there would be time to make things
right between them, to make her truly happy.

He had been hardened for so long, embittered
by what had happened to his father, so he could
see nothing but his status, his wealth, the protection it gave him. But it was no protection in the
end. He could never buy the one thing he truly
needed, his wife's love, and now that could be

slipping away for good. He had never felt such raw despair.

And he realised that if he could not leave the past behind, could not change, he would lose Alex, and she was the most precious thing he'd ever had in his life. What was control, coldness, beside what she had given him? It was nothing. And now all his control was gone. He couldn't save her, no matter how much money he offered. And that was the worst realisation he could ever have.

He laid her gently on her bed, Mademoiselle LeClerc hurrying before him to pull back the sheets. Alex was as pale as her lace-edged pillows, her gown stained a terrible red. Her eyes fluttered open and she stared up at him.

'I can't die like this,' she whispered. 'So many things…'

'You won't die, not for a very, very long time,' he said fiercely.

'With our grandchildren around me?'

The doctor finished washing his hands in the boiling water the housekeeper brought and stepped close to the bed with a hypodermic of morphine. It pierced Alex's arm and her eyes closed again, and she lay still.

'I can assist, if needed, Doctor,' Emily said and the doctor nodded.

'Very good,' he said gruffly. 'Mr Gordston, if you could wait outside?'

Malcolm started to protest, but he felt Chris Blakely put a hand on his shoulder. 'They can work much faster without interruptions, Gordston.'

Malcolm nodded reluctantly. He looked once more at Alex, lying so still there. So pale. 'It's not goodbye.'

'Of course not,' Chris said gently. Malcolm remembered the man was Alex's cousin, that he had reputation for being a terrible, careless rake. But his face was filled with nothing but kindness now. 'We will see her again very soon.'

Malcolm picked up her blue-silk scarf from where she had draped it over her dressing table and followed Chris into the corridor as Emily unfastened Alex's bodice and peeled away the bloodstained cloth. He found a pair of chairs outside the door. The staff was gathered silently on the stairs, Mademoiselle LeClerc sniffling into her handkerchief, the housekeeper's lips moving in prayer. He realised he was far from the only one who would miss Alex, who loved her.

He sat down heavily, his face in his hands. He'd been able to control so much in his life, to claw his way up in the world, build a vast business out of nothing. But now, when it was the most important, the most vital of all, he could control nothing. There was only waiting. He wound Alex's blue scarf around his hand and breathed in the trace of her perfume.

Chris held out a silver flask to him and Malcolm took a deep swallow of the brandy. Chris drank, too, and for a long moment they sat in silence, the only sound Mademoiselle LeClerc crying. They could hear nothing from inside the bedchamber.

'When we were children,' Chris said, 'we were a harum-scarum lot, my brother Will, Charlie and I, but not Alex. She was quiet, always off reading somewhere. But whenever one of us was in trouble, she was the first we would go to. No one was more understanding than Alex, no one more gentle or kind.'

'Yes,' Malcolm muttered. Kind, always. That was his Alex. Always caring about others, always smiling. Those days they had together were the best he had ever known. Life had been completely transformed with her.

But the image of their bright day on the Versailles canal, at the Eiffel Tower café, strolling through the opera, was replaced by what had just happened—Alex in the power of a man like Nixson and of Mairie. What had they told her?

Was her last memory of him to be of betrayal and pain?

No, he thought fiercely. He would not lose her now. There was too much in their future. He would make her understand the past, would build a new family with her. Give her everything she ever wanted. *Truly* wanted, not things, not possessions, but his love and care.

At last, after what felt like an eternity of agonising time, the doctor emerged from the bedroom, his shirtfront stained red, his eyes tired. There was a glimpse of Alex in her bed, Emily tucking the blankets around her, then the door closed again.

Malcolm rose shakily to his feet, hope warring with despair in his heart.

'I have stopped the bleeding and sutured the wound, and she is resting quietly now,' the doctor said. 'But I fear she lost a lot of blood. She will need a great deal of rest and must be kept still and carefully watched for any sign of infection.'

Malcolm nodded. He would do anything to see her get well again. 'May I see her?'

'Just for a moment. I will send a nurse to stay the night and will call again first thing in the morning.'

Malcolm hurried into the chamber. The curtains were drawn, casting the room into shadows, and the air smelled warm, stuffy, medicinal. He could hear Emily and Chris whispering in the doorway, but all he could pay attention to was his wife. Alex lay very still on her bed, her hands tucked at her sides, her breath shallow, her skin so white.

He took her hand, holding it gently, as if she might break. 'I am so sorry, Alexandra, my fairy queen,' he whispered. 'So very sorry. Just come back to me now and I will spend the rest of my life showing you how much I need you.'

Chapter Twenty-Four

Malcolm stepped softly into Alex's chamber, nodding to the nurse who sat watch just outside the door. It was dark, lit only by the fire in the grate, smelling of the sickly-sweet scent of opium, the tang of blood. He knew it was ridiculous to tiptoe, she still slept and wouldn't hear him, yet still he felt he had to be so careful around her. As if anything too loud, too shocking, too sudden, would make her slip out of his hands too fast, to disappear for ever.

Anything too shocking—like love.

Malcolm sat down on the chair beside her bed and stared down at her sleeping face. She was still on the doctor's morphine, though less all the time as her shoulder slowly knit back together, and her breath was quiet. She smiled a bit, as if her dreams were good ones, yet she was still so very pale. So fragile, her face as white as the lace frills of her nightdress. If once she had been his fairy queen, now she was like a snowflake, perfect and unique and so white.

If he held her too tightly in his desperation, would she melt away?

Malcolm leaned his elbows on the edge of the bed and buried his face in his hands, remembering that terrible moment when she fell to the ground, her dress stained with blood. All his doing, all because of his own business dealings, his own past with Mairie, he had almost lost the most precious thing in the world.

But he would never let her be hurt again. Even if he had to send her away, he would make sure she was safe and happy. And wherever she went, she would take his heart with her. A heart he had thought he didn't even have to give.

After he watched his father disintegrate after his beloved mother died, Malcolm had been sure he would never let himself feel that way. Work would be enough, would be his life. Until Alex. Her sweetness, her kindness, her enthusiasm for life, it had changed him. He could never see the world the same way again.

Then he thought he had lost her. Had failed her. He wouldn't do that again.

He reached out and touched her hand. It was so small, so delicate against the blanket, her cameo ring loose on her finger. 'I'm sorry, *m'eudail*,' he whispered. 'Don't worry, all will be well now.'

Her eyes opened and she stared up at him. At first, her gaze was hazy, as if she was lost in dreams, and then she smiled. He'd thought she would be angry with him, would rightfully blame him for what had happened to her, for keeping secrets from her. That she might then turn from him, send him away.

But her smile was only full of tenderness. 'Malcolm, you're here.'

He kissed her hand, feeling so flooded with love, with gratitude. 'Of course I'm here. I only went down to talk to the nurse who waits outside your door all day, like Cerberus. She's quite the starchy dictator and vows you cannot move from your pillows for at least two more days.'

Alex frowned. 'Oh, the doctor and his battalion of nurses! They are like a pack of autocrats, worse than any Russian tsar. I am sure I feel quite well enough to sit in the garden tomorrow.'

'Not until the doctor says so.'

'Maybe then, just maybe, if neither of us tells, we could open the window just a crack.'

'Very well, maybe just a bit.' He went to push open the window and let in some of the cool evening air, driving out the medicinal stuffiness. He glimpsed the Artemis fountain in the moonlight, her bow raised fiercely, fighting just as Alex did. He smiled and came back to plump Alex's pillows, smooth her sheets.

'That is better,' she said with a happy sigh. 'I have been longing for fresh air. And to read some news of the outside world. Mademoiselle LeClerc refuses to bring me any newspapers.'

'It's just as well. I'm sure you don't want to see Nixson's beady eyes staring back from the headlines.'

Alex smoothed her fingers across the sheets. 'What has happened to him?'

'He will go on trial, of course. They say his business reversals have driven him quite mad and the authorities are much interested in his smuggling operations.'

'And Mairie?'

'Mairie?' he asked cautiously.

Alex gazed up at him steadily. 'I know that you once knew her, once—cared about her. I remember seeing you together in Scotland. I'm sure you must be very worried about her.'

'She will have to testify, of course, and then I think she plans to go to Switzerland.' Malcolm would help her with the move, of course, see her settled into a new life. But he never wanted to see her again. 'You must never think my old friendship for her has been in any way rekindled,

Alex. It was just that, a youthful infatuation. It's as nothing to…'

To his feelings for Alex. For his wife. He wished he could say it, could find the right words to make her truly understand.

She glanced away, her fingers plucking at the satin edge of the blanket. 'Mairie said my father once ruined your father. Left him to die.'

Malcolm frowned. 'That was not quite true. Your father *did* evict him, but my pa had ruined himself with drink long before. He couldn't bear it after my mother died. I tried to keep him safe, but I could not. He died not long after we left your father's estate.'

'It must have been terrible for you to see my father on our wedding day, walking beside your bride down the aisle, soon to be your father-in-law,' she said softly.

'I long harboured anger for your father, I admit,' he said. 'But all I felt on our wedding day was happiness and—and pride. I had the most beautiful bride that was ever seen. A bride I could never have imagined could be mine.'

'Because she was a duke's daughter?'

'Because she was *you*. My wonderful, kind, sweet fairy queen,' he said, pouring all the love that was overflowing in his heart into the words.

She stared up at him, wide-eyed. 'You are not angry with me?'

Malcolm was bewildered. 'Why would I be angry with you?'

'Because of who I am.' She glanced down at her ring. 'Mademoiselle LeClerc said you never left my side while I was asleep.'

'No. And Miss Fortescue and Mr Blakely have been here, as well.'

'No one has ever been luckier in their friends than me. But I never, ever want to be a burden on you, Malcolm. If you want to be with Mairie…'

'No!' he cried, shocked that she would think so. 'I told you, that was long ago. The only woman I love is you.'

'You—love me?' she whispered.

'Yes. I love you,' he said and the freedom of saying it aloud was astonishing. He felt so light he could float up to the ceiling. 'I love you.'

'I love you, too,' she answered, the sweetest words ever said.

'You do?'

'I think I have since I was a child, since you taught me to fish in Scotland,' she said. 'Now it is so much more, it is *everything*.'

Malcolm laughed. 'What fools we've been. I thought I had lost you, that the only way to keep you safe was to let you go.'

'Don't you dare!' Alex said fiercely. 'If you try to send me away, I will just come back. Again and again, for ever.'

'And I can't let you go.'

Alex reached for him, her hand gentle on his. 'I think you should kiss me now.'

'Your arm…'

'Nurse can't see us. I *need* you to kiss me, Malcolm. To know we are truly here, together. That we belong to each other.'

'Oh, Alexandra, my fairy queen,' he said roughly, taking her into his arms. 'Don't you know I am yours through anything at all? Yours and only yours, always.'

She smiled, like the sun coming out after all the storms. 'Yes. Always and for ever.'

* * * * *

Author Note

I've had the most fun working on this series, and visiting my favourite place in the world—Paris! Even if it's only vicariously, on the page! I also love the Belle Époque period, a time of such beauty and innovation and optimism. It seemed like the perfect place for my three vivacious debutante heroines and their handsome heroes.

The Exposition Universelle ran from May the sixth to October the thirty-first 1889, celebrating the one hundredth anniversary of the storming of the Bastille, and was a highwater mark in modern Europe. It also gave us one of my very favourite spots, the Eiffel Tower!

Covering two hundred and thirty-seven acres, the Exposition featured pavilions and villages from countries all over the world, including Java, Egypt, Mexico, Senegal and Cambodia, introducing Europeans to a wide array of music, food, art and languages.

There was a railroad to carry the fairgoers between exhibits, the Galerie des Machines featuring modern inventions—including a visit by Thomas Edison to show off his new-fangled light bulb and gramophone—Buffalo Bill's Wild West Show with Annie Oakley and the art pavilion with works by Whistler, Munch, Bonheur and Gauguin.

Another popular exhibit was the Imperial Diamond, also known as the Jacob Diamond, in the French Pavilion. It was one of the largest stones in the world, previously owned by the Nizam of Hyderabad and then by the government of India. I used it as my inspiration for the Eastern Star.

The fair's main symbol, of course, was the Eiffel Tower—the entrance arch to the fair. By the time the Exposition opened, workers were still putting in the finishing touches and the lifts weren't quite working, but people swarmed up its stairs to take in the dizzying views and shop at the souvenir counters and eat at the cafés.

It wasn't entirely loved, though. A petition sent to the paper *Le Temps* read:

We writers, painters, sculptors and passionate devotees of the hitherto untouched beauty of Paris protest with all our strength, in the name of slighted French taste, against the erection of this useless and monstrous Eiffel Tower.

The tower was meant to be temporary, but it grew on the population of the city and is now one of the most visited and beloved landmarks in the world—a symbol of the beautiful city itself.

One of my favourite aspects of researching historical backgrounds for my stories is looking into the fashions of the day! The end of the nineteenth century and beginning of the twentieth seems like a particularly elegant period to me and the most famous of all the purveyors of fashions of the day was the House of Worth.

Opened in 1858 by an Englishman, the house on the Rue de la Paix was soon *the* place for ladies of fashion to shop. Empress Eugénie, Sarah Bernhardt, Lillie Langtry, Jenny Lind, Princess Alexandra and a variety of royalty and American millionaires patronised the elegant, comfortable salon, ordering their wardrobes for each season. Lush fabrics, unique designs and impeccable service made it famous and its designs are still well known.

I also had a lot of fun using the real-life visit of Edward VII—then the Prince of Wales—in my story! On June the tenth, Bertie, Alexandra and their five children arrived at the Eiffel Tower. It was a 'private' visit—Queen Victoria couldn't countenance the celebration of a country throwing off its monarchy!—but Paris was Bertie's lifelong favourite city and he wasn't about to miss a look at something as grand as the Exposition.

They arrived at the Tower at ten-thirty in the morning, entourage and press in tow, with the Princess wearing a 'simple' blue-and-white-silk gown and bonnet trimmed with lilies of the valley, and were conducted on a tour by Monsieur Eiffel himself. I've expanded the trip, with a few more parties and excursions for the royal group, but I'm sure the fun-loving Prince wouldn't mind!

I hope you enjoy exploring the beauties of Paris as much as I loved writing about it!

Here are a few sources I used in researching the period:

Jill Jonnes, *Eiffel's Tower* (2009)

Amy de la Haye and Valerie D. Mendes, *House of Worth: Portrait of an Archive* (2014)

Claire Rose, *Art Nouveau Fashion* (2014)

Jane Ridley, *Heir Apparent: A Life of Edward VII* (2013)

Richard Hough, *Edward and Alexandra: Their Private and Public Lives* (1992)

COMING SOON!

We really hope you enjoyed reading this book. If you're looking for more romance, be sure to head to the shops when new books are available on

Thursday 27th December

To see which titles are coming soon, please visit **millsandboon.co.uk**

MILLS & BOON

Coming next month

THE EARL'S IRRESISTIBLE CHALLENGE
Lara Temple

'And so we circle back to your agenda. Are you always this stubborn or do I bring out the worst in you?'

'Both,' Olivia said.

Lucas laughed, moving forward to raise her chin with the tips of his fingers.

'Do you know, if you want me to comply, you should try to be a little less demanding and a little more conciliating.'

'I don't know why I should bother. You will no doubt do precisely what you want in the end without regard for anyone. The only way so far I have found of getting you to concede anything is either by appealing to your curiosity or to your self-interest. I don't see what good begging would do.'

He slid his thumb gently over her chin, just brushing the line of her lip, and watched as her eyes dilated with what could as much be a sign of alarm as physical interest. He wished he knew which.

'It depends what you are begging for,' he said softly, pulling very slightly on her lower lip. Her breath caught, but she still didn't move. Stubborn *and* imprudent. Or did she possibly really trust him not to take advantage of the fact that they were alone in an empty house in a not-very-genteel part of London?

It really was a pity she was going to waste herself on that dull and dependable young man. What on earth did she think her life would be like with him? All that leashed intensity would burn the poor fool to a crisp if he ever set it loose, which was unlikely. A couple of years of being tied to him and she would be chomping at the bit and probably very ripe for a nice flirtation. He shook his head at his thoughts. Whatever else he was, he had never yet crossed the line with an inexperienced young woman; they were too apt to confuse physical pleasure with emotional connection. It wouldn't be smart to indulge this temptation to see if those lips were as soft and delectable as they looked. Not smart, but very tempting…

Continue reading
THE EARL'S IRRESISTIBLE CHALLENGE
Lara Temple

Available next month
www.millsandboon.co.uk

LET'S TALK
Romance

For exclusive extracts, competitions
and special offers, find us online:

facebook.com/millsandboon

@MillsandBoon

@MillsandBoonUK

Get in touch on 01413 063232

For all the latest titles coming soon, visit
millsandboon.co.uk/nextmonth